## Novels by L.J. Sellers

### Detective Jackson Mysteries
Secrets to Die For
Thrilled to Death
Passions of the Dead
Dying for Justice
Liars, Cheaters & Thieves

### Standalone Thrillers
The Sex Club
The Baby Thief
The Arranger
The Suicide Effect

### Nonfiction
Write First, Clean Later:
Blogs, Essays, & Writing Advice

**LIARS, CHEATERS & THIEVES**

Cover art by Gwen Thomsen Rhoads
Copyedit by Jodie Renner

ISBN (ebook): 978-0-9840086-0-5
ISBN (print): 978-0-9840086-1-2
Published in the USA by Spellbinder Press

# Liars, Cheaters & Thieves

A Detective Jackson Mystery
By L.J. Sellers

# Chapter 1

*Thursday, Nov. 10, 10:17 p.m.*

Prez woke with his face in a puddle of vomit. He remembered getting sick, but not much else of the afternoon. Darkness engulfed him, and he shivered against the damp frigid air. He never got used to the cold no matter how much time he spent outside or how many layers he wore.

A whistling noise caught his attention and he sat up. From his cardboard tent, he peered across the grassy strip that separated the little canal from the tavern's parking lot. A figure in dark clothing moved quickly toward the vehicle in the corner. He'd seen the Jeep parked there many times before, but this time the driver was inside, hunched over the steering wheel. By his size, Prez assumed it was a man, but the distance and darkness made it impossible to tell if the tall person approaching was a man or a woman. Prez had a fleeting moment of disappointment. If they'd both been women, he would have hustled over and hit them up for money. But two men in a tavern parking lot could be trouble.

The intruder stopped whistling as they neared the car and tapped on the driver's side glass. In the quiet, Prez heard the hum of an electric window, then the muffled sound of a brief conversation. The person on foot leaned in and put their face next to the man in the vehicle, and Prez realized they were probably lovers. His body relaxed. A couple was

4

not likely to harass him. He looked around for the pint of Jim Beam he'd bought earlier, wanting to wash the sour taste from his mouth. He found the bottle wrapped in a dirty blanket, swallowed one of the last mouthfuls, and looked back at the couple in the parking lot.

The man in the Jeep laid his head back, and the woman reached in her pocket for something. Maybe they weren't a couple, Prez thought. More likely a drug buy. It only mattered because he considered himself an astute observer of human interaction ...when he was sober. He'd taken sociology during his one year of college and much of it had stuck with him, although it hadn't prevented him from derailing his own life through a series of bad decisions. And a drinking problem he'd come to accept.

The woman gripped something in her hand and stared at the relaxed man for a long moment. She whispered something, a soft hiss in the night, then plunged a blade into the man's throat, and in one smooth motion slashed it open. The move was so violent, so unexpected, Prez jerked back under his cardboard cover. *What the hell? Maybe it wasn't a woman.*

Footsteps pounded toward the canal and Prez held his breath, hoping the attacker wouldn't look over at his little camp in the brush. He prayed that in the dark and in their rush, they wouldn't see him. He took the last swallow of Jim Beam and closed his eyes. When he opened them, he didn't see the person. Maybe he'd imagined the whole thing. His mind sometimes played tricks on him.

Prez heard a tiny splash as something hit the water, then the footsteps retreated. After a moment, he leaned out and watched the figure hurry across the parking lot toward West 11th Avenue. He glanced at the Jeep. The man was not moving, and blood flowed from his throat. Prez decided it was time to find a new camp. He didn't want to be here when the cops came.

*Friday, Nov. 11, 11:05 a.m.*
Molly Pershing's mouth fell open and she stared at the bank teller in disbelief. "What do you mean my account is below the limit?"

The young woman glanced at her computer screen. "You made an automatic transfer to the Veterans Relief Fund in the amount of $7,000, leaving only $312 in the account. So we charged you the monthly maintenance fee of $5 because your account fell below the $5,000 minimum."

"That's a huge mistake!" Molly raised her voice, something she rarely did, and her heart pounded erratically. "I didn't give them all of my money. Who would do that?"

"You set up a monthly payment online last month," the teller insisted, even though her pudgy young face was starting to show alarm. "Then it looks like you increased the amount Tuesday evening before the scheduled payment went through on Wednesday."

"No!" Molly's legs shook and she gripped the counter. "I mean, I set up the donation, but it was for $50." She'd only been using a computer for a few months, and online banking had seemed like such a convenience. Her friends had warned her it wasn't safe. Why hadn't she listened?

"Did you give someone access to your account?"

"No." A sharp pain tore across her chest. Molly gulped in air. "My daughter has access, but she's been on the account for years." Every breath hurt, and it took too long to get the words out. "She didn't do this, but I think I know who did."

"Who?"

Molly couldn't remember his name. Her brain felt foggy, and she thought she might lose her balance. Bolts of shock ripped down her left arm and she lost her grip on the counter.

"Mrs. Pershing!"

The room spun and her pain-ravaged heart struggled to keep beating. Molly opened her mouth but nothing came out. The beating stopped; her knees buckled. As she hit the floor, her last thought was: *But he seemed so nice.*

# Chapter 2

*Early Friday morning*

"Swing your end wide, then tilt it." Detective Wade Jackson called out instructions to the young man carrying the other end of the couch.

Harlan looked confused, then nodded and shuffled left. "Of course. I've only helped one other person move and he didn't have a couch." The boy grinned, a wide full-toothed expression meant to charm. "I like to help people. I volunteer at Food for Lane County too, but I suppose you knew that."

Harlan kept talking but Jackson tuned him out. The sixteen-year-old was Katie's friend—Jackson couldn't bring himself to say *boyfriend*—and the kid was helping them move. Harlan was clean-cut, got good grades, and didn't do drugs. What else could a father want for his fifteen-year-old daughter? Yet Jackson couldn't stand him. More important, didn't trust him. He couldn't decide if he was just being an overprotective father or if his cop instinct had picked up that the boy was hiding something. Jackson smiled to be polite. Neither Harlan nor Katie knew how he really felt.

They lugged the couch out through the doorway and nearly collided with the two professional movers he'd hired. Semiprofessional, Jackson corrected. He'd found them on Craigslist and had rented his own U-Haul, saving more than half the cost of a moving company. The goal was to get everything into the new house today and unpacked over the weekend, so Monday he could go back to work feeling settled and normal. As if selling his home of thirteen years and moving back into the house where he'd grown up was just another transition in his hectic life.

They carried the couch up the loading ramp without mishap, set it down, and headed back into the house.

"Can I start carrying my clothes out?" His daughter's voice echoed in the nearly-empty living room.

"Sure." They'd started early and had already loaded most of the big stuff. "We're making good time."

Again, Jackson was taken aback by Katie's appearance. In the last eight months, she'd grown taller and thinner and had started wearing her curly hair pulled back in a sleek style. His round-faced, carefree little girl had morphed into a confident teenager who resembled his ex-wife—and sometimes looked at him with the same disapproval. Too many changes were happening all at once, and it was like walking on shifting ground. Sometimes he had flashes of dread that a major upheaval was coming in his life but he had no idea what.

He pushed away the thought and focused on carrying boxes from the kitchen. Getting out of this house and closing the mortgage that linked him to his ex-wife was a welcome break. Although moving in with his brother was not ideal, it was a great temporary landing place. Derrick had recently started driving a long haul truck and was only home four or five days a month, so he'd offered his house to Jackson and Katie when theirs sold.

After ten minutes of making trips to the U-Haul, he realized Katie had disappeared. Worried, Jackson found her in her bedroom, staring out the window.

"I'll miss our dinners on the back deck," she said, turning to him with tears in her eyes.

Jackson pulled her in for a tight hug and she didn't resist. "We'll have backyard dinners at the new house." He leaned back so he could see her face. "We're family, sweetheart. Whenever we're together, we're home."

"You're right. I'm just being silly." Katie wiped her eyes, and he noticed she was wearing mascara, a new development. "I'm kind of excited about the change," she added. "My new bedroom is bigger." She smiled, picked up a stuffed panda that had been left on the floor, and placed it on the windowsill. "I'm leaving this for the little girl who's moving in here."

Jackson's throat closed and he couldn't respond. Katie was saying goodbye to so much more than a familiar bedroom.

His cell phone rang and Jackson braced himself. A mid-morning call on his day off could not be good. He pulled the phone from his pocket and recognized the familiar number. He looked over at his daughter.

Katie scrunched up her freckled face. "It's work, isn't it?"

"Yes."

"Go ahead. I'll keep things moving here." His daughter craved responsibility the way her mother craved alcohol. And yes, those things were connected.

The phone rang twice more. "Thanks, Katie. I'm sorry." Jackson stepped into the hallway as he answered.

"It's Sergeant Lammers. I know you're moving today but I need you. With McCray retired, Bohnert out on sick leave, and Quince rotating between units, you're the man."

"What have you got?"

"A homicide in the parking lot of Pete's Pad on West 11th. A man in a vehicle with his throat slashed. It probably happened last night. So we've got a cold body in an empty parking lot, and my gut tells me this one will be difficult. I need you down there ASAP."

Jackson's pulse quickened. It complicated his personal plans, but the thought of a tough homicide case challenged him. "I'm on my way." He pocketed the phone and gave his daughter an apologetic look.

"A homicide?" She couldn't hide her disappointment.

"Yes. I have to go."

"Don't forget we're supposed to meet Mom and Ivan for dinner tonight."

"Oh shit."

"You realize you said that out loud?"

He laughed. "Sorry. I'm not looking forward to meeting your mother's boyfriend." Jackson scrambled to decide whether to cancel now or wait until the last minute.

Katie glared at him. "Don't blow this off. I want to spend some time with Mom, and you said I can't stay at her place until you meet Ivan."

"I know. But today was not a good day to plan this for, and now I have a homicide to deal with."

"You're saying you won't make dinner?"

"I'll try. Will you make sure the movers put everything in the right rooms at the new house and give them the check I wrote?"

"Of course. Don't worry. We'll get your bed set up too."

Harlan came into the room but for once kept his mouth closed.

"Thanks, sweetie. I'll call you later." Jackson stepped toward her for another hug, but she turned toward the scrawny boy. *Crap*. Why did his job often make him feel like a bad father?

Jackson backed out of the driveway, thinking it might be the last time. He braked at the street and took in the view. The giant oak and birch trees had shed leaves all over the lawn, and the house needed paint. But it was no longer his responsibility. Yesterday, he'd signed the property over to the new owners.

Driving down Hilyard, he started to feel relieved. Within a week, he and Renee would split the equity from the sale, and it would end his legal connection to the woman who'd nearly ruined his life with her drinking. She was out of rehab for the second time in eighteen months, but he wasn't holding his breath. If not for Katie's connection to her mother, he wouldn't care. He had a wonderful new woman in his life and was moving forward.

He turned left on 11th Avenue, a main artery, and headed west. A thick canopy of trees, vibrant with yellow and red leaves, hung over the street, and the air was crisp and cool under a fleeting blue sky. He was grateful it wasn't raining. Working an outdoor homicide in wet weather could be a bitch. But Jackson had lived in, and loved, his hometown of Eugene, Oregon, for more than four decades, and rain was just part of the scenery.

Pete's Pad, made of cinderblock and painted a disturbing rust color, sat near the street with parking in the back. Two patrol cars and a blue unmarked Impala much like his own occupied the driveway and cut off the crime scene from street traffic. Jackson pulled into the Shari's parking lot next door. The restaurant seemed unaffected by the adjacent crime, yet the tavern would be shut down for most of the day. But after the homicide hit the news that evening, drinkers would come pouring into the bar out of morbid curiosity.

Jackson hustled across the dirt strip that separated the parking lots as two uniformed officers stretched crime-scene tape across them. Another officer stood near the patrol cars blocking the entrance, and a dark Jeep sat parked in the back near the canal. The only other car in the tavern lot was a beat-up burgundy Subaru, probably belonging to the employee who'd discovered the body. Neither the medical examiner nor the assistant DA had arrived yet. Lammers hadn't called out the mobile command unit either, most likely because there were no witnesses to interview at the scene. He hoped to find people from the night before who could tell them what had happened.

Jackson hurried across the lot and found Lara Evans scraping something from the door of a midnight-blue Jeep Wrangler. The paint was custom, he knew, because it was the same as his '69 GTO, a vehicle he'd painstakingly restored.

"Hey, Evans. What have you got?"

"I'm not sure. It's sticky, and I don't think it's been here long." She looked up, and the sight of her heart-shaped face and blue eyes made him smile. Evans didn't look like a cop, but she was sharper than the male detectives in the unit, and he'd learned recently that she practiced Brazilian Jiu-Jitsu and could probably beat most of them in hand-to-hand combat.

"Who called in the body?" he asked.

"The bartender. He showed up for work at nine, saw the Jeep, and thought the guy was still sleeping it off." Evans buttoned her pale blue jacket against the wind. "He went over to roust him and found him dead."

"Where is the bartender now?"

"Inside. After I questioned him, he said he had to prep for lunch. I didn't see any reason to make him stand here."

"Have you ID'd the victim?"

"I didn't see a wallet, but if the perp didn't steal it, then it's probably in the vic's back pocket and he's sitting on it." She held out a plastic bag. "The registration and title belong to Rafel Mazari."

Jackson pulled on latex gloves, then slipped the paperwork out of the bag. He jotted down the owner's address, a street name he didn't recognize, then slipped the evidence into his shoulder bag. The man's name was a little unusual, and he was curious about its cultural ancestry. Jackson took several wide shots of the Jeep with his digital camera, then moved closer to the vehicle. It was time to see the body.

The driver's side window was down and rain from the night before had soaked the edge of the upholstery. He stepped forward and took a quick photo through the windshield to get a full frontal image, then took several more through the open side window. Even in his seated position, the victim looked taller than average. His shoulders were narrow, but he made up for it with thick arms that stretched the fabric of his denim jacket. He had dark wavy slicked-back hair, and facial skin that had absorbed a lot of sun but was now a shade of gray. Jackson opened the door and leaned in, careful not to touch anything. The gash across the victim's throat was deep and violent, but not jagged. Blood poured freely, congealing on his jacket collar and white T-shirt in a dark sticky mess. Its rich, metallic scent permeated the vehicle's cab. Under the rust smell of blood, a mix of cigarette smoke and alcohol oozed from the victim's skin and car seats.

As disturbing as the moment was, it didn't fill him with dread the way some victims did. Examining the bodies of women and children never got any easier, but male victims generated less emotion for him.

What had this guy done? Had he simply refused to hand over his wallet or keys to a thug? Or had he been involved in something shady?

"It looks like revenge," Evans said, vocalizing his thoughts. "He pissed off someone big time."

"Could be. The stereo is intact, and the assailant didn't steal the vehicle, but we need to see if his wallet is still here."

"Gunderson won't want us to move the body."

"I know." Jackson gently probed the pockets of the man's jacket. He pulled out a red lighter and a sliding-style knife and handed them to Evans. "Bag these, please." Squatting next to the vehicle, he searched along the edge of the Jeep's floor, looking for something the killer may have dropped. The interior was surprisingly clean, as if it had recently been detailed.

"All I found was an empty Coke can," Evans said. "But I didn't search under the seat on the driver's side because his legs were in the way."

"There's very little blood except on the body. No spatter that I can see."

"You mean no struggle?"

"Not just that. The way he's leaned back makes it look like he was sleeping when he was attacked." The thought made him inwardly shudder. Most murders were crimes of passion. This looked cold and calculated. "The lack of blood indicates a slow heart rate at the time of death."

"He could have come out here drunk and passed out.

Maybe someone followed him and took advantage." Evans shifted in her black sensible shoes and scowled. "But the window was down, and it was near freezing last night. Maybe the victim opened it when the attacker approached."

"He doesn't seem to have a cell phone unless it's in a back pocket. That's unusual." Jackson knew the lack of it would make their job more difficult.

"The perp could have taken it."

"But nothing else?" Jackson heard a car start behind him and turned. A patrol officer was moving his vehicle so the medical examiner could pull through. Rich Gunderson parked and climbed out of a white station wagon, a stark contrast to his black pullover and black jeans. Gray hair pulled back in a ponytail, he looked like an aging musician, minus the sunglasses. It was November in Oregon; they wouldn't see much of the sun again until February.

"What have we got?" Gunderson's voice boomed in the morning quiet. "A bar fight gone bad?"

"I don't see any signs of a struggle inside the vehicle. I think it happened fast," Jackson said.

"Lammers told me his throat was slit. That's rather unusual."

Jackson thought so too. "We haven't seen that since the coke-war murder back in '92."

"Give me twenty minutes before you ask any questions, okay?" Gunderson set down his tool kit and pulled on gloves. "At that point, we'll move the body to a tarp and see what else we find."

"I'll be back in ten." Jackson gave a grim smile and headed for the patrol officers coming his way.

They met in the center of the parking lot. "Let's start a search around the area in case the perp tossed the weapon.

We're looking for a knife or other sharp instrument. Or anything else the perp may have dropped."

Rob Schakowski strode over from the adjacent lot. His military-cut hair, wide chin, and barrel-shaped torso made him look a bit like Buzz Lightyear, and Jackson had bought him the little toy once as a joke. "Hey, Schak. I'm glad you're here. How's the student assault case?"

"Slow and tedious. I needed a break from it."

"Are you up for searching the area, particularly over by the canal?"

Schak bristled. "Hell, yes." Schak had suffered a heart attack during the takedown of a murderer eight months before, and Jackson still worried about him. Schak hated that worry but didn't hold it against him.

Jackson turned to Evans. "Let's go talk to the bartender and find out who was here last night."

The bartender had thin graying hair, a dark mole on his forehead the size of a dime, and a beer belly that hung out under his T-shirt in an ugly display of flesh. Jackson saw Evans grimace as the man reached up for a hand towel and flashed even more of his stomach.

"This is Clayton Grimes," Evans announced as they came into the narrow kitchen. Pots and utensils hung from every available wall space, leaving no room for a window.

Jackson's body tensed from the proximity. He introduced himself, then suggested they go to a table in the bar, still a dark space but bigger. He chose a spot near the door, which he'd propped open on the way in. Without any windows, the room was gloomy, even with recessed lights over the long bar counter.

"Tell me what happened this morning."

"As I told the gal"—the bartender gestured at Evans—"I saw the Jeep in the corner and realized it had been there overnight. So I went over to see if someone was sleeping in it. We discourage that." He caught Jackson's eye, as if he wanted approval. "Seeing him cut open like that about made me sick. And I was in Vietnam."

"You said you realized the vehicle was here overnight. Did you work last night?" Jackson had his notepad ready.

"No, but I came in around nine this morning. And I've seen that Jeep parked there a lot."

"Who drives it?"

"I don't know his name. He's quiet. But he drinks with a couple of buddies sometimes, and one of them is named Jake."

"Were his buddies here last night?"

"When I saw him, he was alone, but it was early."

"Did you see the victim leave?"

"No, I just came in to pick up my check and have a quick beer." Grimes made a scoffing sound. "I don't like to be here when I'm not working."

Evans cut in. "Do you know Jake's last name?"

"I don't know the night crowd that well. You should talk to Mila. She works the evening shift and knows everyone."

"What's Mila's last name and phone number?"

"Mila Kruz." The bartender pulled a cell phone from his jeans pocket, looked up the number, then read it out loud. Jackson dialed it immediately. After five rings, Mila Kruz picked up, sounding groggy. "Call me back in an hour. I'm still sleeping."

"This is Detective Jackson, Eugene Police. I'd like you to come down to Pete's Pad immediately. There was a murder in the parking lot last night and we need your help."

"Oh shit. Who's dead?"

"I'll tell you when you get here. Please hurry. Time is critical to our investigation."

"Give me forty minutes to shower and grab something to eat."

"Skip the shower and eat something on the way. I need you here now."

"Okay. I'm moving. Tell Clay to put on some coffee." She clicked off.

"Kruz is on her way down. Do you have coffee brewed?"

"Of course. Do you want some?"

"No, thanks. Anyone else I should talk to who might have seen something?"

"There's a homeless dude named Prez who camps right behind the parking lot." Grimes looked skeptical.

Jackson thought it unusual he knew a transient's name. "Do you know him personally?"

"I give him leftovers sometimes," the bartender explained. "Don't tell my boss. He'd fire me. He hates the vagabond traffic we get around here."

"Describe him, please."

"That's hard." Grimes rubbed his chin. "He looks about fifty-five, but he could be younger. You know how it is with homeless people. His hair is shoulder-length, a mix of light brown and gray. I'm not sure what else to tell you."

"Height and weight?"

"About my height, I think. Five-nine or so. And skinny, but it's hard to tell because he wears a long brown coat with a fake fur trim. It's a little weird."

"Thanks for your help. I'm sure we'll have more questions later." Jackson handed the bartender a business card. "Call me if you think of anyone else I should talk to."

As they walked out of the dark bar, Jackson blinked at the sun streaming through a narrow gap in the clouds. He looked over at the Jeep where the medical examiner was laying out a sheet of thick gray vinyl with the help of a crime scene technician. Tall, thin, and ageless, Jasmine Parker wore black today too, and they both looked the part of death-scene attendants. They were getting ready to move the corpse out of the car.

"Hey, Parker. I'll take the other end of the body. He looks heavy."

"I'm sure I can handle it." Her tone was neutral and her dark eyes expressionless. Parker would make a great poker player, he thought.

"Okay. But I'm right here if it gets awkward."

"Thanks." A tiny smile. They'd worked together for years, and in their own quiet way were friends. He also trusted Parker with vital evidence more than anyone else at the lab.

Gunderson, in a waterproof jumpsuit, stood next to the corpse, still seated behind the wheel. The ME tugged until the body fell stiffly toward him. He caught the victim under the shoulders and pulled. Parker stepped in and grabbed the body under the knees. They squatted in unison and plopped the corpse down on the vinyl, where it hit with a heavy thud.

"Complete rigor mortis?" Jackson asked.

"Yep," Gunderson said, not looking up. "He's probably been dead at least twelve hours."

"I'd like to empty his back pockets," Jackson requested.

"I'll do it." The ME rolled up Mazari's jean-covered hip and pulled out a leather wallet. He handed it to Jackson, then checked the other pants pockets and found nothing.

In the distance, a siren wailed. The sound jangled Jackson's nerves. They all paused, listening for the direction.

It was coming their way.

Gunderson grabbed his thermal probe, opened the man's jeans, and jabbed the device into the victim's hip.

Jackson flipped through the wallet while he waited for a temperature and approximate time of death. The driver's license matched the registration: Rafel Mazari, age 32, brown hair, brown eyes, motorcycle endorsement, and organ donor. The wallet was thin and held no cash. Jackson flipped through the cards and quickly spotted a National Guard ID. Rafel Mazari had been a sergeant.

"He's National Guard," Jackson said, not sure if it would matter.

Gunderson grunted. "It's Veteran's Day, but there's not much honor in this death."

Jackson turned to Evans. "Can you get online and see what you can find on the victim? I need to contact the family."

"I'm on it." Evans pulled her iPad from her shoulder bag. She liked being connected, no matter where she was, and Jackson was thinking of following her lead. The price tag on the device held him back, so he was grateful to have Evans and her enthusiasm on his team. After two years of training, she'd finally been made a permanent member of the unit. But he still kept an eye on her because she could be a little impulsive.

Another card in the wallet caught Jackson's eye. Kera Kollmorgan, volunteer nurse with the Veterans Recovery Clinic. At first it startled him to see his girlfriend's name in another man's wallet, but if Mazari was a vet, it made sense. Kera had lost her son in Iraq and did volunteer work with wounded veterans. He would have to ask her what she knew about the victim.

He looked over at Gunderson. "What's his core temp?"

"Seventy-two point five degrees." The ME dropped from his squatting position to his knees. "It got down to thirty-five last night and it's only about forty-five right now. If he dropped two degrees an hour out here, my best guess for the moment is that he's been cooling since ten or eleven last night."

"That's well before the tavern closed."

Evans spoke up. "It's hard to believe no one saw him as they came into the parking lot."

"He was in a dark corner." Jackson felt like swearing. Starting the investigation the night before would have made a huge difference. They would have had a whole tavern full of people to question. Now they would have to track them down one by one. He looked at Gunderson. "What else can you tell me?"

"The wound is clean and likely made with something very sharp. Maybe a utility knife or a scalpel. Also, there's not much blood for a severed jugular. He had to be nearly comatose when the blade went in."

"No defensive wounds?"

"None that I can see."

"Right- or left-handed perp?

"The cut runs from right to left, so I'd guess left-handed." Gunderson stood next to the Jeep to demonstrate. "But leaning in the window, it would be difficult to use your right hand effectively. The killer may have been forced to use his left hand. It could be someone with equal dexterity."

*Like a soldier.* The thought popped into Jackson's head, and it seemed significant enough to write down. "Anything else for now?"

The siren was now screaming up the street, only a half-mile away. He recognized the wail of a patrol car and fought the urge to rush to the sidewalk.

"Dog hair on his jacket and tobacco stains on his fingers," Gunderson reported. "I suspect he rolled his own cigarettes."

Jackson wished he'd taken a couple more minutes with the body, but its position in the confines of the vehicle had made it difficult to take in the details.

"Nothing else is obvious," Gunderson continued, "but we'll send the blood work out this afternoon and do an autopsy first thing tomorrow."

Jackson barely heard him over the noise of the siren. He turned and saw a patrol unit swerve into the Northwest Federal Bank across the street.

# Chapter 3

Involuntarily, Jackson moved toward the sidewalk for a better view, and so did Evans. They watched a patrol officer run into the white bank building, weapon drawn. A robbery? Adrenaline flowed in Jackson's veins.

"Let's send an officer over to find out what's going on," Evans said.

Jackson thought the same thing but he didn't respond. He had his own case, and the victim had been dead for twelve hours already, losing a chunk of their window of opportunity. An ambulance screamed up the busy street, forcing traffic to the side, and swung wide into the bank's parking area. Two paramedics trotted into the building with a gurney.

Jackson stopped next to the officer guarding the tavern's lot. "It looks like someone's hurt over there."

"Shit." Evans vibrated next to him, like a hyper dog on a leash. "Do you suppose the crazy guy who's been robbing convenience stores is branching out?"

"Could be." Jackson turned to the uniformed officer. "Go over and see if they need help. Find out what's going on."

"Good call." The officer trotted out into the traffic, which had slowed to gawk at the cop cars on both sides of the street.

"Let's get back to work until we hear from her." Jackson spun toward the parking lot, where the victim lay on the gray vinyl tarp. Was the incident at the bank connected to this homicide? The timing and proximity were certainly odd, but he figured it was likely a coincidence, like the time two Eugene banks were robbed on the same day, but by different people. A desperate day in the meth culture.

Parker and Gunderson hunched over the corpse, picking trace evidence from Mazari's clothes, while Schak hurried toward him carrying several plastic bags.

"I found a syringe in the grass just beyond the asphalt and a fresh cigarette butt with what looks like a bloodstain." Schak sounded more wound up than his usual deadpan delivery. "And one of the patrol officers found signs of a recent homeless camp."

"Is the transient's stuff still there?" Jackson looked at his notes for the name.

"No, but there's a fresh pile of puke. He was probably out here last night."

"His name's Prez and we need to find him." Jackson reached for the bag with the syringe. Made of clear plastic with a light-blue stopper, the needle was different from the ones handed out by the HIV Alliance. It might not have been dropped by a local junkie.

"We'll need patrol help to find the dude," Schak said. "But I have a snitch who might know something."

"I'll get them going on it now." Jackson looked past Schak. The two patrol officers he'd sent to search the perimeter were headed back. When they reached him, he asked, "What can you tell me about the homeless camp?"

The older officer shook his head. "Not much. Whoever it was cleared out recently and didn't leave much trash." He handed Jackson a large plastic bag. "An empty bottle of Jim Beam, two Luna bar wrappers, and a piece of tissue. I only collected items that might hold DNA."

"Speaking of body fluids." The younger officer held out a smaller plastic bag. "I have a present for you."

Jackson took the evidence, realizing it held the vomit Schak had mentioned. "Lovely." He grimaced. "If this is the worst of my day, I'll consider it a success."

"A transient puked on my pants once," the older officer added. "Right down the path from here. We were hauling him out of the canal."

"Speaking of the path," Jackson echoed, "I need you guys to find Prez. I'm guessing he didn't go far. He may be just on the other side of the canal in that wooded area. There's a few camps back there."

"And when we find him?"

"Don't question him. Just bring him back here to me." Without a uniform, Jackson would be less intimidating and get more information. "If I've moved on from here, call me and take Prez into headquarters and give him something to eat and drink."

The older cop raised his eyebrows, and Jackson realized he thought the transient was a suspect. And he could be. They'd had a lot of homeless-on-homeless violence lately. "He's more likely a witness than a perp. Nothing was stolen that we know of."

The officers headed for their cars. They would have to drive to City View to cross over the canal. The water was shallow and only five to ten feet wide, but why get their boots wet?

Not wanting to put the vomit in his shoulder bag, Jackson locked the evidence in his car, then checked in with the medical examiner. "What else did you find?"

"He has a prosthetic leg." Gunderson rapped Mazari's left

26

thigh, and it made a sound that was clearly not flesh and muscle. "I'll know more this afternoon when I process him."

A wave of sadness rolled over Jackson. The dead man had served his country and likely lost his leg to a bomb, then he'd come home and been slaughtered like an animal. Tragedy on tragedy. Some people seemed doomed.

Two men in dark suits approached from the Shari's parking lot where Jackson's car was. Detective Michael Quince was tall and boyishly handsome, while Jim Trang, the assistant DA, was short with grumpy, furrowed features. Both would be useful on this case.

"About time you got here."

Quince grinned and Trang scowled.

"I can't stay," Quince said. "Lammers called me just as I arrived and said to head across the street. It looks like a case of fraud."

"Why the ambulance?"

"An old woman had a heart attack." Quince paused for effect. "Right after she learned her account had been nearly cleaned out."

"Another double tragedy." The personal fraud and resulting death were far worse than a bank robbery.

"What's the homicide scene?" Trang wanted to know.

"Thirty-two-year-old male with his throat slit while he sat in his vehicle. Rafel Mazari, National Guard sergeant with a missing leg. Killed between ten and eleven last night and found by the tavern bartender this morning at nine." Jackson paused to let Trang catch up with his notes. The ADA used a black leather binder with a yellow legal tablet. The EPD all scribbled on little notebooks that fit in their pockets. "We're looking for a possible witness-slash-perp, a homeless guy named Prez."

"Do you have a task force meeting planned yet?" Quince asked. "Lammers wants me to work both cases."

"Let's meet at six in the conference room. If something shakes loose before then, I'll call you."

Quince headed for the sidewalk as Evans came this way. They high-fived each other in passing. Jackson had thought if Quince hadn't been married, those two might have hooked up when Evans first joined the unit. Then more recently when they were working his parents' murder case, Jackson and Evans had experienced a little moment and he'd wondered if she had feelings for him. Now she was dating Ben Stricklyn, an IA detective, so it was a moot point. Lucky Ben.

Before he could feel guilty about the thought, his phone rang. It was Kera.

"Hey, Jackson. I thought I would check in and see how the move is going. Should I bring you guys some lunch? Or am I too late?" His girlfriend treated him better than he deserved. They'd met when the Planned Parenthood Clinic where she worked had been bombed and had been dating just over a year

"A sweet thought, but I got called out to a homicide. So Katie and the movers are handling it without me."

"I'm sorry to hear that. A tough case?" She was asking if any kids had been killed. As a nurse, dealing with injured or victimized children was the hardest part of her job too.

"Emotionally no, but logistically yes." Jackson recalled finding Kera's card. "Do you know a veteran named Rafel Mazari?"

He heard a sharp intake of breath. "Don't tell me Rafel is dead."

"I'm sorry, Kera." He paused, giving her a moment to

process the news. "Did you work with him?"

"Yes." She choked back a cry. "He was murdered?"

"Last night."

"That poor man."

Jackson heard her distress and knew it wasn't just about Rafel Mazari. Kera's son Nathan had been killed in Iraq less than two years ago. Her grief was still raw at times. "I'm sorry to be the one to tell you about him. Were you close?"

"I cared about him."

Jackson hated what he had to say next. "I'll need to talk with you later today or tomorrow about this case."

"You mean question me."

"Just gathering information so I can solve this."

"I know. I have to get off the phone now." She hung up without saying goodbye. Jackson tried not to take it personally, knowing she was upset by the death. But it worried him. Kera had been a little distant since he'd decided to move into his parents' old house instead of settling in with her. He felt guilty, but Kera still had her daughter-in-law and baby grandson living with her, and he couldn't handle the chaos. Their family lives were both too complicated to attempt to mesh them together right now.

Jackson stared at the phone, wondering if Kera was mad at him or just upset about Rafel. When the case was over, they would do another getaway. A weekend at the coast or maybe Belknap Hot Springs.

A horn blast from the street caught his attention. A little red car was trying to turn into the tavern's parking lot, and a patrol officer was waving it on. The female driver gunned the engine and pulled into Shari's next door. Jackson hoped it was the night bartender.

The woman climbed out of her car and marched over. She

was forty-something and almost as wide as she was tall. She wore her dyed-red hair in a twisted bun on top of her head and looked like an angry bird. Jackson hoped she'd lose the attitude. He was not in the mood to be patient. He intercepted her on her way into the tavern and introduced himself.

"Mila Kruz," she said, brushing past him. "But you knew that. I have to get some coffee before I can even be civil."

Jackson followed her into the building. The windowless space felt smaller this time and he hoped to get through the schematics quickly. The day bartender was slicing onions and pickles for a lunch crowd that wouldn't get through the perimeter. The pungent smells made Jackson's stomach growl. Kruz poured herself a tall mug, added a little cold water, and downed half her coffee standing in front of the kitchen sink.

"That's better." She met Jackson's eyes for the first time. "Who got killed?"

"Rafel Mazari."

"That's fucked up." Her muddy brown eyes slid away. "He was a war veteran, you know. He lost a leg in Afghanistan."

She knew something she wasn't telling, and he would have to pry it out of her. "Can we sit down?"

"Sure."

They went to the same table near the front door, which Jackson propped open again. He took out his notepad.

"It's a little chilly," Kruz complained.

"I need the fresh air." He also wanted better light on her face, so he could detect any signs of deception. Not that she was a viable suspect—unless she'd snuck out on her break to commit murder—but she might protect someone else. "When did you come into work?"

"Five p.m."

"Was Mazari here?"

"You mean Rafel? No, he came in around eight or so."

"Was he alone?"

"Yes, but his buddy Jake came in soon after and joined him."

"Jake who?"

She shrugged.

"Where did they sit?"

She pointed at a table in the corner near the entrance to the kitchen. "He always sat there."

"How often did he come in?"

"Two or three times a week."

"How long did Jake sit with him?"

"I'm not sure. Maybe an hour." She gulped the rest of her coffee.

"What happened last night? I can tell you're avoiding the subject."

Her shoulders tightened. "Things got a little tense between Rafel and his wife, but I don't know the particulars. I was behind the bar."

"What's his wife's name?"

"Sierra Kent."

"When did she come in?"

"No clue. I only noticed her when things got loud." The bartender pushed up from the table. "I gotta get some more coffee."

Jackson went with her and grabbed himself a cup. This would be a long day.

When they returned to the table, he said, "Tell me what happened from the time Jake sat down with Rafel."

"They had a couple beers, then another guy joined them

for a while. Then I heard a commotion and looked up." She stopped suddenly and yawned. "Excuse me." A pause. "Rafel's wife, Sierra, was at the table and they were arguing. I saw Jake leave, then I got busy. Next time I looked over, they were all gone."

Jackson took a moment to catch up his notes. He would expand them later. "What time was that?"

"I'm not sure. Maybe around ten."

"What was the argument about?"

Kruz hesitated. "I didn't hear anything they said."

"But someone did. And you heard them gossip about it."

"An old guy named Zack said Rafel accused her of cheating on him."

"What's Zack's last name and how can I reach him?"

The bartender rolled her eyes. "You can come back tonight. He'll be sitting right there on that third stool." She pointed toward the bar.

"Who else was here that might have overheard it?"

"A woman named Nikki. She's here every night too and knows everybody. She comes in around seven."

Jackson tried to mask his frustration. Spending the evening in a bar, talking to daily drinkers, was not an ideal investigation. But he would get more information in this environment than if he dragged them into headquarters. "What can you tell me about Rafel's wife?"

"She's blond and pretty and rarely comes in here."

*Not helpful.* "What do you know about Jake?"

"Nikki can help you with that. I'm busy working when I'm here."

Jackson hoped Evans' computer search had come up with something. He needed to find Rafel's wife and speak with her immediately. "Thanks for your time. I may have more questions later. If you think of anything in the meantime, call me."

"I can go now?"

"Yes." Jackson stood, handed Kruz a business card, and strode outside. The sky had turned an angry gray, but Jackson was still happy to see it.

Evans sat on the hood of her car, intently perusing her little iPad. He was eager to see what she'd discovered, but Gunderson was loading up the body, so Jackson hurried over to him. "Did you find anything else I should know?"

"The victim is wearing a chain under his T-shirt with a little locket. I found this key inside." The ME held out a small plastic bag with a small silver locket and key.

Jackson brought it close to his face. It looked like it might open a diary or miniature lockbox. "Thanks. What time is the autopsy?"

"Eight o'clock. The deck is clear for him."

"I'll see you then."

Evans called to him from her car, so Jackson headed over.

"I can't find much on Mazari, but his wife, Sierra Kent, is a veterinary assistant. She works at the Animal Care Clinic and volunteers with Pro-Bone-O, the group that treats homeless people's pets. She might be at the clinic now." Evans looked up. "Should we go see her?"

"We have to split up and cover a lot of territory fast. I'll go see the wife, and I need you to track down Mazari's friend Jake and another guy that was with them last night. The wife was here too, and witnesses say Mazari and his wife argued."

"So it could be a domestic." Evans looked disappointed.

Jackson mentally mapped out a strategy to keep his task force moving forward. "After you run down the witnesses' names, head out to Mazari's house and wait for my call. I'll go see the wife at work and get her permission to search the house. If I can't, I'll send Schak to get a warrant."

"Is Quince with us on this homicide?"

"Part-time." Jackson took out his phone. "What's the number of the wife's clinic?"

He keyed it in and saved it, deciding not to call ahead. He found Schak in his cruiser, eating a sandwich. "Where'd you get that?"

"I brought it from home and was lucky enough to be at my desk when Lammers called. My wife packed an apple too. You want it?"

"Sure." It was better than nothing, and he'd never seen Schak eat fruit anyway. "I'm going out to inform and interview the wife. Evans will head for the victim's home. I'll try to get permission for a search, but if I don't, I need you to round up a warrant ASAP, then join her. I'll come out as soon as I can."

"Will do." Schak put down his lunch. "After the Walker family, I thought I'd seen it all. But this kill looks so cold, it creeps me out."

"I know what you mean."

# Chapter 4

The Animal Care Clinic near 28th and Willamette had once been a Mexican restaurant, and its beige stucco exterior and arched entry gave it surreal look, as though it belonged on a movie set. The interior, however, didn't smell like enchiladas. Instead, a pungent mix of wet dog and harsh antiseptic assaulted Jackson's nostrils.

A worried woman with a cat in a plastic carrier sat in the small lobby. Behind the reception counter, a young woman stared at an oversized monitor, chewing gum. "How can I help you?"

"I'm here to see Sierra Kent."

"Can I tell her who's asking?"

Jackson hesitated. If the wife was their perp, he didn't want to give her a chance to scoot out the back door. But without the proper incentive, she might ignore him. "Detective Jackson."

The receptionist gave him a long look up and down, and he imagined what she would report to Sierra: *He's forty-something, six feet tall, with dark hair and nearly black eyes. He's dressed nice, but he's got a scar above his left eye, and he's kind of scary-looking. He might even be wearing a gun under that suede jacket.*

Jackson gave her a friendly smile before she turned away.

In a moment, the receptionist came back, followed by a

gorgeous woman. Sierra Kent was as tall as him, but with a face like a model: wide-spaced, sky-blue eyes, prominent cheekbones, and lush pouty lips. The white lab coat couldn't hide her full breasts, and Jackson felt a tug of attraction.

"This is Sierra Kent," the receptionist said, then plopped down.

"I'm Detective Jackson, Eugene Police. Can we go someplace private?"

Her eyes widened in alarm. "Is Rafel hurt?"

"Let's go sit down somewhere." He stepped forward, hoping she would comply rather than panic.

She pivoted and strode down a narrow hallway. Following, he noticed her hair: long, ash-blonde dreadlocks pulled together in a thick ponytail. It surprised him. Dreads were somewhat common in Eugene, but not usually on professionals.

They entered a small cluttered office with two desks and an arched window. Jackson sat in the visitor's chair as Sierra plopped down on the other side of her messy desk.

"Please tell me what happened," she begged. "Rafel didn't come home last night. I know something's wrong."

"Rafel Mazari is your husband?"

"Yes."

"I'm sorry to report that he was found dead in his Jeep this morning."

Her hands flew to her mouth. "Oh god, no."

Jackson gave her a minute. As the spouse, she was automatically their primary suspect, but her surprise seemed genuine. He walked a fine line in this situation and even had to be careful about how much he told her. Sierra cried for minute, shoulders shaking, then abruptly looked up. "Was it an overdose?"

Jackson jotted a quick note. "Was Rafel a drug addict?"

"No, but he drank too much sometimes after taking his pain pills. Tell me what happened."

"He was attacked in his vehicle in the parking lot of Pete's Pad."

Sierra looked confused. "Attacked how?"

The wife was either a skilled liar or she really didn't know how her husband had died. But he couldn't give her the details yet. He had to hold back to see if she would reveal information only the killer would know. "He was killed with a knife."

She sucked in her breath. "But why?"

"We don't know yet. We'd like to go through Rafel's personal items and see if we can learn anything that will help us."

"What do you mean?"

"We want to look at his computer and check through his drawers for a journal or appointment book, for example."

Sierra pulled her shoulders back. "That seems so invasive. I don't think so." She shook her head. "This is all too sudden."

"Then we'll get a warrant. Excuse me." Jackson sent a text to Evans and Schak, updating them to get the paperwork. He looked up and caught Sierra's eyes. "Why didn't you report your husband missing when he failed to come home last night?"

"I didn't know anything was wrong."

"He often stayed out all night?"

"No." Sierra started to cry again.

Watching family members grieve was the toughest part of his job. It made him feel like a callous voyeur.

"He was gone for so long," she said between sobs. "Ten

months in Afghanistan, then four months in the Madigan Army Medical Center. And now he's gone for good."

Jackson steeled himself against her pain, starting to think she might not be their suspect.

"Can you give me a minute, please?" she begged. "Alone?"

If she was innocent, her request was completely reasonable. If she'd killed her husband, a minute alone would give her time to destroy files, warn others, or hide evidence. He glanced around her cluttered office as she sobbed. Finally, he said, "I'll be right outside."

He left the door ajar and stepped out of her line of sight. Across the hall, an open door revealed an examining room, and Jackson glanced in. Not being a pet owner, he'd never been inside a veterinary clinic. It looked much like a doctor's workspace, only the table was stainless steel. The metal counter was lined with a similar assortment of gauze, steel instruments, and syringes. A tingle shot up his neck. He slipped into the room and took a quick look at the two syringes lying there. Long and thin with blue stoppers, like the one from the crime scene. He pulled his camera from his carryall bag and took close-up photos. The pictures would help him get a subpoena to confiscate a few syringes for comparison.

Jackson hurried back across the hall into Sierra Kent's office. She was on her cell phone, whispering, her tears gone. When she saw him, she abruptly cut off the call.

"I have to ask you some important questions." Jackson stayed on his feet to be intimidating. Sierra was a high-priority suspect now.

"Can it wait? I need to call Rafel's family."

"No, it can't. Please put down the phone."

She started to argue, then relented.

Jackson wanted to take her into the interrogation room at the department, but he suspected she wouldn't go without being cuffed and dragged. With his luck, the receptionist would take a picture with her cell phone and post it online, and the department would take a public beating for abusing a grieving widow.

"What did you and Rafel fight about at the tavern last night?"

"It was nothing." Her face hardened, a little beauty slipping away.

"You arrived at the tavern after he did. Did you know he was there?"

"Of course. He called me and asked me to come down."

"When was that?"

"Around eight-thirty."

"Is the call in your cell phone?"

"Yes. I can show you, if it's important." She scrolled through her data, looking for the call.

"What did he say?"

"He said he missed me, but he sounded drunk and depressed."

"Was that normal behavior for him?"

A sob burst from her throat. "I don't know. Since he came back from Afghanistan, he's been different. Angry, depressed, suspicious."

Jackson sat down and softened his tone. "Was he getting counseling?"

"He went a few times to make me happy, but he hated it."

"Were you cheating on him?"

Her frosty-blue eyes sparked with anger. "I resent that."

"Tell me what you fought about."

She sighed. "He accused me of cheating. He'd become

obsessed with the idea." She met Jackson's eyes. "Rafel was paranoid. The war changed him."

Jackson thought the war changed everyone who went over. "Where did you go when you left the tavern?"

"I stopped to see a friend, then went home."

"What friend?"

"Madison Riley. She works in another bar."

"What bar and what time did you get home?"

"Game Day, over on Highway 99. I left at ten-thirty and got home around eleven."

*Plenty of time to kill her husband.* "I'd like you to come down to the department and make a statement."

"What do you mean?"

"We'll record your version of events for clarity."

"You think I knifed my husband?" Her hands clenched into fists. "Don't waste your time with me. Get out of here and find the real killer."

"I can't do that without your help." Jackson leaned forward, earnest. "I need to know more about your husband's life. Tell me who his friends are and who he'd spent time with lately."

"I want to see him first."

"He'll be in the morgue later. You can call the medical examiner and arrange it."

She bit a trembling lip. "He has two close friends, Jake Pittman and Cody Sawyer. They've known each other since grade school. Rafel also has some army buddies he gets emails from, but they don't live here."

Jackson jotted down the names. "Has anyone new come into his life recently?"

"Not that I know of."

"Have his finances changed?"

A hesitation. "I don't know. We kept our money separate." She suddenly sucked in a quick breath. "Oh no."

"What is it?"

"Adam. Rafel's son." Her eyes signaled panic.

Jackson realized there was more to the situation. "Is he your child as well?"

"No. He's from Rafel's first marriage, but he lives with us."

"Where's his mother?"

"She's dead."

That piqued his curiosity, but the details could wait. "How old is Adam and where is he now?"

"He's eight and in school." Sierra glanced at the clock on the wall. "He'll be home soon on the bus, and I'll have to tell him." She looked distressed.

"I'll be there with you if it helps."

Sierra closed her eyes and tears rolled down her cheeks. "What am I going to do now?"

## Chapter 5

As a civilian, Lara Evans loved River Road because, unlike the new cookie-cutter subdivisions, many of the homes here were distinctive, with large lush lots. As a police officer, she hated the area because parts of it were in her jurisdiction and other parts were considered county, and it was difficult to keep straight. Houses sitting right next to each other could be under different law enforcement.

She finally located Mazari's address on Santa Rosa and parked at the end of the driveway, wondering how long she'd have to wait for Schak to get the paperwork. She studied the home to see if it would tell her anything about the occupants. The first thing she noticed was a skateboard on the front porch, making her wince. The victim had a kid. She didn't feel compelled to have any of her own, but she had a soft spot for all the poor children whose parents ended up in trouble . . . or dead.

The house—painted lavender with an overgrown perennial garden for a front lawn—was unusual, even in this area. Had she not known, Evans would have bet her paycheck a military man did not live there. So much for stereotypes. It made her wonder about his wife though. Evans climbed out of her city-issued Impala and took photos of the house. Feeling pumped, she decided to take a quick look around. What could it hurt?

The path to the front door was a series of rough-cut stone steps, embedded in ornamental moss, surrounded by tangled vegetation. If Mazari and his wife were homeowners, they weren't trying to keep up with the neighbors. The front porch held a stack of empty ceramic planters, a stool made from a tree stump, and the skateboard she'd noticed earlier. Just as she spotted some muddy dog prints on the gray concrete, loud barking began. A dog was in the house. Great. She'd check around back.

Evans found a path in the vegetation that led around the side of the house. She reached over the short gate and let herself into the backyard, moving cautiously in case the dog was free to come and go from the house. The barking stayed inside, so she took a few more steps along a sawdust path, then stopped and stared. The oversized yard had been turned into a miniature farm. Chickens roamed freely from the coop in the back corner and a thirty-foot greenhouse took up half the property. A dog run occupied a fair amount of space as well, and three beehives sat in a patch of clover. Evans steered clear of the hives and scanned the area directly behind the house. A huge woodpile sat on one side of a narrow wooden deck, and a small generator was on the other.

*Were they survivalists?* These people looked like they wanted to sustain themselves in case everything went to hell and they had to live off the grid. She'd bet they had a stockpile of weapons too. Seeing nothing potentially connected to the murder, Evans left the surreal backyard and trotted to her car.

She checked her cell phone to see if Schak had called or sent a message about the search warrant. Since he hadn't, she walked next door to a neighbor, where she saw a PT Cruiser in the driveway. Might as well start gathering information. She knocked on the door and was pleased when it opened seconds later. The cranky-looking middle-aged man was not who she expected.

"Detective Evans with the Eugene Police. I'd like to ask some questions about your neighbors."

"The loud ones in the purple house?"

Lara suppressed a smile. "Yes. Can I come in?"

"For a few minutes. My granddaughter will be home from school soon, and it's our time together."

"What's your name?" Evans asked, as they sat down on padded dining room chairs.

"Sam Regal." He seemed rigid, his thick torso straining the buttons on his Levi work shirt.

"You said your neighbors were loud. What kind of loud?"

"They argue a lot. Is that why you're here? To investigate the noise complaints?"

"It's more serious than that. Do you know what they argue about?"

"Money mostly. And the kid. I don't think the stepmother likes him very much."

Evans took notes as quickly as she could. "Did you ever see them strike each other?"

The man pursed his lips and shook his head. "No, but I wouldn't be surprised by it."

"What kind of car does the wife drive?"

"A green Jetta. Why?"

"What time did she come home last night?"

"I have no idea. I was watching the game."

Lara had no idea what game. "Did you know Rafel or ever talk to him?"

"Not really. He deployed about six months after they

moved in, then he was gone for a year."

"How long has he been back?"

"About six months. It's been rough for him."

"How so?" Evans could imagine, but she needed specifics.

"He once told me he worried he'd never find a job or work again. He seemed depressed."

"Do you know any reason someone might want him dead?"

The neighbor looked startled. "No. Is he dead?"

"He was killed last night. Was anyone here while you watched the game?"

"Of course. My daughter and my granddaughter. Why?" He pushed up from his chair.

The move unnerved her, and Lara jumped up too. Her right hand came up reflexively, ready to reach for her weapon. He grabbed the back of his chair and she relaxed. "I'm just doing my job. We have to question everyone connected to the victim."

"I understand but I can't help you. I didn't know them that well. I'd like you to go now before my little girl gets home."

"Thanks for your time." Evans gave him a business card. "Call me if you think of anything that might help us solve this crime."

As she headed for the door, he called out, "Wait."

Evans turned back. "Yes?"

"Two weeks ago, on a Saturday I think, they were fighting. I heard his wife threaten to kill him."

Lara's pulse quickened. "What exactly did she say?"

"They were getting into her car and yelling back and forth. She said something about how worthless he was. Then he said something I didn't understand. She screamed, 'I should kill you myself!' Then she slammed the car door and they drove off."

Lara walked away with mixed feelings. Finding a solid suspect early in an investigation meant they'd likely get a conviction, but it also meant the chase was over and the tedious case building would begin.

## Chapter 6

Jackson arranged to meet Sierra Kent at her home, noticing he thought of her as Sierra, instead of Kent, the way he referred to male suspects. Even female co-workers got last-name treatment. Depersonalizing was how they made their job bearable at times. It was Sierra's beautiful face, he realized, and he knew he had to get past the distraction.

He jotted down the license plate of her Jetta as she left the parking lot, torn between following her home to make sure she arrived and taking a quick detour to the crime lab to drop off the syringe for dusting. He still needed Sierra's prints for comparison, and unless she'd been arrested, he would likely need a court order to get them.

On instinct, Jackson climbed in his cruiser and followed the Jetta. Her refusal to let them search her husband's possessions made him distrust her. And the fact that she hadn't thought about her stepson until late in the conversation also made him wonder what kind of mother she was. Yet she volunteered her free time to treat the pets of homeless people. Killer or not, Sierra Kent was an unusual woman

Two unmarked blue sedans took up the space in front of the house on Santa Rosa, and the green Jetta was in the driveway. A patrol unit would arrive soon for backup.

Jackson parked in front of the well-kept home next door and walked over. Evans, Schak, and Sierra were on the front porch, engaged in a heated debate. As Jackson hurried up the slick stones, he realized only Sierra was being loud.

Schak, warrant envelope in hand, patiently explained his position. "Time is critical to solving this murder. The killer already has a twelve-hour head start."

"Twenty minutes," Sierra pleaded. "I just want you to wait in your cars until Adam comes home and I have a chance to tell him what happened. He'll freak out if he walks in the house and sees cops searching through his dad's things."

As Jackson neared the group, a dog started barking. *Crap.*

Evans asked over the noise, "Do you have weapons in the home?"

Jackson tensed again. Evans didn't ask idle questions.

Sierra stiffened. "A few. What difference does it make?"

Jackson cut in. "Ms. Kent, we appreciate your concern for the boy's feelings, but we have to proceed with our investigation. We'll stay out of the living room until you've had a chance to talk to Adam. Open the door."

She didn't move.

"It will look even worse to the boy if you're handcuffed and locked in the back of a patrol car." Jackson didn't enjoy threatening people, but he had to treat this woman more like a suspect. If she was only a grieving widow, he would have to live with this decision.

"This is my mother's property. She'll sue you."

Nobody responded. They'd heard the threat every day as patrol cops and still heard it all the time from suspects.

"We have a warrant. Open the door and get control of the dog." Jackson raised his voice. Gorgeous or not, Sierra Kent was a pain in the ass.

"Heartless bastards!" She spun toward the door.

Jackson followed his teammates inside, inhaling the acidic aroma of recently canned tomatoes. The small house had pale yellow walls, threadbare puke-green carpeting, and a barking black Lab. Sierra kneeled, grabbed the dog by the collar, and tried to soothe the whimpering animal.

"Where is Rafel's computer?" Jackson asked.

"We share one, and it's in the dining room." She pointed at the small area separating the living room from the kitchen. Next to a small table stacked high with newspapers, canning jars, and baskets of vegetables stood a cluttered computer desk.

Jackson looked over at Schak, who nodded and sat down in front of the monitor. His partner, who hadn't used a computer until the department issued him one at the age of thirty-five, had become quite proficient at finding hidden personal files.

"Show me where his clothes and personal items are."

"Let me put Kiesha in her dog run first. You're upsetting her. She can tell you hate dogs."

Jackson only nodded. He didn't hate dogs, he just didn't trust them. He'd nearly lost his left eye to a dog and hadn't made the mistake of getting that close again.

As Sierra took the dog out the sliding glass door, Jackson turned to Evans. "What made you ask about weapons?"

"I think they're survivalists. They've got a mini-farm and a generator out back. Plus, the victim is military."

"Good call. I don't trust the wife. She may be connected to the syringe from the crime scene. Let's pick up the weapons as evidence. I don't want her to have access to them." He moved toward Schak. "Is the warrant specific about confiscating personal items?"

"I wrote it broadly and Judge Cranston signed it, so I think we're good." Schak held out the warrant.

Jackson took the envelope, but stuffed it in his shoulder bag. "I trust you."

Kent came back in and Jackson said, "We want to see the weapons. We'll take them to the lab for documentation."

"This is bullshit. My husband was murdered! He's a victim and you're treating us both like criminals."

Jackson didn't blame her for feeling that way, but he had to follow procedure. He noticed Schak staring at Sierra instead of the computer. Her face was a work of art and hard to turn away from. "I'm sorry," Jackson said, meaning it. "This is just procedure. Everything will be returned eventually, even the guns, as long as they're registered."

She glared, then marched down the short hallway to a bedroom in the back. A huge steel gun safe took up a corner of the room, contrasting sharply with the colorful patchwork quilt on the bed. Sierra pulled a key from a fake candle and opened the safe. "If Rafel wasn't shot with a gun, I don't see how his gun collection is evidence."

Jackson understood her point, but he wasn't backing down. He didn't want their prime suspect to have access to weapons. "Everything is evidence until we rule it out. Everyone is a suspect until we rule them out. Please wait in the living room while we conduct our search."

"As soon as Adam arrives, I'm taking him to his aunt's house. I don't want him to be here for this."

"I understand. Tell me her name, address, and connection to Rafel."

"Sasha Altman. She's Rafel's sister. She lives on Blackfoot, but I can't think of the exact address right now." Sierra seemed near tears again.

Jackson reminded himself she could be a victim too. "Take some time to inform your family, but please keep yourself available to us for further questioning." He'd have the patrol officer follow her until he was confident she wasn't planning to leave town.

Sierra reluctantly left the room. Evans, who'd pulled on gloves during the exchange, yanked open a nightstand drawer and withdrew a large silver handgun. It looked like a Glock. "They do like to be prepared," She commented. "Not that I blame them."

Jackson heard a school bus brake on the street outside. "Bag and tag all of it," he said. "I want to get a look at the kid before she whisks him away."

He hurried up the hall, grateful he wouldn't be the one to tell the young boy his dad had been killed. Jackson's own parents had been murdered when he was thirty, and he'd never forget the look on the face of the sergeant who'd had to break the news. This would be the worst day of Adam Mazari's life.

Sierra rushed outside to intercept the boy on the sidewalk. Jackson would have liked to overhear their conversation, but he watched out the window and left them their privacy. Had he been insensitive? Too insistent on searching the home ASAP?

The boy was small for his age and had light-brown hair over a round face. He must take after his biological mother, Jackson thought, because he sure didn't look like Rafel Mazari. He hoped they would solve the case without having to question the child. Mazari's death in a tavern parking lot, rather than his home, meant his son probably didn't have any relevant information, but Jackson couldn't rule it out.

Sierra put Adam in her car, quickly packed an overnight

bag for the boy, then left without speaking. He noticed she didn't pack a bag for herself. There was so much more he needed to ask her.

After sending the patrol officer to follow Sierra, Jackson and Evans each made several trips to his car, carrying an assortment of hunting rifles, automatic weapons, and an antique revolver. They also bagged twelve knives, nunchuks, and a set of brass knuckles.

"Holy crap," Schak said, as Jackson walked past him for the third time. "Was he expecting the war to come to him?"

"Maybe. It happens sometimes with combat troops." Jackson paused. "Find anything interesting?"

"Not yet. This computer has been scrubbed. As in, no history of internet use. Williams might be able to retrieve the data, but I can't."

"Any personal files? Letters? Bank statements?"

"Sierra has files relating to animal medicine, PDFs with organic farming information, and emails from her mother, but Rafel doesn't have anything."

"That's odd."

"It's almost like he knew something was going down and deleted his personal stuff." Schak pivoted to face Jackson. "What do you think of the wife?"

"A little cold and a little defensive. If she's the killer, she's stopped bothering to put on a phony show for us."

"Stunning to look at too, but those dreadlocks are freaky."

"They are."

Jackson took the last two rifles and locked them in the backseat of his car. Next, he and Evans searched every inch of the master bedroom, trying not to leave a mess. Evans found a vibrator in a zipped case in one of the dressers, but nothing related to the murder. The master bathroom proved more fruitful. The top shelf of the medicine cabinet was lined with pill bottles, all prescribed to Rafel Mazari: Oxycontin, Xanex, Klonopin, Zoloft, Neomycin, and Flexiril. Jackson recognized them as mostly pain pills and mood stabilizers. He searched the small trash next to the toilet, hoping to find an empty syringe, but instead came up with several small bloody bandages. He bagged and tagged one in case it contained relevant DNA, then changed his gloves, stuffing the old pair back in his bag.

He conducted a cursory search of the boy's room, while Evans dug through the closet at the end of the hall. He crossed to the third bedroom and found it locked. "Crap."

"What's wrong?" Evans trotted toward him.

"This room is locked, which means I really want to know what's in there."

"No problem." Evans grabbed her carryall, which she'd left on the floor in the hall, and came up with a lock pick.

As she worked the mechanism, Jackson joked, "Did you learn that in juvie?"

"I wasn't in long enough." Evans laughed in an odd way, and Jackson realized he'd hit a nerve. She popped the lock, opened the door, and grinned. "One of my snitches taught me the skill in exchange for a pass on a pot possession charge."

They looked into the room and said in unison, "Holy shit."

Only a narrow path separated the ceiling-high stacks of boxes and crates. Factory food labels were obvious on many of the containers, but others were taped closed and labeled with a black marker: *Medicine, Reference Books, Blankets, Coffee, Batteries.*

"They're prepared for the apocalypse," Evans said, no humor implied.

"Let's open a few to be sure the contents match the

labels."

Jackson reached for a cardboard container marked *Medicine*. He set it on the floor, and Evans handed him a utility knife.

"You must have been a hell of a Girl Scout."

"Nope. Just a child of alcoholics."

Jackson wondered if his own daughter felt the need for that level of preparedness. He squatted, cut open the box, and found it stuffed with bandages, rubbing alcohol, antibacterial ointment, aspirin, and a hefty supply of Vicodin. He glanced up at Evans. "We may end up opening every one of these, but not today. Let's move the boxes away from the closet and see what's in there."

They worked together for five minutes, clearing a path to the bedroom closet. Every time Evans squatted to pick up a box, Jackson noticed her small tight butt. Sweat broke out under his arms as he moved cases of canned beans.

Schak came in to see what the commotion was about. "What the hell?"

"Survivalists," Evans said. "They're probably preparing for social breakdown. Or maybe just extreme weather."

Jackson moved the last case of chili con carne and pulled open the closet doors. Inside sat a dark trunk with a musty, faintly familiar smell. A trickle of fear ran through his chest. Gently, he pushed open the lid and leaned forward for a closer look.

*Oh god.* He turned to Schak in the hall. "Call the bomb squad, please."

# Chapter 7

*Friday, Nov. 11, noon*

Michael Quince walked through Northwest Federal to a small office in the back. The bank's internal investigator stood, introduced himself, and shook Quince's hand. The man's flush-red cheeks made him look uncomfortable, even though his voice was confident.

"Detective Michael Quince, Eugene Police." He still got a kick out of saying that, even after five years at that rank. A decade ago, he'd started as a dispatcher with the department, thinking it might be more interesting than factory work. If someone then had told him he'd end up a detective, he would have asked what they were smoking.

The two men sat down and Quince got right to the point. "We seem to have a tragic case of fraud, and as you know, cyber thieves disappear quickly. I'd like to access Molly Pershing's records and begin an investigation immediately."

"Because Mrs. Pershing dead, I can give you the relevant information. But her daughter is also on the account, so for extensive records, I'll need a subpoena."

"Fair enough. For starters, I need to know where the money went."

After a moment of clicking through files on his computer, the bank investigator said, "It was transferred to an account in an online bank called American Heritage. To a business account with the name Veterans Relief Fund. It was her second transfer to that account."

Quince wanted to get out his Netbook and google the name, but it could wait a few minutes. "How much was the first transfer?"

"Fifty dollars."

"And today's transfer?"

"Seven thousand."

Quince made a whistling sound. "Wow. How was the transfer made?"

"Molly set up an automatic monthly payment, initially in the amount of $50." The banker paused as he scanned a file on his computer. "The amount was changed late Tuesday night, and the $7,000 transfer went through on Wednesday. If we'd had more time, we would have caught it and notified her."

"Will you give me a printout of those transactions?"

"Sure." The banker clicked a few keys. "What can I do to help the investigation?"

"Type up a statement summarizing what you just told me. I'll need it to get a subpoena to access the data from the perpetrator's account."

An hour later, Quince sat on a bench outside Judge Marlee Volcansek's office, waiting for her to take a break from court. Netbook in his lap, he keyed in *Veterans Relief Fund* and a website came up. Surprised the perp hadn't taken down the site yet, or at least renamed it, Quince clicked through its simple pages. The website hosted photos of injured soldiers and appealed to people's sympathy. It asked for donations and offered three ways to send money: through PayPal, by setting up an automatic monthly donation, or by mailing a check to a post office box. He determined the internet protocol address, then logged into the American Registry of Internet Addresses. He clicked *whois* and keyed in the IP address for the charity site. While he waited for the search to complete, he crossed his fingers and hoped the website was hosted by a legitimate company he could subpoena for information about the site's owner.

Nothing came up. The site wasn't hosted in North America. Quince swore under his breath, then looked around the wide courthouse hall to see if anyone had heard him. If the website had free hosting from a provider out of China or Russia, he had no chance of tracking the owner. He keyed in the IP address again to make sure he hadn't typed it wrong. This time, the name Gorilla Social Services came up, and he heaved a sigh of relief. It was a new provider he hadn't heard of yet, but at least he could contact the company and ask them to release the name of the person who paid for the website service. It could be a ten-minute task or turn into a ten-day ordeal while he waited for callbacks, wrote a subpoena, and pressured them for a response.

He quickly found the host's contact information and made the call. An answering service picked up, which was not a good sign. Quince left a message, stressing the urgency of a callback. While he talked, he spotted the judge coming down the hall. Damn, she was good looking. Too bad about the ugly robe. He wondered when that silly tradition would go away. As the judge came near, he stood and smiled. "Can I have a minute of your time, Judge Volcansek? I have an important subpoena."

Back at his desk in the department, Quince called the online bank, American Heritage, got a manager on the phone, and explained what he needed and why.

"Fax me the subpoena," the banker said. "We're not releasing information about our client without it."

Quince got the fax number and wrote it down. "The two-page document will be there in a moment. Please call me right after you read the subpoena."

"I'm on my way to a meeting, and this is Friday afternoon. I appreciate the importance of your investigation, but you may not hear from me until Monday." The banker clicked off before Quince could press his case.

*Well, hell. That sucked.* Maybe the website hosting company would come through for him. For now, it was time to track down Molly's connections. Earlier in the bank, a patrol officer had found the dead woman's cell phone in her purse and called her daughter, so at least he didn't have to deal with that issue. But he needed to find out how the perp had come into contact with Molly and somehow accessed her banking information. What if there were other victims out there?

Quince pulled into Rosehill Estates, surprised by the number of cars in the parking lot. The senior community in south Eugene contained both independent apartments and an assisted living center, but he hadn't expected many of its residents to still be driving. Molly Pershing had lived here, and accessing her personal records was an important step in tracking what had happened to her money.

Cold rain plopped on his head as he jogged across the parking lot. His short hair offered little protection, but he rarely wore a hat. Too much to keep track of.

A receptionist led him to the director's office, where she barged in with only a knock and made a breathless introduction. "Mrs. Fowler, this is Michael Quince, a detective with the Eugene Police."

The director, a fifty-something woman, stood and shook his hand. "What can I do for you?"

"I'm sorry to inform you that one of your residents, Molly Pershing, died of a heart attack this morning."

"Oh no." The director's face fell and she sat back down. "Molly was so sweet. We'll miss her dearly."

"I have more bad news. She was the victim of fraud, and that's why she had the heart attack."

"Oh that's terrible. What kind of fraud?"

"I'm still investigating and I need to look through Molly's personal documents and computer, if she has one."

The director hesitated. "I should contact her daughter. She's listed as Molly's next of kin, and I think I need her permission."

"Another officer called her this morning, so she already knows what happened."

She looked relieved. "That's good. I've notified a lot of families about the death of their loved ones. It never gets easier."

"I tried contacting the daughter about entering Molly's apartment but she's not answering her phone. It would help my investigation if I didn't have to wait. Other residents may be at risk or have already been conned."

"That concerns me," the director responded, "but privacy issues are so important these days. We have to wait until we hear from Molly's daughter."

Frustrated, Quince said, "Will you at least send out an announcement to everyone in the facility? If anyone has had dealings with the Veterans Relief Fund, I'd like them to contact me." Quince handed her a business card. "Or if they have information about how Molly came into contact with the fraudulent charity, I'd like to hear it."

"I'll print up a notice and have our volunteer deliver it this evening."

"Any ideas how Molly met the con man?"

"She spent a lot of time at the library and at the Hartford Senior Center, but if she had guests in her home, I didn't know about it."

"I'll check out the senior center." Quince stood. "They took $7,000 from Molly. I suspect they'll close out their account and disappear if we don't act quickly."

"I'll get the memo out now."

"Call me the minute you have any information." Quince thanked her and left. In the lobby, he checked his cell phone for email messages. Jackson had notified him of a task force meeting at six. He still had some time.

"Mr. Quince," the director called out, as he headed for the main door.

He turned around.

"Molly's daughter says to do everything you can to catch the bastard."

## Chapter 8

In the forty minutes it took the Explosives Disposal Unit to arrive, Jackson's team searched every drawer, cupboard, and dark space in the house and the garage, which held mostly tools and more food supplies. They'd debated the merits and risks of staying in the house and continuing their search, then decided to proceed. Knowing the dynamite and blasting caps were in the back closet made them all a little jittery, but the family had lived in the home with the knowledge, so the fear was mostly psychological.

As long as nothing dramatic—like an earthquake or a falling tree—occurred while they were inside, they rationalized it would be fine. Once the EDU arrived, the experts would evacuate not only the house, but likely the neighbors as well, while they moved the explosives into the containment unit for transfer and disposal. So Jackson and his team made the most of the few minutes they had, gathering up personal papers, the family computer, and most of the knives in the kitchen for comparison to the victim's wound.

Finding nothing else of significance in the house, Jackson headed out the sliding door to see what surprises awaited outside. The black Lab began barking excitedly, but it was penned in a long run parallel to the greenhouse, so Jackson ignored the raucous sound. Evans hadn't exaggerated the mini-farm setup. He even spotted a goat under a tree near the back fence. The side-by-side sheds on the left were what interested him. One was padlocked, so Jackson opened the other and found it full of split wood. He paused in front of the second green metal building. Bashing in the door wouldn't be wise, considering what they'd found in the closet. Long-handled metal cutters would do the job, but he didn't carry those in his car. The bomb squad would have to handle it. He hoped the shed held only power tools. Why had they kept the explosives in the house? Fear of them being stolen? Or fear of that fir tree falling on the shed and setting off an explosion that might take out the back of the house?

He heard Schak yell from the back door, "You gotta come see this."

Jackson hurried inside, wondering what new oddity they'd found.

The coat closet in the living room was open, and the access to the crawl space under the house had been exposed. Schak handed him a flashlight. "Take a peek."

Jackson kneeled and leaned his head down into the cool damp air, praying he wouldn't have to crawl under the house and retrieve whatever it was. The beam of the flashlight showed dozens of small wooden barrels sitting in the spaces between the foundation supports under the house. Mingled with the wet dirt smell was the rich aroma of aged whiskey. His body relaxed and he rocked back.

"Why take on the apocalypse without a good buzz?" he joked. "They seem to have thought of everything."

"What the hell do you suppose the dynamite was for?" Schak asked, scratching his nearly buzzed head.

"Blowing up bridges to keep outsiders from entering the county." Jackson stood and stepped away from the closet.

He'd been hearing rumors of such plans for decades but had never seen proof of it before now. They wouldn't know for sure what these people had in mind until they questioned Sierra Kent again. Why hadn't she warned them? He'd bet money the ice goddess knew about the explosives.

Evans walked up and Jackson figured it was a good time to plan their next moves. "Once we leave here, we need to split up and cover as much ground as we can." He looked at Schak. "I need you to find Prez, the transient who had his camp behind the parking lot. I have two patrol officers looking as well, so connect with them first. We need to know if Prez saw anything. Bribe him with food and be gentle."

Schak laughed. "You know I'm good with the subcultures."

"Must be all that sensitivity training."

"What's my assignment?" Evans asked, sounding eager.

"Locate and question Cody Sawyer. He's one of the victim's friends who was at the tavern last night and apparently hangs out with Mazari on a regular basis. Bring him in if you have to. This wasn't a random act of violence, and someone knows what happened and why."

"I'm on it."

Jackson nodded. "I'll track down and question Jake Pittman, the other friend who was drinking with the victim. We'll meet back at the department at six and start the whiteboard. After that, we'll head to the tavern to question everyone who was there last night."

"What about the wife?"

"I've got a patrol officer following her, and the DA's office is writing a subpoena for her fingerprints." Jackson dug the syringe from his bag. "The animal clinic where she works uses this exact type, so I'm dropping it off at the crime lab to dust."

"You think she drugged him, then cut his throat?" Evans asked.

"It's the most likely scenario."

"Why a public parking lot?" Schak added.

"To throw us off and make it look like a transient or an angry drunk did it."

They heard the big EDU unit pull up outside, so they grabbed their carryall bags, stuffed full of small evidence containers, and headed outside. The overcast sky had started to drizzle, and Jackson considered grabbing his coat from his car. But the EDU sergeant and his team weren't wearing raingear over their steel chest plates, so the group of them stood on the sidewalk getting wet while Jackson briefed the bomb-squad leader on what he knew about the explosives, the whiskey kegs under the house, and the padlocked shed in the back. Around the perimeter, the EDU team was pounding on doors and told residents to leave the area, eliminating their chance to interview the neighbors that afternoon.

"After we transport the known devices, we'll search the property for more." The sergeant was ready for the detectives to leave so he could get a team member suited up and into the house.

"Be safe." Jackson turned to his task force. "Update me if you learn anything significant. Otherwise, I'll see you at six."


Jackson pulled into the crime lab, a two-story gray-brick building with no signs to identify it and no windows on the first floor. The size and newness of it looked out of place in an otherwise rundown area near the train tracks. The Eugene Police Department's facilities were spread out over the city's core, and driving from one place to another was a pain in the ass sometimes. The city had just bought a new building for their headquarters, which everyone was excited about, but it would need to undergo nearly a year of renovations and wouldn't resolve the spread-out issue.

He flashed his ID at the gate camera, parked in back, and climbed from the car. The door on the big processing bay was just closing down, and he caught a glimpse of the Jeep from the crime scene. The drizzle had become a steady downpour so he dashed for the building. As he reached the door, he realized he hadn't felt any pain when he ran—for the first time in nearly a year. The prednisone he'd been taking for months was finally working to suppress the fibrotic growth wrapped around his aorta from his heart to his pelvis. Retroperitoneal Fibrosis. He'd been diagnosed last spring, then flayed open like a fish to save his kidneys. His doctor had informed him he was lucky to still be functional. Others with the disease often ended up on dialysis or with colostomy bags. The thought of either fate filled him with dread and made him diligent about taking his meds, despite their side effects.

Inside the lab, he took the stairs up to the second floor and hurried to Jasmine Parker's office. The technician was just taking off her coat, and her long black hair was wet enough to stick to her back.

"Hey, Parker."

"Already? I just got in from the crime scene." She shook off like a wet dog and sat down.

"Why were you out there so long? Did something significant come up?"

"Not really. I spent some time searching the area, then the tow truck was two hours late."

"I saw the Jeep in the bay. Thanks for staying with it."

"It's my job."

Jackson sat on the edge of the chair, not planning to stay long, and put the evidence bag with the syringe on her desk. "Schak found this near the edge of the parking lot. It might just be an addict's trash, but the victim's wife works in an animal clinic and they use this type of syringe."

Parker reached for the little bag. "And you want me to log it in for you and dust it immediately?"

Technically, he should have left it in a locker downstairs, but the syringe was a priority. Jackson tried not to feel guilty. Forensic evidence in homicide cases always took precedence. "Knowing it actually has prints will help us get a subpoena for the wife's to compare."

"I'll do what I can."

"Thanks, Parker. When you have the prints, call Trang in the DA's office too. He's working on the subpoena."

"I will." A look of concern flashed across her stoic Asian features. "Are you okay, Jackson? You look tired."

He laughed. "I always look tired. But I feel better than I have in months."

Back downstairs, he and another technician carried in the weapons and noncritical evidence from his car. Schak had the victim's computer, and Jackson had Mazari's wallet and other personal items. They'd examine them more thoroughly after they questioned witnesses—which always came first.

After leaving the lab, Jackson took Delta Highway toward Springfield, their sister city, where Jake Pittman lived. Jackson had called him earlier and left a message, but hadn't heard back. He put in his earpiece and tried again. After two rings, a gruff male voice said, "Who is this?"

"Detective Jackson, Eugene Police. I need to talk to you

about your friend, Rafel Mazari."

"I just heard he was murdered, and I'm upset, so it's not a good time."

"I'm sorry for your loss, but this can't wait. You were one of the last people to see him alive, and I want to find his killer. Are you at home or at work?"

"I'm just leaving a job site. I can meet you at Terry's Diner on Centennial for a few minutes."

Jackson would have preferred to see the man's home, especially if he was anything like Mazari, but he didn't want to press the issue. Pittman seemed reluctant, maybe even a little hostile. Jackson started to ask how he would identify him, but he'd already hung up.

The diner was nearly empty at four in the afternoon, so finding the witness was easy. Besides two older women, the only other customer was a man of about thirty, sitting at a table near the front. Jackson approached him cautiously. If Pittman was the killer and liked weapons as much as his friend did, he could be dangerous. The man at the table wore jeans and a black sweatshirt, and his bearded face was streaked with dirt.

He stood as Jackson approached. "Jake Pittman." He didn't offer his hand.

Jackson introduced himself and gestured that they should sit. "I'm sorry for the loss of your friend. How long had you known Rafel Mazari?"

"Since fifth grade." Pittman looked past him over his shoulder.

He was either uncomfortable making eye contact with another male, or a liar, Jackson thought. "You went to school together here in Lane County?"

"Junction City." Pittman squeezed his hands together on the table.

"And you've stayed in touch with Rafel since then?

"Yep."

"Where do you work?"

"I'm a self-employed tree cutter and landscaper. I worked for Emerald's Yard Care for years, then got laid off during the recession."

"How's business?" Jackson kept it casual, hoping Pittman would relax.

"Slow."

"You drank with Rafel last night at Pete's Pad. What did you talk about?"

Pittman gave a small shrug. "The usual. Not finding jobs. Watching the game on Saturday. Nothing special."

"Rafel was unemployed?"

"Since he got back. Before he deployed, he worked at Universal Tires, but they don't need him now." Bitterness made his voice harsh.

"How did Rafel seem to you last night? Anything different from the usual?"

"He was pissed off." Pittman met his eyes for the first time. "He thought his wife was cheating on him."

"Did he say with who?"

"He didn't know, but he suspected it might be the vet she works for."

"When did he call Sierra and ask her to come down?"

"I don't know."

Jackson waited, but Pittman didn't add anything. "What happened when Sierra arrived?"

"Rafel asked her who she was screwing. She denied it and got mad. They started yelling at each other so I left."

"Did they fight a lot?"

"I don't know. Maybe."

"Did you spend time with the two of them together?"

"Not really."

"You don't like Sierra much, do you?"

He shrugged again. "She was okay until she cheated on him."

"But you don't know who she was seeing?"

"No." Pittman shifted in his seat.

Jackson thought he'd just been lied to. He made a mental note to follow up. "Did you suspect someone?"

"I don't know Sierra's people."

"How long had she and Rafel been married?"

"Two years. But he spent half that time in Afghanistan and the hospital."

"How did they meet?"

"He took his dog into the animal clinic where she works and fell hard." A flash of regret. Or maybe grief.

It was time to pin down the important details. "What time did you leave the bar?"

"I'm not sure. Maybe nine-thirty or so."

"Was Sierra still there?"

"Yes. She and Rafel were arguing."

"Where did you go after that?"

"Home. Why?"

"I'm just trying to establish where everyone was at the time of Rafel's death."

Pittman shook his head. "I was home with my wife."

"What's her name and number?"

"Hailey Pittman. But I want you to leave her out of this."

"The sooner I verify your alibi, the sooner I cross you off my suspect list."

"Fuck you." Pittman jumped to his feet. "Rafel was my best friend. I loved him like a brother."

"Then help me find his killer."

Pittman was already walking out, and Jackson let him go.

## Chapter 9

*Friday, Nov. 11, 3:48 p.m.*

After a couple of calls, Evans learned Cody Sawyer was living with his parents in South Eugene. She drove out Hilyard, past the ball fields, community pool, and jogging trail. Even in the rain, die-hard runners pounded down the sawdust path. She knew Jackson lived in the neighborhood to the left. Just thinking about him made her smile. Evans suddenly remembered that Jackson was supposed to be moving that weekend. She'd asked if he was moving in with Kera, and he'd said no and changed the subject. Her surge of joy at the news made her realize she wasn't over him. She'd been dating an Internal Affairs detective for a couple of months and really liked him, but she'd realized a while back that she *loved* Jackson. Maybe she always would.

Turning right on East 39th, she found an odd chunk of Dillard Road that was separate from the rest, and moments later, she located the Sawyers' address. Tall evergreens surrounded the two-story, cedar-plank house, and the roof was dotted with skylights that weren't doing much good among the trees. A stylish sixty-something woman with shoulder-length gray hair opened the door. She looked as if she'd been crying.

Evans introduced herself and asked to speak with Cody.

"Is this about Rafel?"

"Yes."

"I'm Susan Sawyer, Cody's mother. He's in his room. I'll go get him."

She came back, followed by a pretty-faced, wiry man who looked younger than his thirty years. His green eyes were bloodshot with spent tears.

Evans introduced herself again, and Sawyer responded with a handshake. His grip was weak, but he was grieving, so she tried not to judge him. "Let's sit down someplace private." She didn't want the mother hovering. If Sawyer still lived at home at thirty, his parents were probably overprotective.

He led her through a perfectly-appointed and unused living room into a den in the back of the house. The dark room had thick carpet, soft recliners, and a giant flat-screen TV.

Evans pulled up a footstool to sit on. "You heard the news about Rafel?"

Sawyer nodded. "Sierra called me."

"How long had you known Rafel?"

"Since grade school in Junction City."

"What about Sierra? Did know her well?"

He shook his head. "I only met Sierra after her and Rafel got together."

"How did they meet?"

"At the animal clinic where she works." He pulled in a deep breath. "Sierra said Rafel was killed with a knife. Do you have any idea why?"

"I was hoping you could tell me."

He shook his head. "No idea. Rafel didn't have a lot of friends, but the people he knew loved him."

"Did he have any enemies?"

"Not that I know of."

Time to jolt him. "What about the guy Sierra was cheating with?"

"What are you talking about?" His voice seemed surprised but his eyes didn't.

"Last night in the tavern, Rafel accused his wife of cheating. Did he ever talk about it with you?"

"I knew he was worried." Sawyer smiled a little. "Have you met Sierra? Guys come on to her all the time. It made Rafel a little paranoid."

"What about you? Did you come on to her?"

"No." His forehead furrowed with distress. "I have my own girlfriend."

"What time did you arrive at Pete's Pad last night?"

"Around a quarter to nine."

"What made you show up?"

"I figured Rafel and Jake were there, and I was bored."

"What time did you leave?"

"Around nine-thirty."

"Why such a short visit?"

"Rafel was being weird. Then Sierra showed up and they argued, so I left." He looked down, as if ashamed of his friends.

"What did they argue about?"

"The usual. Whether she was cheating. Rafel couldn't let go of the idea."

"Was she?"

"I don't think so, but I wouldn't know."

"Where were you between ten and eleven last night?"

Startled by the question, his voice squeaked. "Right here in this chair, watching a movie."

"What movie?"

"Inception. It's my favorite."

"Can anyone verify that?"

"My parents went to bed, but they knew I was home."

"Tell me about yourself, Cody. Where do you work? And why do you live at home at the age of thirty?" Evans knew it was blunt, but someone had to ask him.

His jaw tightened, and shame and anger flashed across his face.

"I was a successful real estate agent with Windemere. My dad wasn't happy with my career choice, but I owned a house and made good money. Then the housing market collapsed and I was let go." He leaned toward her, his voice rising in pitch. "I tried finding work as a waiter, which I'd done in college, but no one was hiring. I finally managed to sell my house at a loss, and I moved back in here because my parents couldn't stand to see me living in Jake's unheated garage."

Evans had a moment of guilt about prejudging him. "Sounds like it's been a rough couple of years."

"It was. But I landed a job at Royal Caribbean Cruise Lines a couple months ago. It's phone work and I hate it, but I've saved enough to get my own place soon."

Evans looked at her notes. "You said Rafel was being weird last night. What do you mean?"

"He hugged me, which he never does, then he seemed depressed. When Sierra came in, he got angry and paranoid. He was like that sometimes when he drank."

"Did Rafel take drugs?"

"No." Cody touched his chin and leaned back.

"I think you just lied to me." Evans softened her tone "He's dead and can't get into trouble. But if he used street drugs, then he had a dealer. And that might help explain who killed him."

"There is no dealer. He had a prescription for Oxycontin. I think he was taking a lot. He'd been losing weight."

"Who's his doctor?"

"Someone at the VA Clinic. Although he was getting physical therapy from a volunteer at a different clinic."

Mazari kept morphing in her mind—from a wounded veteran victim, to a crazy weapons-loving survivalist, now to a pain-riddled, pill-popping mental case. Had his friends known about the explosives? "Tell me about the dynamite."

"What?" Sawyer practically sputtered.

"The explosives Rafel and Sierra kept in their house. What were they for?"

"They kept explosives?" His expression changed from shocked to hurt.

Evans found it puzzling. "Why does that bother you?"

"I thought I knew Rafel."

"What about Sierra? Would she kill her husband?"

Another stunned look. "No. What a horrible thing to say."

"Is there anything else you'd like to tell me?"

"I don't know what it would be."

Evans gave him a business card. "I'll probably want to talk to you again, so stay available. In the meantime, call me if you think of anything important."

On her way out, Evans stopped to speak briefly with Mrs. Sawyer. She confirmed that her son had come home around ten, but admitted she'd gone to bed shortly after. She tried to convince Evans she would have heard if Cody left later, but Evans only nodded. Sleeping parents were easy to get past. She'd done it a dozen times as a teenager.

# Chapter 10

*Friday, Nov. 11, late afternoon*

Sophie Speranza caught sight of her editor coming toward her cubicle and reflexively tensed. He was either going to call her into his office and lay her off or give her an assignment she didn't want. The newspaper had been stable for a few months—not making money but not losing it either—and the small group that was left had started to hope they might survive.

"I've got a feature you're gonna love." Karl Hoogstad leaned against her half-cubicle wall.

*Yeah, right.* She hated the do-gooder stories he forced her to cover occasionally. She much preferred the crime stories and even the court proceedings, which could be batshit crazy sometimes. "I'm listening."

"An ex-National Guard soldier was found murdered this morning."

He had her attention now. "What's the story?"

Hoogstad looped his hands in his belt and rocked back on his heels. Short, lumpy, and balding, he was surprisingly confident. He continued, "The soldier was wounded in Afghanistan and received some kind of medal. Now he's the victim of a heinous crime. I want you to dig into this guy. Talk to everyone who knew him. There's an emotional and meaty feature here. I can feel it."

"I'm all over it." She couldn't help but be jacked about the assignment, and it made her feel guilty about her reaction to a tragic death. "How did you get the information so quickly?"

"A bartender I know gave me a call. The guy was killed in his vehicle in the parking lot of Pete's Pad last night."

"I'm intrigued. Thanks for letting me have this one." The assignment could have gone to several senior reporters instead.

"You'll dig harder. This is your kind of piece."

"What the guy's name?"

"Rafel Mazari."

Sophie jotted it down and spelled it back to make sure she had it right. "I'll get going on it right away and work through the weekend. Let's beat the TV people with this story."

"Get Brian if you need a photographer." Hoogstad gestured at her cube neighbor. "Where are you going to start?"

"I'll call my detective contact and see what I can find out."

"Good girl."

*Fucker.* He would have to ruin an otherwise pleasant exchange.

"I heard that," the City photographer said, popping up over their shared cubicle wall as the editor walked away. "It was so loud inside my brain, I worried you'd directed it at me."

"Be glad your mind is that open. I'm sure the sentiment bounced off Hoogstad. You heard the assignment?"

"I'm stoked. Will they let us get a photo of his corpse?"

"I doubt it." She shook her head. "I'm going to keep this tasteful."

He laughed. "There's always a first."

"Bite me."

Sophie turned her focus back to the domestic-shooting story, impatient to wrap it up and move on. The name Rafel Mazari was familiar to her. Where had she heard it? She wrote a few more sentences, and the information popped into her head. A woman she'd dated years ago had gone to school with Rafel and knew his first wife, who'd died in a freak car accident. That was the only reason Sophie remembered the name. Her girlfriend had talked about the accident for days, and another reporter on the paper had covered it. Sophie hit Save and closed the piece she was writing. It could wait.

She called Kim Bradley, the woman who'd known Rafel and his wife, and left her a message to call back. Sophie considered contacting Jasmine Parker, her current lover, who worked for the police department's crime lab, but she resisted. Jasmine's information was confidential, and her girlfriend resented when Sophie tried to pry out details. But every once in a while, Jaz volunteered a juicy nugget of information. Sophie decided to be patient, find out what she could, and not ask Jasmine unless she got desperate.

Instead, she called Detective Jackson, a senior investigator in the violent crimes unit who always got the best cases—the bizarre crime stories she liked to cover. Over the last year, they'd developed a half-assed working relationship. Sophie understood and accepted that he hated giving her information, but she almost always had something solid to offer in exchange. Jackson had come to accept that Sophie was a pretty damn good investigator too, and people often told her things they wouldn't tell a police officer. So now, he often returned her calls, and sometimes gave her exclusive on-the-record comments.

Jackson didn't answer—no surprise—so she left a message: "Hey, it's Sophie. I've been assigned to write a profile about Rafel Mazari's life, and I'd love to know more about his murder. Anything you're willing to share would be helpful, and of course, if I find anything interesting, I'll pass it along. Be in touch." He might not call her until he needed something, like a news archive search, but she'd keep trying. Their jobs were similar, but their goals were different. He wanted to keep the scoop all to himself, and she wanted to share it with the world.

She ran Rafel Mazari's name through the newspaper's digital archive. Two stories came up. One was about his unit returning from Afghanistan, and the other was a short piece about his ex-wife's accident, which had happened on Prairie Road, just south of Junction City. Sophie studied the photo—a pretty blond woman who looked fresh out of high school—then scanned the story:

*Friday morning, Joanna Mazari's life was as good as it gets. Married to her high school sweetheart, their son had started kindergarten and Joanna had landed a terrific job with an advertising agency.*

*But on her way to work, tragedy struck in the form of a wasp. Highly allergic, Mazari carried an EpiPen with her everywhere, according to her sister, Laura McKinsey. That morning when the yellow jacket in her car stung her in the upper arm, Mazari's body reacted instantly, swelling and cutting off her air supply.*

*Mazari managed to pull off Prairie Road, not far from her Junction City home, and dial 911. The paramedics arrived too late and found her dead of anaphylactic shock. They also found an epinephrine injector on the floor of her car.*

*Joanna Mazari is survived by her husband, Rafel Mazari,*

*28, a sergeant in the Oregon National Guard, her son, Adam Mazari, 5, her sister, Laura McKinsey, and her parents, Chester and Sue McKinsey of Seattle, Washington.*

A bizarre story and not well-written, Sophie thought, and it wouldn't add much to Rafel's feature, except to expand the idea that he'd experienced more than his share of grief and trauma in his short lifetime. Sophie found Rafel on Facebook, but his page was sparse, like someone who'd signed up, then forgot about it. He'd listed very little information about himself, except for his National Guard service and his favorite music—Coldplay and Nickelback—and he'd posted only once a week or so, usually a political comment about government excess. Rafel had also uploaded a collection of photos, most of his second wife, Sierra Kent. Gorgeous woman, Sophie noted, but the dreadlocks were a bit much. Sophie clicked through and found Sierra's Facebook page, which held more information. Sierra posted regularly about an interesting mix of subjects: caring for animals, nutrition, holistic health, and preparing for the end of civilization when all the resources ran out and everyone had to fend for themselves. A bit paranoid, Sophie thought, but maybe with good reason.

Before she had a chance to google Mazari's late wife, her phone rang. It was Kim Bradley, the woman she'd dated before falling half-assed in love with a male college professor. That disastrous relationship had taught Sophie to stay away from men. They weren't worth the great sex.

"Hey, Sophie," Kim said, "I was surprised to hear you're still at the paper. But I'm glad."

"And you're still not reading the paper or you would have seen my byline," Sophie teased.

"Busted." Kim laughed. "So why are you asking about Rafel and Joanna?"

"Rafel was murdered last night, and I'm working on a feature story about him."

"Oh my god. That's awful. Do you know who killed him?"

"Not yet. I'm looking for background stuff, people who knew him well and can give me some insight into who he was."

"If you want to hear the good stuff, talk to Rafel's sister, Sasha. If you want the dirt, talk to Joanna's sister, Laura. She thinks Rafel killed Joanna for cheating on him."

## Chapter 11

Jackson checked his watch: 5:05 p.m. He had just enough time to stop at the Sixth Street Grill and fulfill his obligation to meet his ex-wife's new boyfriend, then slip out before his task force meeting at six. They'd invited him and Katie to dinner weeks ago, and he'd reluctantly agreed. In theory, he wanted to be a reasonable, politically correct, divorced parent. In reality, he hated the idea. After scheduling the dinner, his house buyers had closed their loan two weeks early and offered him cash to let them move in right away. He'd obliged by stepping up his moving plans, only remembering his dinner engagement after it was too late. This would work out for the best, he decided. He'd get his social obligation out of the way without having to sit down for meal with a woman he no longer cared about and a man he didn't want to know.

He took the expressway toward Eugene, popped in his earpiece, and hit speed dial #1.

"Hey, Dad. How's the case going?"

"It's interesting, but still unsolved. How's the moving?"

"We finished around four, I gave the movers their check, and now we're getting ready to meet everyone for dinner."

"What do you mean *we?*"

"Me and Harlan. He's coming to dinner. It's only fair, since he helped us move all day."

"You and Harlan are at the new house by yourselves?" *Had Katie taken a shower with the boy in the house?* Jackson's heart missed a beat.

"Yeessss." She drew out the word in exaggeration. "We've been setting up the beds so we'd have somewhere to sleep tonight." She burst out in a nervous giggle. "I mean you and I. Harlan's going home after dinner."

Had he not been driving, Jackson would have closed his eyes in horror. "Today was an exception, but as a general rule, I don't want Harlan in the house when I'm not there."

"Got it. Are you coming to dinner?"

Jackson avoided a direct answer. "I'm headed to the restaurant now."

"Thank you. I'll see you soon."

Katie clicked off before he could offer to pick her up rather than have her ride with Harlan, a sixteen-year-old boy, the riskiest of all drivers. *Crap. You can't have it both ways,* a voice in his head chided. You can't treat her like an adult when it's convenient, then act like she's still a little girl when you're worried. Why not? he countered. It was a time-honored parental tradition.

Jackson found a parking spot in the tiny lot behind the restaurant. Renee had likely chosen the venue because it was a few blocks from police department headquarters. She also knew it was one of his favorites, and they'd eaten a few meals together here during their sixteen-year marriage. He hurried inside, glad it had stopped raining but worried about Katie and Harlan driving in the dark.

A few minutes early, he stepped into the lounge and spotted Renee and her date. A wave of apprehension rolled over him, like a body block from an invisible linebacker. If

Renee was drinking again, he wasn't staying. From a distance, he sized up Ivan Anderson: older, with salt-and-pepper hair and a thick body. No gut though. A nice face, Jackson had to admit, and a nice dresser too. The turtleneck was a little much, but what did he care? Renee looked the same as the last time he'd seen her. Dark curly hair, cut short, but skinnier than she'd ever been during their marriage. And still pretty, despite years of alcohol abuse—if you didn't look too closely.

He strode over to their high-topped cocktail table and tried to smile sincerely. But the glass of wine in front of Renee made him wince.

"Don't worry. It's nonalcoholic," She said, reading him.

Jackson was only semi-relieved. Beverages that looked and tasted like alcohol seemed like a bad idea for an alcoholic. Renee made introductions and Jackson shook Anderson's hand, pleased the man had a good grip.

"Should we go into the restaurant?" Renee asked. "Katie and Harlan will be here soon."

"Sure." He would wait until the last minute to announce he wasn't staying.

Once they were seated in the other half of the establishment, they chatted about Katie for a minute. But Jackson had little time and soon looked at Anderson. "What do you do for a living?"

"I'm an investment banker with Pierce and Waterson."

*So the guy had money.* Jackson hated him a little. "Sounds like a secure position."

"I've been with the company for six years." Anderson smiled. "I was in Denver before that. After my wife died, I moved out here to be close to my daughter."

Knowing the man had a child he was close to gave

Jackson a little peace of mind. "How old is your daughter?"

"Twenty-four. She graduated from the University of Oregon last year and got a job with KRSL news. Dakota Anderson. She's on at eleven. Maybe you've seen her."

"I think I have." Jackson hadn't, but he would now.

Katie and Harlan walked up, and Jackson breathed a sigh of relief. His daughter was safe and he could leave soon. He snuck a peek at this watch. Katie noticed but didn't say anything.

Renee asked about the move, and his daughter filled in the details.

"Your dad wasn't with you?" Renee scowled.

"I picked up a homicide case this morning." Jackson tried to sound casual, but he felt defensive.

"Your work must be fascinating, yet emotionally challenging," Anderson commented.

"That's exactly right." Jackson gave him points for schmooze, but he had to get out of there. "I have a task force meeting at six, so I have to run."

"That's typical," Renee said, rolling her eyes.

*And you'll be drinking again in three weeks*, Jackson thought. *Typical.*

He shook Anderson's hand, then decided he might as well be gracious and shook Harlan's too. "Thanks for your help today." He kissed Katie's cheek. "Have a good time at your mother's."

It was all he could do not to run from the restaurant.

Jackson drove the five blocks to City Hall, parked in the lot underneath the white brick building, and ordered Chinese food for his team. At least he wouldn't be eating in his car, which he often did, while driving to interview witnesses or get search warrants signed. He looked forward to the day he could submit the paperwork online, get a judge's electronic signature, print it and go.

Upstairs, department activity was winding down, as the day-shift patrol officers filed their reports, and the property crimes and vice detectives left for the day. He ran into Michael Quince as he entered the area where the violent crimes detectives had their desks crammed together in a too-cozy-for-comfort way. The wooden slats over the outside of the windows gave the room an eerie quality. He couldn't wait for the move to the new building.

"Hey, Quince. Glad you could make the meeting."

"Why not? I've had dinner at home every night this week. My wife was starting to get suspicious."

Jackson laughed. "I have to check my voicemail, then I'll meet you in the conference room. I ordered food."

At his desk, he sat long enough to see if a witness in a domestic-shooting case had called on his office line. She hadn't. No surprise. The sister had failed to report the abuse for years.

He checked his cell phone too and found a message from Sophie Speranza, asking for details about the homicide. How the hell did she know about it already? He suspected Sophie had a source in the department that gave her just enough information to send her in the right direction. But then, Eugene only had 140,000 people inside its borders, so word spread quickly among the key players.

He also had a message from Jackie Loomis, the department's new spokesperson, asking for a statement about the homicide. If Sophie already knew, then the TV stations would cover the story on their late-night news. Jackson called Loomis back and she picked up.

"Thanks for getting back to me. Media people are ringing my phone nonstop. What can I tell them?" She sounded frazzled, and he didn't envy her job.

"Rafel Mazari was found dead in the parking lot of Pete's Pad this morning. We believe he was killed some time late last night, but the cause of death has not been officially determined. We're looking for witnesses and you can give them my desk number."

"The reporters know about the victim's military service, and they're going to milk it for all they can. Anything we should add or detract from that?"

"Not yet. I have to go. Good luck." Jackson clicked off and hurried down the hall. He would have liked more time to organize his notes and figure out a game plan, but he'd made time for his daughter instead. He was happy with that decision. His relationship with his girlfriend worried him though. He'd call Kera after the meeting.

Schak and Evans were already in the small conference room. The city had finally given them a table, but the chairs were still cheap and uncomfortable.

"Sorry I'm late," Jackson said, sitting down. "To make my daughter happy, I had to meet my ex-wife's new boyfriend." He grimaced, surprised he'd shared that. Kera's openness must be rubbing off on him.

"Sweet." Schak grinned. "Next, you'll all be in counseling together."

"You're a good man." Evans leaned over and clapped him on the shoulder. "Now, what's for dinner?"

"Chinese food, but let's get something done before it arrives. Evans, will you take the board?" She had the best writing and the best sense of organization.

Evans jumped up and wrote the victim's name at the top

of the long, erasable board. "I'll make a column for each of the three people who were with him prior to the attack." She drew three lines down the board, then put names and tags on the four columns: *Rafel Mazari: victim, Sierra Kent: wife, Jake Pittman: friend, Cody Sawyer: friend.* Under the victim, she wrote: *TOD: 10–11 p.m.,* and under that, *National Guard, Afghanistan.*

Jackson turned to Schak. "Did you find the homeless guy?"

"No, but I have a good lead. Two people told me he shows up at the Dining Room every day and waits in line for it to open at three-thirty. He was gone by the time I got there today, but I'll try again tomorrow."

"Is that the free restaurant run by Food for Lane County?" Quince asked.

"Yep. A pain in the ass to the surrounding businesses." Schak's voice was matter-of-fact.

Jackson looked up at Evans. "What did you learn from Cody Sawyer?"

"He and Rafel went to grade school in Junction City together and have been friends ever since." Evans jotted brief notes in the last column. "Sawyer lives with his parents after a period of unemployment, but just started work at Royal Caribbean. He says he was home last night at ten. His mother supported the claim, but she went to sleep and can't swear he didn't go back out."

"Pittman says he was home with his wife, but I haven't had time to verify it," Jackson added.

"Mothers and wives," Schak scoffed. "No alibis at all, as far as I'm concerned."

"Would your wife lie for you?" Evans asked.

"Depends on how recently I'd pissed her off." Schak

grinned, enjoying his own humor.

Jackson wanted to get back on track. "Sierra says she stopped at another bar, then got home by eleven. I haven't verified her story yet either. That's my priority for the morning." Jackson paused, knowing he was missing something. "After the autopsy, that is."

"What else did the wife say?" Evans wanted to know.

"She said her husband had been moody and paranoid since he got back from Afghanistan and kept accusing her of cheating." Jackson checked his notes. "The boy is Mazari's child from a previous marriage, and his biological mother is dead."

"Do we know anything about that?" Quince spoke up for the first time.

"Not yet, but it's worth looking into." Jackson added *dead first wife* to his to-do list as Evans wrote it on the board. "Also, Pittman mentioned Mazari was unemployed, and he sounded bitter about it."

"Do you think it's a factor?" Evans looked back over her shoulder.

"I don't know. Let's brainstorm motive."

"We have the cheating issue." Evans made a narrow fifth column on the board. "If the wife had someone on the side, she could have killed Rafel to be free of her husband."

"Jealousy," Schak added. "Maybe Mazari was the cheater, and the jilted husband killed him. A slit throat looks like rage or revenge to me."

"We thought so too," Jackson said. "Women are known to kill with knives but not usually the throat. And there was no sign of a struggle."

"If he was drunk or passed out, he would have been an easy target for anyone." Schak gestured toward the board.

"Add *random violence.* We can't rule out the crazies who camp out in the trees on the other side of the canal."

"Homeless people aren't usually violent unless they're provoked," Jackson argued, but Evans was talking too.

"Mazari was taking Oxycontin and Vicodin, among other things." Evans wrote *Drugs* in the motive column. "He had prescriptions, but if he got addicted and needed more than his doctor was willing to give him, he may have gone to the street."

"Or escalated to a stronger drug." Jackson made a note. "Evans, will you track down his doctor tomorrow, see if he'll tell us anything?"

"What about money as a motive?" Quince asked. "I've been investigating the fraud all day, so it's on my mind. I see a pattern of unemployment and financial frustration with these guys." Quince was a floater. He'd worked sex crimes, financial crimes, and violent crimes, and had even trained with the bomb squad. Their captain wanted flexibility in the detective rank, in case one unit got overloaded or had too many officers out at the same time.

"How would that lead someone to kill Mazari?" Evans stared at Quince. "We need to see the victim's bank records."

Jackson was curious about the incident across the street that morning. "What happened over at the bank?"

Before Quince could respond, a young records clerk knocked on the door and stepped in. "Jade Palace delivered your food." She had two heavy plastic bags in each hand.

Schak moved to take them. "Thanks."

"No tip?" Deadpan tone.

They were silent for a moment, then Jackson reached for his wallet.

The clerk burst out laughing. "Kidding. I brought forks

and paper plates from the break room. Don't work too hard."

They dug into the food, passing it around and eating quickly, so they could get back to their discussion. When they had a case like this, it became an obsession, and they worked it like a geek with a Rubik's cube.

After a few minutes, Quince said, "An older woman, Molly Pershing, had a heart attack as she stood at the bank counter. She'd just learned her account had been cleaned out of $7,000. The money had been transferred to a charity called Veterans Relief Fund." He paused and wolfed half a spring roll. "Molly, or someone, had set up an automatic monthly payment of fifty dollars. After the first transfer, the amount was changed to $7,000 on Tuesday night, and the money went through Wednesday. I suspect the perp helped her set up the auto payment and learned her bank login and password. He or she then accessed Molly's account and changed the amount just before the next transfer. I've subpoenaed the charity's banking data, and I have a call in to the web hosting company, but I'm not optimistic about getting information before Monday."

"A fake veteran's charity? That's low." Schak shook his head in disgust.

"Until they stole the seven grand, they may not have done anything particularly illegal," Quince said. "Unless they violated Oregon's charitable institution laws."

"I wonder how many other seniors they conned." Jackson put down his fork and looked at Quince. "You're looking for the source of the marks?"

"I found it. Someone got a hold of a senior center email list and sent out a solicitation, asking for donations. I found the email on Molly Pershing's computer.

"Keep us posted on your case," Jackson said. "The

military angle intrigues me."

"You think there's a connection to the homicide?" Quince arched his thick eyebrows.

"I'm open to the idea. People kill for love, money, or fear."

Evans tapped the board. "Do we know what Mazari did for a living before he shipped out?"

"He worked for a tire store," Jackson said.

"Sawyer was a real estate agent who's now doing telephone service," Evans added. "What about Pittman? What does he do for a living?"

"He's a self-employed tree cutter and landscaper whose business is slow."

"None of these guys seem to possess the computer skills to pull something like that off." Evans took a sip of her coffee.

"It doesn't take much," Jackson argued. "Let's get back to the homicide."

"I like the wife for it," Schak said, dripping sweet-and-sour sauce on his white shirt.

"You just like the wife," Evans mocked. "She is stunning."

"I hate the dreads though." Schak shook his head. "They're a deal breaker. I couldn't do her."

"Dreads?" Quince hadn't met Sierra.

"Yep. A shame." Schak wiped at the sauce with a napkin. "Tall gorgeous blonde with big boobs and dreadlocks."

"Let's move on," Jackson cut in. He was with Schak on this one, but the discussion was off-limits with Evans present. "I dropped off the syringe at the lab, and Trang is writing a subpoena for Sierra's prints for comparison. The animal clinic where she works uses the same style of syringe, which is distinctly different from the ones passed out by the HIV alliance."

"See, it's the wife." Schak nodded, mockingly smug.

"And if we get a match?" Evans cut in. "What's the theory? She drugged him first?"

"It would explain the lack of struggle and the low blood flow." Jackson pushed his plate aside and glanced at his notes. "For tomorrow, Schak, you're still looking for Prez and any other parking-lot witnesses. Evans, dig up everything you can on the two friends. Quince, if you have time, get Mazari's bank records. I'll verify alibis and bring Sierra in for prints and extensive questioning. I want to know more about the explosives."

"What are you talking about?" Quince was still not up to date.

"We found dynamite and blasting caps in a closet in the victim's home. Along with a year's supply of food, medicine, and whisky. They were preparing for something."

"There's a group here in town that operates on that premise," Quince responded. "Paranoid hippies who call themselves Territory Defenders."

"Schak, if you have time, look into it, please." Jackson thought he'd covered everything. "After this, we'll head out to the tavern and question everyone. We need to pin down the exact times our four players left the premises."

"Now you're talking." Schak pushed aside his plate. "Ready when you are."

They each took their own car, with the idea they'd head home afterward. Jackson planned to return to the department for a while and get his notes organized, but he wanted to be home by midnight. He climbed in his car and sat for a moment. Where was home? His bungalow on Harris Street was empty and soon would be occupied by a strange young couple. His daughter was at her mother's, and his furniture—the bed he would sleep in soon—had been moved into the house he'd grown up in and co-owned with his brother Derrick. In some ways, the house would be familiar and comfortable, yet without his parents, it would never seem quite like home again. He didn't understand how Derrick had lived there all those years with all those memories. Jackson looked forward to fixing up the place and getting it sold. Then he and Derrick would both start fresh in their own places, hopefully with a little cushion of cash. Beyond that, he couldn't form a plan. He might just rent a place for a while and see what happened with Kera and her entourage.

He drove down Oak Street, pleased to see the rain had driven the transients and idle teenagers out of the downtown area, at least for a while. The only people on the sidewalks were couples headed for a night out at a theater or lounge. The city's core was making a slow, steady comeback, but the transients, druggies, and homeless teenagers still kept a lot of people away. The whole police department wished the city council would let them roust the loiterers the way they did in other cities. But not in *sensitive* Eugene. In fact, other states like Texas sometimes sent their mentally ill homeless people to Eugene with a one-way bus ticket.

His resentment made him feel like an old curmudgeon. Jackson turned right on West 11th and put in his earpiece. He called Kera but she didn't answer. Disappointed, he set his cell phone on the seat next to him, in case she saw the missed call and got right back to him.

After a short drive, he reached the tavern and again had to park in the lot next door. As he'd predicted, Pete's Pad was jam-packed. Every regular who'd caught the evening news had come out to the tavern tonight to gossip and grieve. The noise was overwhelming.

Evans was already in the mix, notepad in hand, questioning two mid-thirties women. He caught sight of Schak at the counter, talking to a middle-age man and sipping a beer. Jackson didn't blame him. They were working late, and Schak wasn't in uniform. The beer was also a prop to get people to open up. Most serious drinkers didn't trust nondrinkers.

Jackson headed for the other end of the counter to speak with Mila Kruz, the bartender he'd questioned that morning. He glanced at his notes, then hollered over the back of two men seated at the bar. "Hey, Mila, Detective Jackson again. You mentioned the names Zack and Nikki to me this morning as witnesses. Is either of them here now?"

"Zack's right here." She grinned at the gray-haired guy between them.

The man slowly turned. "What can I do for you?"

Missing an eye and part of an ear, the old guy was hard to look at. Jackson introduced himself, raising his voice above the din. "You were here last night between eight and eleven?"

"Every night."

"Did you know Rafel Mazari or talk to him last night?"

"He was a vet, like me. Damn shame what happened to him."

"I agree. And I need help finding his killer. Tell me about the argument you heard between Rafel and his wife." Jackson wished they could go somewhere quiet to talk. But it was raining outside, and the man on the barstool wasn't going anywhere.

"I was on my way to the john, and I heard Rafel say, 'I know you're seeing someone. I've smelled him on you.'" Zack shrugged. "Then Sierra yelled, 'You're crazy!' That's all I

95

know."

"Did you see Sierra leave?"

"Nope."

"What about Rafel?"

"Nope. I'm usually right here, minding my own business."

"But you knew Rafel was a veteran. Had you talked to him recently?"

"We talked one time. He asked me about my eye, and I told him I'd lost it in Vietnam to a spook with a bayonet. He told me about the landmine that took his leg."

"Did he mention any other explosives?"

"I'm not sure what you mean. But Rafel's eyes sure lit up when he talked about all the IEDs over there in Afghanistan."

"Any idea who would kill him?"

Zack's bloodshot eye glistened with an unshed tear. "Nope."

Jackson gave up. He caught Mila's attention. "What about Nikki?"

"Over there. In the red leather jacket." She pointed to a blonde woman seated at a table with two men.

Jackson made his way through the crowd. This was probably the busiest the tavern had ever been. A laundromat where someone had been murdered would not fare so well.

At Nikki's table, he introduced himself, then looked at her male companions. "Will you excuse us for a moment?"

One was already leaving. The other squeezed Nikki's shoulder. "I'll be back."

"You're here about Rafel's murder, aren't you?" She was pretty in a used-up kind of way. Too much makeup that didn't hide the dark circles under her eyes and dark roots that were overdue for a touch-up.

"Did you talk to Rafel last night?"

"For a while, when he first came in." Her hands shook as she twisted her cocktail napkin.

"How did he seem? Was he worried or anxious?"

"No more than usual."

"What was he usually worried about?"

"Not having a job or future. He was kind of sad." She bit her slick-red lower lip. "But he'd been in Afghanistan, so he was a hero and I respected him."

"What can you tell me about last night?"

"Not much. I heard him and his wife had an argument, but I missed it. Must have been in the ladies room when it happened."

*Snorting a little coke or meth,* Jackson thought. "Did you see Mazari leave?"

"Yeah. I waved at him as he walked by."

"Was he with someone?"

"No, but he got into a shoving match with a guy at the door."

That grabbed his attention. "What guy? Do you know his name?"

"No. He's not a regular."

"What happened exactly?"

"The guy was coming in as Rafel was leaving and they brushed shoulders. I think Rafel was drunk and bumped him. The guy shoved him and Rafel shoved back. Then Rafel stumbled out the door."

"Did the guy follow him?"

"I don't know. Someone started talking to me and I looked away."

*Crap.* "Describe the guy in as much detail as you can."

She touched a shiny red nail to her lip and thought for a moment. "He was medium height and stocky with a shaved head and a beard."

"You said shaved, not bald?"

"Yeah, I got that sense, like he didn't have any hair on his head."

"Beard color? Eye color?" Jackson took notes, glancing up as he talked. "Anything distinctive like a tattoo?"

She bit her lip. "I don't know. I was a kind of drunk."

"What was he wearing?"

"Maybe a leather jacket?" Nikki looked frustrated. "I only saw him from here to the door and it happened fast. Sorry."

"Who else might know him? I need a name."

"I'd never seen him before so I have no idea."

Jackson tensed with frustration. "Would you be willing to work with a sketch artist to create an image?"

She looked worried. "I don't think it would help. It's dark in here and he was twenty feet away."

Jackson took down Nikki's phone number and gave her his card, not letting go of the idea that she could be more helpful. He made his way through the crowd and found Schak and Evans to give them the details of the new lead.

They spent another hour in the tavern, asking everyone if they'd seen the guy with the shaved head, but came up with nothing.

Frustrated, Jackson finally rounded up his team and they headed outside. They stood in the dark wet parking lot trying to decide what to do next.

"We have to find this guy," Jackson said. "What if he followed Mazari out and killed him in a meth rage just for bumping into him? We know it could happen."

"We have to get our witness to work with the sketch artist, then run his picture on the news and put posters up around the bar." Evans' voice still held energy, and it made

Jackson feel old and tired.

"Okay, let's call it a night. I'll be in touch about a meet-up tomorrow."

Back at his desk, Jackson transferred all his notes into a Word document. He'd recently learned to use the Notebook layout, and it made grouping the information much easier. Once he had the file updated, he printed four copies and set one on the desks of each of his task force members, holding one back for Sergeant Lammers, in case she wanted an update. He grabbed a new case folder, labeled it, and transferred all his paperwork to the binder. It was midnight and time to go home, but he was stalling. The new house would feel empty without Katie and would still be stacked with boxes. He didn't know if he could even find his toothbrush. At least the kitchen was set up because his brother had been living in the house all along. Only now, Derrick was on the road, driving a truck three weeks out of four and would be a very part-time roommate.

Jackson really wanted to head for Kera's and crawl in bed with her, but it was too late to call and too late to just show up. He stared at his phone. Kera hadn't called him back. What was going on with her?

## Chapter 12

*Saturday, Nov. 12, 5:30 a.m.*
Jackson woke to the high-pitched sound of his cell phone alarm, and his pulse accelerated to match the beeping. *What the hell?*

It took him a moment to realize he was in his childhood home, in the bedroom that long ago was occupied by his parents. He stumbled into the bathroom and stood in the shower until he was fully awake. As he dried off, he spotted his prednisone on the back of the sink. Katie had unpacked it and left the medicine where he could find it even half asleep. Damn, he loved that girl.

He swallowed a pill, searched for the box holding his underwear and socks, and tried to think of something special he could do for Katie in return. She'd probably get all their stuff unpacked before he was home long enough to help. Unless he got lucky, and Mazari's killer came in and confessed that afternoon.

Maybe one of the new tablet computers on the market, Jackson thought. Katie had wanted one for months, and now that the prices had dropped, he could afford it. Hell, maybe he'd get one for himself too.

In the kitchen, he made toast and brewed coffee, discovering that his brother drank the same fresh-ground blend he did. What else did they have in common, despite going nearly ten years without talking to each other?

Jackson stepped out on the porch and found the local newspaper in the box. He didn't have time to read it this morning, but he liked to at least glance at all the headlines before he walked into the department.

Mazari's murder had made the bottom half of the front page, but the story was short on details. The Willamette News had shown a photo of the victim in his military uniform, along with information about his service in Afghanistan. Jackson was glad he'd missed last night's TV news coverage. Broadcasters always played up the emotional or sentimental angle as much as they could, then the public called the department and pressured them for a solution. He gulped his coffee while scanning the other headlines, then bolted from the house. The autopsy wasn't until eight, but he wanted to be in the department early to make some calls and look over some of the evidence they'd picked up yesterday.

At his desk, Jackson clicked on his computer but resisted checking his email. He pulled on gloves and removed the victim's wallet from its plastic evidence bag. Plain, worn brown leather, the wallet itself told him nothing about the victim. But the thinness of it made Jackson think Mazari might have been a paranoid type who processed or discarded anything extraneous. There were no receipts, no scraps of paper, and only two business cards, one of which was Kera's and one was for Jake Pittman's tree-cutting business. No cash. That was odd, unless the killer had taken the money. But putting the wallet back into the dead man's pocket after pilfering it would have been challenging for anybody, and unusual for a street thug.

Mazari had also carried a driver's license, a credit card,

an ATM card, and his military ID. For a man who kept a year's worth of food his house, his wallet was a skinny comparison. It made him think of the computer in the victim's house and Schak saying it had been scrubbed. If he'd gotten involved in something illegal recently, Mazari may have been afraid to keep information that could be used against him.

He put the wallet away, planning to have it dusted for prints, and grabbed a pile of mail he'd picked up from the victim's counter. Nearly every piece was from someone wanting money, including a stack of medical bills, some of which were Sierra's. Jackson assumed Mazari's service-related medical expenses had been paid for by the military, but maybe not all. A letter from a medical lab caught his eye. Included with the hefty bill were the lab results from a DNA paternity test. As best as Jackson could tell from the stilted medical language, the two samples—Adam Mazari and Rafel Mazari—had not matched. Adam was not Mazari's son.

Jackson leaned back in his chair, feeling the weight of that news for Mazari. He must have been devastated to learn the boy he loved was not his own. Jackson recalled seeing Adam outside the house the day before and thinking he didn't look anything like his father. Maybe Mazari had suspected for a long time. But did the paternity issue have anything to do with his murder?

It seemed unlikely. But the shaved-head guy from the bar was still a priority. Jackson called the department's sketch artist and left messages for her at work and at home. She probably had the weekend off, but knowing Officer Rice, she would come in and do the sketch if she was available. Jackson was less optimistic about getting the witness to cooperate. He called her anyway and left Nikki a message to be on standby for the sketch artist.

He glanced up at his computer clock and realized it was time to go.

The parking lot at North McKenzie was less crowded than he'd ever seen it. The main hospital operations had moved out of the university-area building to the massive new facility, River Bend, at the edge of Springfield. One of Eugene's biggest financial losses. Jackson hadn't been inside the new hospital yet, and he considered that a good thing. For now, autopsies were still conducted in the basement of the old medical building in a room called Surgery 10.

He took the elevator to the lower level and found his way to the small white room with the big stainless steel drawers. The medical examiner and pathologist stood near the counter talking, and Rafel Mazari's body lay on the narrow table, covered by a white sheet.

"You're on time." Rudolph Konrad's voice held no sarcasm. The pathologist was a no-nonsense type who simply liked to run a well-ordered lab. His blond hair and padded cheeks made him look younger than his forty-something years, but Jackson imagined he'd been born with an old soul.

"I do my best." Jackson grabbed a gown, mask, and booties from a shelf near the door.

As he suited up, Rich Gunderson, the medical examiner who'd been out at the crime scene, stepped over and whispered. "Wait'll you see this guy."

"Ready?" Konrad glanced at the clock. It was time to start.

The three stepped up to the table, with the medical people on either side and Jackson at the foot, a familiar routine. Jackson would move in closer if he wanted to see something in detail, but he preferred to listen more than look.

The pathologist removed the sheet, folded it carefully, and set it on the stainless steel counter.

Jackson's eyes were drawn to the victim's prosthetic leg, a mix of high-tech plastic and shiny metal. At the top of the prosthesis was an area of gnarled pink scar tissue that used to be the man's groin and lower abdomen. Rafel Mazari had not only lost his leg in the IED explosion, he'd also lost his penis and testicles. Jackson winced, his body contracting to protect his own privates. *Jesus Christ.* No wonder the man had been angry and jealous.

"I knew you'd flinch," Gunderson said. "I did too. Poor guy."

Disgust and rage battled for Jackson's emotions. "Who would murder a wounded, dickless veteran?" *Except maybe his wife.*

"Let's see what we find." The pathologist interrupted their conversation and began an inch-by-inch search of the body, starting at Mazari's feet.

"What are you looking for under his toes?" Jackson asked.

"Needle marks. Some addicts hide their addiction by shooting up in their feet."

"What makes you think he might be an addict?"

"Doesn't he look like a man who had a lot of pain?" Konrad's voice was deep and monotone. He made no judgments about the dead.

The search was slow and tedious, so Jackson made a mental list of things to do next. Check alibis, get Sierra's fingerprint subpoena signed, and go see Kera. Because she knew the victim, he could justify the trip over. It had been too long since he'd seen her.

The two medical men gently rolled the body over. After

probing with a gloved finger, Konrad said, "Fixed lividity in the area of his glutes indicates he died right there, sitting up in his vehicle."

Jackson knew he was referring to the reddish-purple pooling of blood in the corpse's butt and the back of his one leg.

The pathologist continued his careful search of the victim's skin. "This is unusual." Konrad grabbed a magnifier with a built-in light and examined an area on Mazari's back. "He has faint, old scarring, probably from childhood."

"What kind of scars?"

"I think he was beaten. Maybe struck with a lash. He has similar scars on his legs too."

Another wave of disgust. What the hell kind of life had this man had? Jackson started to understand Mazari's survivalist mentality, the hoarding of food and weapons. But he didn't understand how the soldier could have kept explosives in his home after a landmine had taken a chunk of his body.

After another five minutes of searching the victim's hands and arms, they rolled the body back over, and Konrad began to examine the neck wound. Yesterday, the medical examiner had cleaned up the excess blood before putting the corpse in the drawer.

Konrad measured the length and depth of the wound, then used the magnifier again to examine the tissue. He looked up at Jackson. "This incision was made with a long sharp instrument, possibly even a scalpel. The wound is deeper on the right, so I believe the perpetrator started there and cut deeply enough to sever the carotid artery."

"So the attacker was likely left-handed?"

"Most likely."

Gunderson cut in. "But considering the victim's position in the vehicle, a left-handed strike may have been essential. So the assailant could have used his left hand even though it's not his dominant one."

"This was a clean, strong, confident assault," Konrad countered. "Not likely made by someone using their non-dominant hand."

For Jackson, that conflict meant that in court the assailant's primary hand would be a moot point.

Konrad continued his examination of the neck, then paused and said something Jackson didn't hear.

"What did you find?"

"A tiny puncture mark, on the left side." He put down his magnifier and reached for a photo on the counter. "That might explain the small volume of blood."

"He was drugged first," Gunderson said. "I thought so."

"We won't know for sure until we get the blood toxicology report in a few days." Konrad set down the photo. "But this victim had something injected into his neck before he was cut open."

Jackson's thoughts went immediately to the syringe they'd found at the crime scene. He was eager to call Parker and see if she'd found prints on it.

"We'll begin the internal examination now." Konrad picked up the Stryker saw and clicked it on. The humming sound as it cut through the breastbone often made first-time cops pass out.

"I need to take off now," Jackson said, over the noise. "We found a syringe at the crime scene, and I need to get some prints ASAP. Call me if you find anything significant." He pulled off his gear and hurried out, glad to be leaving the windowless death room.

Jackson called Parker at the lab as soon as he was on the main hospital floor and had cell service. "Did you print the syringe?"

"Yes, and good morning to you too."

"Sorry, but I just discovered our victim had a puncture mark."

"Interesting." He heard a drawer open, then Parker continued. "The syringe has an intact thumb print and a partial index finger. I'm just getting ready to run them through the local database."

"Call me if you get a hit."

"I planned to."

"Thanks."

Jackson called the assistant district attorney as he walked to his car. The dark sky was breaking up, revealing patches of blue. A surge of optimism about this otherwise bleak case quickened his step.

After the short drive from the hospital to department headquarters, Jackson pounded up the stairs, feeling physically better than he had in months. His surgery site was now just a long white scar from pelvis to sternum, and as long as he took his prednisone, he had little pain. He was due for a CAT scan soon, and he hoped to discover that the white fibrous tissue *cloud* had stopped growing. It was probably wishful thinking.

At his desk, he pulled out the case file and started making calls. First, he left a message with Hailey Pittman, Jake's wife, asking for a return call. Evans had already determined Sawyer's alibi was iffy, so that left Sierra's to check. He called Game Day Sports, looking for the bartender Sierra had claimed she'd visited Thursday night. Madison Riley wasn't there so he asked for her cell number. They wouldn't give it to him but said they'd pass along his message.

Evans stopped by his desk. She looked sharp in a mint-green blazer and black slacks. Knowing her, she'd already run five miles that morning.

"Anything interesting from the autopsy?" she asked.

Jackson wanted to tell her about the abuse Rafel's body had suffered, but it felt too personal. He would wait and tell everyone at the same time at the task force session that afternoon. "Yes, but it probably doesn't have any bearing on the case. I'll update you at the meeting today."

"Okay." Her face fell a little. "I've got some stuff to report too, but nothing critical yet. I'm headed out to talk to people who know the three friends. Anyone you want me to question in particular?"

"Pittman's wife, if you can find her. We still need to verify his alibi."

"She's first on my list. When's the task force meeting?"

"We'll say four and see how it goes."

Evans squeezed his shoulder and walked away. She moved like a trained athlete, completely in tune with her body. He envied her self-discipline. Kera was like that too. Jackson vowed to start running more than twice a week.

He looked at his notes, then called Rafel Mazari's sister, where Sierra had taken his son. Adam was not biologically related to either of the people who'd been raising him, Jackson realized. He felt sorry for the boy and wondered if Sierra would continue to make a home for him.

A soft voice answered. Jackson introduced himself, then said, "Is this Sasha Altman?"

"Yes. Are you investigating my brother's murder?"

L.J. Sellers

"I am, and I need to ask some questions."

"I understand."

"Where were you Thursday night?" As long as she was being understanding, he might as well get the ugly question out of the way.

"I was home with my family."

"Was Adam with you?" It was a guess. The boy was too young to stay home alone while his parents drank in a bar.

"For a while. Why does it matter?"

"I'm trying to establish a timeline. Who brought him over and what time did they pick him up?"

"Sierra dropped Adam off around eight-fifteen and said she'd be back in an hour. But she didn't pick him up until around eleven. That's too late for him to be up on a school night."

But plenty of time to have killed her husband in the parking lot before going home. "Do you know where Sierra is now?"

"Probably at the Saturday Market. She has a booth there and likely couldn't find someone to handle it for her at the last minute."

"Is Adam with you?"

"Yes. Sierra asked if he could stay with us for a few days while she works through the details in dealing with Rafel's death."

"Did Rafel ever talk to you about the boy's paternity?"

"What do you mean?"

"Did he ever mention that Adam might not be his son?"

The sister drew in a sharp breath. "No. That can't be true."

"I may need to talk with Adam eventually, but I'll call you first."

"You wouldn't dare mention that ugly gossip!" Her tone

rose half an octave. "Adam is grief-stricken about his father."

"Of course I wouldn't. I hope not to have to question him at all." But if Sierra went to trial, Adam might be called to the stand. "Sasha, can you think of any reason someone would kill your brother?"

"No." She cried quietly. "He was a good man."

"What is Sierra's booth at the market?"

"She sells braided dog leashes and baked dog treats."

"Thanks for your time." Jackson clicked off.

At first it seemed odd Sierra would be at the Saturday Market the day after learning of her husband's murder. Yet everyone reacted differently. Some people collapsed and took to their beds. Others kept moving forward, afraid if they slowed down or thought about it too much, the pain would be unbearable.

Jackson grabbed his coat but left his shoulder bag. The craft market was a half block away, nestled into a park-like area on either side of Oak Street, and he wanted to round up Sierra while he could. Hopefully, the subpoena for her fingerprints would come through shortly. He walked down 8th Avenue, passed by the county court building, and stopped at the market's information booth. In the courtyard beyond, a group of ragtag drummers kept up a loud steady beat.

After a five-minute discussion with the cheerful, older woman manning the directory, they finally determined that Sierra's merchandise was near the fountain across the street. Hundreds of eight-foot booths jammed a two-block area, selling jewelry, ceramics, candles, wooden carvings, wind chimes, yard ornaments, and tie-dyed T-shirts. Jackson hadn't visited the market since Katie was young and didn't think he would again anytime soon.

The smell of pot smoke rolled off a young man wearing a kilt who crossed the street in the other direction. He seemed oblivious to Jackson's suit jacket with the gun bulge. But then, possession of marijuana was a misdemeanor in Oregon, punishable by a small fine.

The crowd seemed thin, but it was the end of the season, possibly the last day of the market until next March. Jackson made his way past college students, hippies, and groups of female shoppers. He spotted Sierra in a booth near the fountain. She was talking to a couple and pointing to a tray of cookies on the narrow counter. As he approached, she listed the ingredients, and he realized they were for dogs.

Sierra spotted him, cringed, and excused herself from the couple.

"I'm sorry to bother you, but I need to ask a few more questions. Please come with me to the department"

"I can't leave my booth."

"This is important. Can you call someone to come down and watch it for you?"

"You think I didn't already try? If I didn't need the money, I wouldn't be here today." Distress filled her voice, and he noticed dark circles under her eyes. She was still beautiful.

Jackson's phone rang. He glanced and saw it was Parker from the lab. "Excuse me, I have to take this." He answered without taking his eyes off Sierra. "Hey, Parker, what have you got?"

"I ran the prints on the syringe and got a match. She was arrested five years ago during a demonstration. Printed, fined, and released."

"Who."

"Sierra Kent."

## Chapter 13

*Saturday, Nov. 12, 4:55 a.m.*

Evans woke before the alarm went off and rolled out of bed. Her thoughts went immediately to the new homicide case. They would get a breakthrough today, she could feel it. She hurried to the kitchen, made a small of pot of Italian coffee, and turned on her computer.

She downed a tall mug of java while catching up on news—mostly about protests around the world, including ones planned for Portland and Eugene that day. She was glad not to be a patrol officer or SWAT member. She didn't sympathize with the anarchists and tree huggers who demonstrated regularly in Eugene, but she could relate to the 99-percenters and their anger at Wall Street. The recession had crippled law enforcement in Oregon, and the county jail was little more than a joke now.

Humming with energy, she changed into workout clothes and headed for the back bedroom. The thick mats on the floor felt cool to her bare feet. She'd padded the walls too, after she'd injured her ex-lover during a sparring match. Evans loaded a mixed file of techno music and began a rigorous thirty-minute kickboxing routine, followed by fifteen minutes of Brazilian Jiu-Jitsu. She missed having a sparring partner and wished Ben, the IA detective she was dating, was more interested in martial arts. So far, he seemed content to keep it casual: dinner and sex once or twice a week, with little or no involvement in each other's personal lives. Sometimes she wondered if he had a secret wife and kids on the side.

Evans laughed at the thought, then went out for a quick run. She preferred long runs after her shift to burn off the tension and calories of the day, but knowing Jackson, they would work late again. That was fine with her. She loved his obsessiveness, among other things.

At headquarters, Sergeant Lammers intercepted her on the way to her desk. "Where's Jackson this morning?"

Evans was surprised to see her boss on the weekend. "He's at Rafel Mazari's autopsy."

"I know it's early in the investigation, but do we have a viable suspect?"

"We're leaning toward the wife, but we don't have anything solid yet. And we're still looking for a guy from the tavern who had an altercation with the victim."

"Shit. The mayor called me last night. He was planning a special event to honor our returning young veterans, and he's taking Mazari's murder rather personally."

"We're doing what we can."

"I know. Tell Jackson to keep me in the loop."

"Yes, ma'am." Evans resisted the urge to grin. Lammers was built like a refrigerator, had no patience for idle conversation, and barked at the male detectives just to remind them who was in charge. But she had promoted Evans a few months back, making her a full member of the team instead of a trainee, and for that she'd always be grateful.

When the boss strode away, Evans turned on her computer and made a quick list of sites to check: their local criminal database, the citizen's database, CODIS (the national criminal database), and Facebook. In the recent past, she'd tracked down a few witnesses on the social networking site, and it sometimes provided key information.

After twenty minutes in the criminal databases, all she uncovered was that Jake Pittman had once had a DUII, and two months later had pleaded guilty to a menacing charge in exchange for a one-year probation. Both incidents were seven years old. Cody Sawyer hadn't even had a traffic ticket since he was nineteen. Pittman was not on Facebook, but Sawyer was. Evans learned his date of birth, place of employment, and favorite music, but didn't find anything indicating he belonged to a survivalist group. She noticed his status said *Single* rather than *In a relationship*, even though Sawyer had told her he had a girlfriend.

Evans heard Jackson come in and settle down as his desk. She glanced over. He looked great in a royal blue shirt under his black suede jacket.

After sifting through Sawyer's friends for a few minutes, Evans found Hailey Pittman, who she assumed to be Jake's wife. The photo showed her in a deck chair and it wasn't flattering. Hailey had limp, ash-colored hair, a narrow face, and only fifty-eight Facebook friends. She worked at Evergreen Insurance, only a short drive from the department, so Evans decided to head over and chat with her. She would verify Jake Pittman's alibi and see what else she could learn about the guys. Evans tucked her iPad in her shoulder bag, stopped to check in with Jackson, and headed downstairs to her car.

The insurance office was in one of the black glass buildings behind Valley River Mall. Shaped like bathtubs, the architecture was a local joke, but still commanded high-dollar leases because of the location. Evans took the stairs to the second floor and found Hailey in the office across the hall. She was behind a tall counter, wearing a headset, and talking rapidly to a customer.

Evans waited for her to disconnect and introduced herself. "Do you have minute, Ms. Pittman? I need to ask some questions about Rafel Mazari."

She looked nervous. "I have to answer the phones."

"I only need a few minutes. We can step out in the hall." Evans didn't want her distracted every time the phone rang. "This is important."

Hailey excused herself, then stuck her head into an office in the back and asked someone to answer the phones.

Out in the hall, Evans realized Hailey was only about five foot one. Evans pulled her shoulders back, feeling tall for a change. "Did you know Rafel Mazari?"

"Yes. He was Jake's best friend."

"Do you know anyone who would want to kill Rafel?"

"No. I can't believe what happened. Rafel was a veteran, a hero, like Jake."

"Jake is in the military?"

"He was in the Army and did a tour of Iraq in 2006." Her pride was evident.

The information seemed significant and Evans wrote it down, but she couldn't make a connection, so she jumped to the meat of the interview. "Do you know anyone connected to Rafel or Jake who has a shaved head and a beard?"

"No."

It was worth asking. "Where were you Thursday night?"

"Me?" Hailey pointed to herself in open-mouthed surprised.

"I have to ask."

"Home."

"What time did Jake come home from Pete's Pad on Thursday night?"

"I don't know." She looked confused.

"But you were home."

"Yes."

"You didn't hear Jake come home or speak with him?"

Hailey gave a tiny shake of her head, as though Evans might be stupid. "I don't live with Jake. I left him months ago and filed for divorce."

Evans was taken aback. "You didn't see him at all on Thursday?"

"No."

"Interesting." She wrote *Pittman lied/alibi* on her notepad.

"Can anyone verify that you were home Thursday night between ten and eleven?"

"My roommate was there."

Evan got the name and contact information, then moved on. "What did you think of Rafel?"

"I felt sorry for him." Hailey glanced toward the office door.

"Did you like him?"

"I liked him before he shipped out, but he was different when he got back."

"How so?"

"I don't want to speak badly about him."

"I'm trying to find his killer. I need to know what was going on with Rafel."

"He was withdrawn and depressed. But that seemed normal, considering his circumstances."

"Why did you leave Jake?"

"We had money problems." Hailey lowered her voice. "Why does it matter?"

"We're looking for a motive for the killing."

"Jake didn't kill Rafel. They were best friends." Hailey started to tear up. "No matter how broke Jake was, he wouldn't let that affect his friendship. He loved Rafel."

"How broke was Jake?"

"I supported him for a year after he got laid off. Being dependent on me made him mean." Hailey looked at the office door again. "I really should get back."

Evans remembered the fraud case with the phony veterans' fund. "Did Jake come into any unexpected money lately?"

Hailey blinked. "I don't know." Her voice vibrated with stress.

"Did you ever hear him mention the Veterans Relief Fund?"

"Maybe."

"Why are you protecting Jake?"

"I don't know anything about his finances now."

She was shutting down, so Evans let it go for the moment. "What do you think of Sierra?"

"She's okay. The whole back-to-nature thing is a little weird to me, but then I'm a city girl."

Evans remembered what the neighbor had overheard. "Did you ever hear Sierra threaten Rafel?"

"No, but I saw her kill a chicken like it was nothing. It kind of grossed me out, and I quit going to their barbeques."

"Would Sierra have any reason to kill Rafel?"

Hailey hesitated, twisting a pen in her hands. "Rafel thought she was cheating on him."

"With who?"

"I don't know. I didn't spend that much time with them."

Evans knew there was more. "If she wanted out of the marriage, why not just leave him?"

Hailey glanced around, then whispered. "Most military men have life insurance. Rafel may have been worth more dead."

# Chapter 14

Jackson took Sierra to the interrogation room and gestured for her to sit. "Empty your pockets and give me your backpack while we talk."

She let out a harsh laugh. "I don't think so."

"Then I'll cuff you and do it myself." If it came to that, he would wait for Evans and let a female search Sierra's pockets, but he wanted to keep this simple if he could.

"You can't cuff me and search me unless you arrest me."

"I'm officially arresting you for obstruction of justice. Turn around and put your hands behind your back."

"Okay. You win, fucker. Take the damn backpack." She tossed it at him and he had to react quickly to catch it. Sierra had already called him a few choice names when he'd threatened to cuff her and escort her past her peers at the market. But she'd grudgingly come along rather than be handcuffed in public. He'd allowed her to make a call, and she'd asked a friend to come down and close up her booth at the Saturday Market. Her lack of cooperation made her look as guilty as her fingerprints at the crime scene.

"Pockets too."

She pulled a tube of chapstick from her front pocket and tossed it on the table, then shoved both hands deep into her jeans and turned the pockets inside out. "Happy now?"

"I'll be back in minute with something to eat."

He left her uncuffed, dropped her backpack in his desk drawer, and ordered two turkey sandwiches and diet Pepsis from a nearby deli. While he waited for the food to be delivered, he called his team and asked them to come in. Next, he conducted a cursory search of Sierra's pack: wallet, keys, knit vest, water bottle, paperwork for her pet-stuff business, and finally, in a small outside pocket, her cell phone. Too bad he couldn't search it without a warrant.

He called the assistant district attorney, who still didn't pick up, and left a message: "We've already got a match on Sierra Kent's fingerprints to the syringe at the crime scene. So skip that paperwork." Jackson started to ask him to write a search warrant for Sierra's cell phone, but wasn't optimistic that Trang was even working that day. They'd handle it themselves.

The food arrived and he took Sierra a sandwich and soda. She wouldn't look at him or speak. He set it down and went back to his desk. His team hadn't shown up yet, so he wolfed down his sandwich and made a quick call to Kera, who answered right away.

"Hello, Wade."

The sound of her warm sexy voice was like a pain reliever kicking in. And she rarely called him Wade anymore because everyone else called him Jackson. "Hey, Kera. Sorry I didn't call sooner. I've been working nonstop on this case, but I've missed you."

"I know you're on a homicide. I didn't expect to hear from you at all."

"We caught a break today, and I think I'll have some time tomorrow. I'd love to see you."

"Don't you still have to unpack?"

"It can wait."

"In that case, I'll get Danette and the baby out of the house tomorrow afternoon so we can be alone."

"I like the sound of that."

"Can you be here for lunch?"

Before he could respond, Evans rushed up to his desk, eyes popping with energy. He had his earpiece in, and his teammate didn't realize he was on the phone. Evans blurted out, "We've got some stuff to catch up on."

"I'll meet you in five minutes," he said quietly, waving her off.

"Sorry," Evans mouthed and walked away.

To Kera he said, "I'll call you tonight to confirm." The line was silent. "Kera?" Had they been cut off or had she hung up? A small stone of worry lodged in his gut. It was time to interrogate his suspect, so he texted Kera and said he'd see her tomorrow.

Operating from the same guilt, he made a quick call to his daughter, knowing she was at her mother's and not likely to pick up. He left a message: "I'm just checking in to make sure everything is okay. Call me if you want to leave for any reason. I love you."

He would have felt better if he'd actually talked to her. He was trying to be less overbearing, but Katie had been through so much with Renee's alcoholism and relapses. He simply didn't trust his ex-wife. If Katie were still ten instead of fifteen, he wouldn't let her be alone with her mother. His daughter had learned long ago not to get into a car with Renee when she'd been drinking, but her mother's mood swings could be damn near as damaging.

Schak hurried up to his desk, and Jackson snapped his mind back to work. "Let's go question our suspect. I want you to watch from the conference room. I called the DA and he said he'd be here soon."

"Will do." Schak headed for the hall and Jackson followed. He liked to have an observer for interrogations when he could. Sometimes it was easier to spot a suspect's reaction if you weren't in the middle of it.

Evans joined them as they moved past her desk.

"What did you find out?" Jackson asked, knowing she had something to share.

"Pittman lied about his alibi, and Mazari may have had a life insurance policy. We need to ask about both."

"We'll add it to our long list."


They stepped into the windowless space, and Jackson immediately felt the closet-sized room begin to shrink. The dingy gray walls lacked a one-way observation window, but two years ago, they'd finally purchased a video recorder for the room. Once he got into interrogation mode, Jackson hoped the claustrophobia would fade and let him work.

Sierra was on the opposite side, facing them, looking gorgeous and defiant as ever. She wore a dark green sweater and faded jeans, and her dreadlocks were gathered loosely behind her neck. Jackson wondered how much her hair weighed and if it gave her headaches.

He sat near the door, making Evans take the inside chair. He'd asked her to participate in the interrogation in case Sierra responded better to a woman. It was important for the whole team to be involved, including the DA, because this interview could prove critical to making their case in court. They needed at least a hint of a confession or an obvious pattern of lying to justify pressing charges against Sierra. Until Mazari's toxicology report came back, they couldn't even compare the residue in the syringe to the substances in his blood. If there was no match, Sierra's prints on the syringe would mean nothing.

He'd left the suspect uncuffed, but she hadn't touched the sandwich or soda.

"I need a glass of water. I don't drink this poison."

Evans offered to go get the water, and Jackson asked her to bring coffee too. This would be another long afternoon.

He stated his name and the date for the camera. "I'm speaking with Sierra Kent, wife of murder victim Rafel Mazari. Ms. Kent has been read her Miranda rights and has declined counsel at this point. Is that correct, Ms. Kent?"

"Yes. I have nothing to hide and no money to pay a lawyer."

"We found unlicensed explosives and unregistered guns in your house. You're facing several serious charges."

"The guns weren't mine, and I didn't know about the explosives." Her chin came up and she pulled her hands to her chest. "I was shocked to come home yesterday and find the bomb squad at my house. I'm still spinning from all this."

"Aren't you a member of Territory Defenders?"

She shook her head. "No, and neither was Rafel."

Jackson didn't believe her but decided to come back to it later. "Let's talk about the night of the murder, Thursday, November 10. When did your husband Rafel leave the house?"

"Right after dinner, around seven."

"Did you know where he was going?"

"Yes. He said he was going to Pete's Pad for a beer. It was pretty typical."

"How did you feel about his drinking?"

"A little worried, but Rafel wasn't an alcoholic."

"Did it make you angry that he spent so much time away

from home?"

"I told him it wasn't fair to Adam, his son, but he didn't seem to care."

Evans came back with a bottle of water under her arm and two mugs of break-room coffee, which they hated but sometimes drank anyway. While Evans silently settled back in, Jackson kept his eyes locked on Sierra. He wanted to talk about Adam, but not yet. He had to establish the timeline first. "What happened next?"

"Rafel called me and asked me to come down to the tavern. He sounded upset."

"What time was that?"

"Maybe a quarter to eight."

"What exactly did he say?"

"He said we needed to talk." A little frustration in her voice. "He indicated he'd made a decision about something important but he wouldn't say what."

"When did you leave your house?"

"Around eight. I took Adam over to his aunt's."

"Where did you go after that?"

"To Pete's Pad to talk to Rafel."

"What time did you arrive?"

"I don't know."

"Tell me everything that happened in the tavern."

"Rafel was sitting with his friend Jake, and I joined them. After a minute, Rafel said something like 'I know you're seeing another guy.' I denied it, as always, because it's not true." She made a point to look him in the eye. "Then Rafel called me a liar and said he wanted to leave me."

It was the first time she'd mentioned that. "Was Jake present when he said that?"

"Yes. Eventually, he got tired of our fighting and left the

table, but I don't think he left the tavern."

"Did you see Jake Pittman again?"

"I'm not sure."

"Did you see a man with a shaved head and a beard at the tavern?"

Sierra looked a little confused. "No. Why?"

"Does Rafel have any friends matching that description?"

"Not that I know of."

Jackson paused, letting Evans know she could step in.

His partner took the cue, leaning toward the suspect. "Were you hurt when Rafel said he wanted to leave you?"

"Of course. I had no idea he was even thinking about it." Sierra looked at her hands.

*Was she distressed or lying?*

"Were you a little angry too?" Evans prodded.

"I was tired of the accusations, tired of the fighting. Maybe I was a little relieved." Sierra bit her plump lower lip.

Evans' next question surprised him. "Did you grow up on a farm?"

"Yes. In southern Oregon. Why?"

"What kind of animals did you have?"

"Chickens, rabbits, pigs. The usual. Why?"

"Did you help slaughter those animals?"

"Sometimes." Sierra narrowed her eyes. "Why are you asking about this?"

"You know how to use a knife? You've cut into a pig and watched it bleed to death?"

Sierra jerked in anger. "I've also treated a lot of animals and saved their lives."

Evans suddenly shifted gears. "Did Rafel carry life insurance?"

Sierra blinked in surprise. "When he was in the military

he had a policy. He bought it before he shipped out to Afghanistan. But I think it was terminated when he was discharged."

They'd have to look into that—and a million other little things, Jackson thought. He took up the timeline again. "When did you leave the tavern?"

"I'm not sure, but I think it was close to nine-thirty."

"Rafel was still there?"

"Yes."

"What about Jake?"

"I don't know." She reached for her water bottle, and Jackson noted she used her left hand.

"Did you see Cody Sawyer at the tavern that night?"

"He stopped at our table and had a beer."

Jackson wondered if Sawyer had overheard the couple's fight. "What did the four of you talk about?"

"Nothing really. Rafel was too moody, so Jake and Cody left." Her voice was clipped, as if she was losing her patience.

Jackson knew they were just getting started. "Did Cody leave the bar?"

"I don't know."

"Then what happened?"

"Rafel started talking about leaving me. It upset me so I got out of there."

"What did you do next?"

"I drove over to Game Day to see my friend Madison."

Evans cut in. "Before you left Pete's, did you walk around the parking lot for a while? Thinking about your pending divorce?"

Sierra shot her a look. "No. I wanted to get away. I left immediately."

"What route did you take to the Game Day bar?" Jackson

knew it was on Highway 99 next to a pizza parlor with miniature golf.

Sierra blinked, then hesitated. "Seneca to Highway 99."

"What time did you arrive at the second tavern?"

"Don't make it sound like that," Sierra snapped. "I went to Pete's to talk to my husband because he asked me to. Then I went to see my friend, who happens to be a bartender, because I was upset. I didn't finish my beer in either place."

"What time did you arrive at Game Day and what time did you leave?"

"I'm not sure. I was only there about ten minutes. Madison was too busy to talk to me."

"But you spoke to her? Will she corroborate your statement?"

"Of course."

"Where were you between ten and eleven?"

"At home."

*A documented lie.* "Rafel's sister says you didn't pick up Adam until eleven."

"Bullshit. She exaggerates to make me look like a bad stepmother."

"An hour is a long time to be unaccounted for."

Sierra was silent.

It was time to get to the heart of it, so Jackson asked, "When did you drop the syringe in the parking lot at Pete's Pad?"

"What?" Alarm darkened her face.

"We found a syringe with your fingerprints about thirty feet from where Rafel was killed."

"That's crazy."

"Tell me how it got there." Jackson kept his voice neutral.

"I don't know. I don't carry syringes around with me."

Her eyes were a little wild now. "I don't believe you. This is a trick."

"The syringe is real, the prints are yours, and the DA is preparing to file murder charges against you."

Sierra sucked in air as if she'd been punched. She gripped the table with both hands. "Rafel must have dropped it."

Jackson cocked his head to express his doubt. "Why would your husband have a syringe with your prints?"

She paused for a long moment, her head down. "I gave him shots of ketamine at home sometimes. For his pain and stress."

"What kind of drug is that?"

"It's primarily an anesthetic, but it can be used for pain and depression."

"Where did the drug come from?"

"The Animal Care Clinic." A shadow of shame crossed her face.

"You stole doses of ketamine from the veterinary clinic where you worked and injected your husband with them?" Jackson tried to keep the disdain out of his voice.

"Only a few times." Sierra sounded scared, but also angry. "Sometimes he had groin pain that was unbearable and it triggered his PTSD. I couldn't stand to see him suffer."

Jackson decided it was time to empathize and give her a way out. "He was a troubled man and you felt sorry for him, didn't you?"

"Yes." She bit her lip again.

"He talked about suicide sometimes, didn't he?" Jackson was winging it.

"Sometimes."

"He faced a life of pain, with no job, no self-esteem, and no penis."

Evans jerked and dropped her pen on the table, and Jackson wished he'd told her earlier. "So you killed Rafel to put him out of his misery," Jackson said softly. "The way you would a wounded animal."

"No." Sierra closed her eyes and shook her head. "I wanted him to get counseling."

"You gave him a dose of ketamine in his Jeep to take the edge off. Then when he relaxed, you cut his throat, like you would a farm animal."

Sierra pushed back from the table and shouted "No!" as she stood up.

Jackson and Evans were on their feet just as quickly. Jackson had his hand on his Taser. "Sit down!" Sierra started to cry, and Jackson wondered if it was all an act. "Sit down or I'll cuff you."

The suspect slumped into her seat. He had a few more questions, then they would give her a break while he conferred with the DA. "Did you know Rafel had done a paternity test on Adam?"

"Yes. What does this have to do with his murder?"

"How did the results affect him?"

"Rafel was crushed, but I think he'd always suspected." Sierra shifted in her seat.

"Did it change things for you two as a couple?"

"It brought back memories of his first marriage, and Rafel got more paranoid and started accusing me of cheating."

"We'll take a break now. Would you like anything when we get back?"

"I want to call a friend who knows a lawyer."

# Chapter 15

Victor Slonecker was putting on his jacket as Jackson and Evans walked into the conference room. The district attorney's suit was expensive, his dark hair perfectly groomed, and his expression hungry, like a man who never quite got what he wanted.

"We can't charge her yet, and if she gets a lawyer, we have to let her walk out of here." Slonecker snapped his briefcase shut. "The prints on the syringe are not enough to convict her, and I don't want any more lawsuits."

"What if the residue in the syringe matches the victim's toxicology, and her alibi falls apart?" Jackson asked. He made a mental note to follow up with her bartender friend.

"Maybe." Slonecker moved toward the door. "But she already admitted to injecting her husband with tranquilizers. We can't prove she's the one who left the syringe."

"We could charge her with theft from the clinic." Jackson didn't want to let Sierra out of custody until the evidence became clear.

"She'd be released almost immediately," Slonecker argued. "And arresting her could prejudice a potential jury against her, giving her a reason for a change of venue."

"Arresting murder suspects on minor charges to hold them is standard procedure."

"Suit yourself. But she'll be released in days. No one does

jail time on minor theft charges."

"What about the explosives?" Schak threw in.

Slonecker spun toward him. "What explosives?"

The DA must have missed the first part of the interrogation.

Schak said, "We found dynamite and blasting caps in the house the victim shared with his wife. She claims she knew nothing about it."

"Oh Christ. Just keep it off the news." Slonecker strode toward the door. "And keep me informed."

After the DA left, they were silent for a moment. Finally, Jackson said, "His staff has been cut, and he's under a lot of pressure."

"He's right about the media coverage," Schak added. "It could get crazy if they find out about the explosives."

"It's probably too late," Evans said. "Neighbors saw the Explosive Device Unit at the house and were asked to vacate their homes, so they're already speculating. And if reporters talk to the neighbors..." She didn't need to finish the thought.

"No one knows the quantity. It could have been a single pipe bomb. The EDU response is the same." Jackson turned to Schak. "Did you notice anything we should know about before we go back in there and try again?"

"The two times where Sierra's body language suggested discomfort were when you asked what the four of them talked about at the bar and at the end when you asked about the kid."

"Thanks." Jackson touched Evans elbow. "Let's question our suspect again before her lawyer gets here. We'll make her take us through the evening backward, and see if we can trip her up."

The second round of questioning was mostly unproductive, even though Sierra's supposed lawyer never showed up. The suspect stuck to her story and refused to discuss the injections she'd given her husband. She wouldn't elaborate on the guys' conversation at the tavern either and became uncomfortable when Jackson asked about Rafel's child from his first marriage. Finally, Sierra admitted she didn't want to raise the boy, but didn't know how to get out of it. After thirty minutes, she simply stopped answering. They gave her a bathroom break, put her back in the interrogation room, then met with Schak in the conference room.

"She's a tough one to read," Schak complained. "I think she's lying about the explosives and minimizing her husband's pain medication use. But her denial about the murder is almost convincing."

"She's a mixed bag," Jackson agreed.

"Are we going to arrest her?" Evans asked.

"It's almost three," Schak cut in. "I've got to run over to the Dining Room and see if our buddy Prez is in line for a free meal."

"I'll go with you." Jackson turned back to Evans. "Would you book Sierra into jail on theft-one charges? I want to keep her out of circulation for a day or so if we can. We'll meet back here in an hour."

"I'm on it." Evans started for the hall, then spun back. "There were moments when I believed her. We have to keep considering other suspects, other scenarios."

"We will." Jackson stood to leave. "I keep coming back to motive. What did she have to gain by killing him? Nothing that seems worth a murder charge. Unless she had simply started to hate him and couldn't bear the thought of a messy divorce."

"What about the shaved-head guy from the tavern?" Evans asked. "How are we coming with that?"

"I have a call in to Officer Rice but she hasn't gotten back to me. She might be unavailable for the weekend. We need to keep asking everyone connected to this case if they recognize the description." Jackson nodded at Evans. "See you in an hour or so."

The Dining Room was four blocks away on 8th Avenue, so they decided to walk. An ominous sky threatened rain again, but they ignored it. Their overcoats would keep them dry, and it wasn't cold enough yet to wear a hat. Jackson started at a brisk pace, then heard Schak breathing a little too hard, so he slowed down. He wanted to ask his friend if was eating better and exercising after his heart attack, but he would never do it. Schak had a wife. That was her job.

"This case seems pretty squirrelly," Schak said, as they crossed the street. "I keep thinking there's something else going on we haven't tapped into yet."

"I know what you mean. I'd love to look at all their bank records." He remembered he'd assigned some of those subpoenas to Quince. "Hold up." He stopped and sent Quince a text: *Task force meeting at 5:00. Bring bank records?* After originally hating getting texts from his daughter, Jackson had come to love the new communication tool. It was fast, silent, and efficient. As he started forward again, he said, "We need more people on this. I miss McCray. I still can't believe he's retired."

"I went golfing with him last month. He looks great."

"Good to hear."

They crossed Lincoln and could see the crowd forming

outside the Dining Room. The concrete building sported a colorful mural on the side. A crowd formed a loose line that snaked through the parking lot, which had only a few cars because most of the patrons didn't own a vehicle. Most didn't have a home to go to either. These people were in survival mode. The free meal, eaten in peace in the dignity of a restaurant atmosphere, was likely the best hour of their day.

They stopped fifty feet away, and Jackson flipped through his notes for Prez's description. "We're looking for a fifty-five-year-old with light brown hair going gray, wearing a long brown coat with a fur trim."

"I see him." Schak nodded, but didn't point. "He's near the front, carrying a green plastic bag. What's our approach? We don't want him to bolt."

"Let's wait until he's inside, then we'll sit down at his table. He won't walk away from a meal, and the public place will make him feel safe." Some patrol cops were less than gentle with homeless people, so transients had learned to be distrustful. On the other hand, Jackson also knew two senior officers who bought clothes and blankets for the homeless every winter.

The restaurant doors opened, and the line of people surged forward. Jackson and Schak strode toward the front, ignoring the protests from hungry people who thought they were cutting in line. The group near the door glanced at their suits and expressions and parted to let them through.

Inside, the bright white interior surprised Jackson, as did the long counter with individual stools. Prez sat on the end, near the front door.

"I'll speak to him while you grab some stools." Jackson moved toward the witness.

Prez turned at the sound of his voice, looking alarmed.

Jackson gave him his warmest smile, one he usually reserved for Katie and Kera. He stepped forward. "Are you Prez?"

"Who wants to know?" The man's cheeks were sunken, and he was missing some bottom teeth, but his eyes were clear and lucid.

"I'm Detective Jackson. You're not in any trouble, but I'd like to speak with you for a few minutes. My partner Schak will join us in a second." Jackson had his digital recorder in the palm of his hand and clicked it on. Legally, he was supposed to inform Prez he was being recorded. He'd wait for the right moment.

"I'm about to get some dinner here. Don't get me kicked out." Prez clutched his bulging plastic bag with bony fingers.

"We won't." Jackson smiled again. "What's your full name?"

"Prescott Sutton."

"I like it. Would you rather be called Prez though?"

"Yes."

"Okay. I just want to ask about your last camping spot behind Pete's Pad. It looked like a safe dry place."

"So?"

"How long had you been camped there?"

"A couple weeks. I didn't make any trouble."

Schak brought two stools, and they sat at the end of the counter. Their presence semi-obstructed the flow of people into the restaurant, and a few diners mumbled as they stepped around. The room filled with muffled voices and the smell of unwashed clothes and hair. Even the fresh-baked bread and meatloaf aroma drifting from the kitchen couldn't mask the pungent odor generated by fifty people without access to hot water.

"The last time you were behind the parking lot was

Thursday. Do you remember that night?"

"Not really."

"This is important, Prez. A man was killed. We need to know if you saw anything, and I need to record your statement."

Prez blinked rapidly and squeezed his hands together. "Maybe I did and maybe I didn't. I don't trust myself after a few belts of Jim Beam."

"This isn't a courtroom. Tell us what you saw."

"Or heard," Schak added.

"I heard whistling, so I crawled out of my tent. Then it stopped."

"Who was whistling?"

"Someone in the parking lot. They walked up to the Jeep in the corner."

A young woman in a long white apron set a plate of food in front of their witness, then served the man next to him. Prez dug in, gulping meatloaf like a man who didn't trust it to still be there if he looked away. Jackson let him eat. He'd learned patience on the job long ago, and this was nowhere near the worst of the situations he'd sat through.

When Prez slowed down and furtively glanced over, Jackson prodded, "What happened next?"

"The window came down, and she put her face next to the man in the Jeep."

"You're sure it was a woman?"

"I think so."

"And what do you mean 'put her face next to his'? Like a kiss?" Jackson found this puzzling.

"Maybe." Prez wiped his hand across his mouth. "It was dark. I couldn't tell."

Jackson decided to just get the whole story down. "Then

what happened?"

"The man laid his head back, and the woman reached for something in her pocket. I thought she was selling drugs, but she wasn't." Prez's attention wandered for a moment, like he was back there, reliving the scene.

"What else happened?"

"She said something, but I didn't hear it. Then she killed him. Like that." He made a knifing gesture across his throat, then looked around, as if embarrassed. Prez's eyes started to water.

"Did you see anything else? Like where the person went?"

"I closed my eyes after that. I didn't want to see."

*Crap.* "Did you hear anything? Like a car start?"

"I heard her run to the canal. I worried that she saw me, but I don't think she did. Then I heard a splash."

*The weapon!* A little tremor ran up Jackson's spine. "Big splash or little splash?"

"A quiet splash. I looked out again and she was running toward the road."

"Was she tall or short? Skinny or good-sized?

"Tall, like a man. But she had a long ponytail."

*Like Sierra's dreadlocks.* "Would you recognize her if you saw her again?"

He shook his head. "It was too dark."

"Thanks, Prez." Jackson reached for his business card, knowing it was a waste of time. "Would you be willing to testify at a hearing?"

"No." The homeless man slid off his stool. "I don't like court."

Jackson wanted to grab his arm and hold him back for a minute, but he knew better. He jumped up and kept pace with Prez as he scurried from the restaurant. Schak was right behind.

"Will you come to my office and make a video?" he pleaded.

Prez didn't even look back as he ran across the street, clutching his green plastic bag.

"I guess we need to put on our waders and search the canal." Schak sounded surprisingly cheerful about it.

"We need a round-the-clock watch on Sierra Kent too." But Jackson doubted he could get the resources for it.

They started back toward the department, moving at a rapid clip. Jackson felt physically lighter. Knowing they probably had the right suspect simplified their investigation. They still had to search the canal and build a case, but a lot of the pressure was off now.

## Chapter 16

*Early Saturday morning*

Sophie hurried across the newspaper's nearly empty parking lot and used her ID badge to enter the building. The lower level was a ghost town of empty cubicles and lifeless copiers. After the massive layoffs, management had moved the remaining staff upstairs, hoping to lease out the office space below. So far that hadn't happened.

On weekends, the upper level was nearly empty too, with only a couple of sports reporters and a single copy editor on duty. The quiet was great for focusing and getting things done, but she thrived on interaction, and the stillness was almost creepy.

Sophie said hello to the sports guys who were watching TV—tough job they had—then brewed a cup of mint tea and settled into her workspace. She made a dozen calls to Rafel Mazari's friends and family, but no one answered. She decided that when she tried again, she'd use her cell phone instead of the paper's line, which showed *Willamette News* as the caller.

After thirty minutes of getting nowhere, she finally connected with Rafel's National Guard captain. During a productive interview, she learned Rafel had served with the 1249th Battalion and been honorably discharged after he returned from Afghanistan. The captain spoke highly of Rafel, calling him a "dedicated soldier who was well-liked and trusted by his team."

He also told her the story of Rafel's injury, giving her a blow-by-blow account of the mission they'd been on when Rafel stepped on a land mine in the Marjah District. He'd almost died twice during the helicopter evacuation to a medic unit in Kuwait, before being flown to Germany. Later, during his stay at the Madigan Army Medical Center, Rafel had been given the Oregon Exceptional Service Award. The captain also made an offhand comment about Rafel not being able to wear his state award on his national military uniform. Sophie realized she didn't know much about how the National Guard functioned in connection with the federal military, but she wasn't sure it was relevant to her feature. Still, she asked a few questions and learned that when the federal military requested state units, those soldiers became part of a larger military battalion and were under federal jurisdiction during their combat service.

Near the end of the conversation, she asked if Rafel had received counseling after his trauma. The captain had given what sounded like a standard line about counseling being "available to all our service men and women," then terminated the interview shortly after.

He'd also given her the names and numbers of two soldiers Rafel had served with, but neither answered, so she left messages. Sophie wrote a lead for her story, then started to outline the basic structure. Her phone rang, sounding surprisingly loud in the quiet building.

"This is Sasha Altman, returning your call."

*Yes! This wouldn't have been much of a story without input from Rafel's family.* "Thanks for getting back to me. I know this must be a painful time for you."

"I'm devastated by the loss of my brother and shocked by

his murder." Sasha had a low, silky voice with an unusual cadence. "But I want people to know the good things about him."

"As opposed to the focus on the bomb squad being called out to his house?"

"Yes. The news last night made him sound like a crazy person."

"My story will highlight his National Guard duty and his deployment, as well as offer readers a full picture of who he was as a person. Can we meet today?"

After a brief silence, Sasha said, "I can give you an hour. I hope you won't dwell on his injury and his struggle to adjust."

Sophie jotted down the phrase with quote marks around it. "I don't plan to. What time is good for you?"

"Around one-thirty is fine. I have a class after that."

"Should I come to your home or would you be more comfortable meeting in public?"

"Please come to my home. I have kids."

After a quick lunch at Café Yumm, Sophie took Beltline to River Road and headed for Sasha's home on Springcreek. She realized the woman lived within a few miles of her brother, so Sophie stopped by Rafel Mazari's house on the way. The City-section photographer was already there, and they chatted on the sidewalk for a minute. No cars were in the driveway, and Sophie wondered where the widow was. She had a feeling Sierra Kent was not likely to talk to her for this story.

It started to rain, so she hopped back in her car and drove out to Springcreek. Sasha's two-story house had been recently built and painted an unusual mix of pink and gray.

The playpen-sized front yard was covered with lush grass that looked like it could be rolled up and moved.

The woman who answered the door had mocha-colored skin, perfectly straight ebony hair, and the whitest teeth Sophie had ever seen. They introduced themselves, then Sasha gestured toward chairs in the front room. The muffled sound of kids playing came from a back room, and a hint of incense wafted from Sasha's loose purple shirt as she walked. Sophie was curious about her nationality and tried to think of the correct way to ask.

As they sat down, she said, "I'd like to know about your brother's name. Where did Mazari originate?"

"A Pashtun tribe. My father was born on the Pakistan/Afghanistan border and came to America when he was a child. I almost kept the family name when I got married, but my husband thought it would be best for our children to have his surname."

"How many kids do you have?" Sophie asked to be polite.

"Two boys, five and three. Rafel's son, Adam, is staying with us for a while now too."

The news of the child surprised Sophie. "This must be terrible for him. Can I ask why he's not with his mother?"

"Adam's biological mother was Rafel's first wife, and she died when he was five. Sierra has been a stepmother to Adam, but she's dealing with detectives and other difficulties right now." Sasha's flawless face remained impassive, but there was so much more in her tone, Sophie couldn't decide what to ask next.

She pulled out her recorder. "May I?"

"All right."

"You said Sierra was dealing with the police. Is she under investigation?"

"They're questioning her right now. She called to request I keep Adam for the weekend."

Sophie had to ask. "Do you think Sierra was involved in Rafel's murder?"

Sasha didn't blink or look surprised. "No. Sierra may be many things, but she's not a killer and had nothing to gain by Rafel's death."

More loaded phrases. "What are some of Sierra's *many things*?"

Sasha gave her a knowing smile. "I don't want to speak ill of my sister-in-law. Let's just say her politics and personal focus are not something I relate to. And it surprised me that Rafel got caught up in all of it."

"Will you elaborate? I don't know much about Sierra." *Except what she'd learned on her Facebook page.*

"I'd rather talk about Rafel."

"Okay. What was he like as a child?"

"He was wonderful fun." Sasha's composure cracked, and she looked like she might cry. But she continued, "We lived on a few acres farther out River Road, and Rafel was always coming up with some new adventure. He and his friends built a fort and a rope swing and dug a hiding pit. We used to play wild versions of hide and seek, and Rafel was always coming up with some new twist."

"What were his friends' names?"

"Cody Pittman and Jake Sawyer. The three of them went everywhere together. Especially after the camping trip where they got lost and survived a night in the woods together. It bonded them."

A light-haired boy of eight or so ran up to them. "Aunt Sasha, can I watch TV in the family room? Your guys are bugging me."

*This must be Adam.* Sophie studied him, realizing he didn't look anything like Rafel.

"Okay, but quietly, please," Sasha said. "We're still talking. And no adult shows."

The boy trotted off, and his aunt apologized for the intrusion.

"No problem." Sophie glanced at her questions. "Were you surprised when Rafel joined the National Guard?"

"Yes and no. I think he saw the guard as another adventure."

"How did you feel about it?"

"I was proud of him, but a little worried too. I knew deployment was a possibility, even though Rafel didn't believe it would happen."

"How did your parents feel?"

"Dad was proud of him too."

"Are your parents still out on River Road?"

"Our father is, but our mother left us when were young."

"That must have been devastating. How old were you?"

"Rafel was twelve and I was ten. We were crushed." Sasha's voice grew quiet. "She left a short note but didn't say a personal goodbye. I took it harder than the guys. They were stoic, and Rafel was quiet for a long time after she left."

"And you've never heard from her?"

"No, but I still think about her sometimes. Her family disowned her when she married my father, then he forced his old-world ideas on her. I think she just couldn't take the isolation anymore."

"That's tragic. Sad for her, and for you and Rafel." Sophie was intrigued by the decades-old family drama and hoped to work it into her story that Rafel had been abandoned by his mother at a young age. "Can I ask if the problem between the families was cultural? Is your father Islamic?"

"He followed many Islamic traditions out of habit, but I think he lost his faith in Allah. Neither Rafel nor I are religious, but we're still Pashtun."

"Was it hard for Rafel to fight the Taliban in Afghanistan?"

"You ask good questions." Sasha closed her eyes for a moment. "Rafel and I are very much American, and my brother never expected to be deployed. He had just gotten married. So he had mixed feelings about his service, but he was loyal to this country and loyal to the fight against terrorism. Most Middle Eastern people hate the terrorists too."

"It must have been difficult for Sierra to be alone for a year right after getting married."

Sasha's jaw tightened, and she reached for the recorder to shut it off. "Sierra is not the kind of woman who can be alone. She dishonored my brother, and I may never forgive her for that."

Sophie understood the subtext and grudgingly let the subject go, despite her burning desire to know who Sierra had screwed while her husband was off fighting for his country. Sophie would ask someone else. Sasha was clearly distressed by the issue and not likely to tell her anyway.

Sophie turned the recorder back on and changed the subject. "The bomb squad was called out to Rafel and Sierra's house yesterday after the police searched it. Do you know what that was about?"

Sasha pressed her lips together. "I don't really want to talk about this, but I also don't want people to speculate and make it worse."

"I'll minimize the subject in my story."

Sasha drew in a weary breath. "Our father worked as a miner when he was young and used explosives on the job. He became a little obsessed and always kept a supply of dynamite. He used it around the farm sometimes, and Rafel became just as obsessed."

Overwhelmed by the irony, Sophie didn't know if she could ask the next question. Still, it worked its way out of her mouth. "How did you feel when Rafel lost his leg to an explosive device?"

"I was crushed by the news but grateful he was alive, just like anyone else would feel." His sister's lips trembled. "Yet I had this sense of the inevitable."

"Did you know Rafel still kept explosives in his home even after his injury?"

"No, but I'm not surprised."

Sophie was freaked out by it. "Were Rafel and his father close?"

"They were when Rafi was young, then over the years, I sensed a distance between them."

"Any idea why?'

Sasha glanced away. "No."

Sophie suspected there was something to pursue. "Will you give me contact information for your father? I'd like to talk to him."

"No." Sasha's tone was unequivocal.

"When is Rafel's funeral service?"

"Monday at eleven. We would have liked to hold it sooner, but they won't release his body until then."

"Is he having a military funeral?" Sophie was thinking of the great photos it would give her for the story.

"No. Our father won't allow it. He's bitter toward the military and wants a simple tribal burial." Sasha gave a sad smile. "Or the American version of it."

Sophie asked for details about the service, thinking she might attend and have a chance to talk to Rafel's father. Or maybe run into Jackson and coax more details about the murder from him. She knew detectives often attended the funeral services of the victims they investigated.

"Is there anything else you want me to know about your brother?"

"He was a loving father. He also loved animals and volunteered in the clinic where Sierra worked. He had a good heart."

## Chapter 17

*Saturday, Nov. 12, 5:43 p.m.*

Back at his desk, Jackson prepped for the meeting by adding his new notes to the main file. He'd already ordered pizza and planned to keep the discussion short. He hated making his team members work late on Saturday. He'd also made a call to the DA and left a message telling him about their eyewitness. Slonecker wouldn't be impressed. If Prez couldn't be counted on to show up in court, he couldn't help them convict Sierra. Jackson knew he had to meet with Sergeant Lammers soon too and let her know they had a solid suspect.

He was pleased to see Quince in the conference room. Quince was young, but he'd made detective early in his career and his experience in the other investigative units made him a good asset. He touched the man's shoulder on the way in. "Glad you could make it. How's the fraud case coming?"

"It's interesting, but I'll wait until the others come in. They'll want to hear this."

"Did you get Mazari's banking records?"

"I did. I went to Cranston's house at eight-thirty this morning, and he read the subpoena in his bathrobe."

"Nice visual," Evans commented as she came in. "Glad it

was you and not me."

"Cranston can be abrasive, but he comes through for us." Quince turned back to Jackson. "The credit union opened at ten, and they made copies for me while I stood there. You gotta love local institutions. Meanwhile, I won't get the charity's records from the online bank until Monday...if I'm lucky."

Schak came in carrying a tall coffee. The rich aroma made Jackson salivate. "You didn't get me one?"

"Sorry."

"You can take the board." Jackson grinned.

"I'm still not letting go of the coffee." Schak dropped his carryall and moved to the long whiteboard, still clutching his cup.

"Let's get started," Jackson said. "I have two major updates. One, we have forensic evidence linking Sierra Kent to the crime scene—or I should say the vicinity of the crime scene." Jackson passed out his updated case notes as he talked. "We also have an eyewitness to the attack. He can't specifically identify the killer, but he thinks it was a woman with a long ponytail. And he heard the person throw something into the canal, so I'll be searching for it first thing tomorrow. You can join me if you want to."

"Should we be out there right now?" Evans was ready to bolt from her chair.

"It's nearly dark. Our time will be better spent in the morning. The eyewitness is a homeless man named Prez who may not ever make it to court, but I want you to hear his statement." Jackson played the recording, and Evans and Quince strained to hear the dialogue over the noisy restaurant background.

When it was over, Evans said, "The whistling is a little

odd. Women don't whistle very often."

"Some do," Schak countered. "What about the attacker putting their face next to the victim? Men don't do that with other men."

"Sierra will sound believable to a jury." Evans gestured with her hands. "Unless she confesses, I say we keep open to other suspects. For example, Pittman lied about his alibi Thursday night. He told you he went home to his wife after leaving the tavern. When I talked to Hailey Pittman this morning, she said she left him months ago. They don't even live together."

Jackson hated being lied to, even though he expected it. "We have to question Pittman again, maybe bring him in this time. He walked out on our last conversation, and now we have a lot more to discuss."

"What about Mazari's autopsy?" Schak asked. "In Sierra's interview, you mentioned he didn't have a penis. Were you serious?"

"Yes. He's got nothing but scar tissue there now." Just thinking about it made Jackson uncomfortable.

"It seems pretty fucked-up for a man who lost his junk to a landmine to keep dynamite in his house." Schak's eyebrows expressed his disbelief.

"It's weird, all right," Jackson said. "I wonder what a shrink would say."

"Maybe he's facing his fears," Evans offered.

"Maybe. But I don't see how it's relevant to the case." Jackson wanted to move on. "What else have we got?"

Schak updated the board as Evans looked at her notes. "I also learned Pittman was an Iraq veteran, so I asked his wife if he'd come into any unexpected money lately. She said she didn't know, but she looked scared and her voice quivered.

She also recognized the name Veterans Relief Fund. I'd love to get a look at Jake Pittman's bank records."

"I would too," Quince said. "My investigation of the fraud involving the charity is still premature, but two of these friends were ex-military, both had money troubles, and one was murdered."

"Did you find anything interesting in Mazari's bank files?" Jackson asked.

"I haven't had time to look. I spent the day tracking down fraud victims." Quince handed Jackson a thick file. "I found seven local people who made voluntary contributions to the charity in amounts ranging from $50 to $300. The scammers targeted senior centers and retirement homes through emails and flyers slipped under their doors. So nobody had direct contact with the charity's founders, and so far, Molly Pershing is the only victim to have money stolen from her."

"I'd like the names of the people who donated to the charity and the amount of the contribution," Jackson said. "I'll cross-check them against Mazari's bank statement."

"The money went to an online bank," Quince said. "Unless Mazari was stupid enough to link the fraudulent charity account to his own, you may not be able to make direct connections."

"You think Mazari and Pittman might have set up the phony charity and conned old people into donating to it?" Evans nodded as she summed up the possible scenario.

"We don't know yet," Quince said. "I'm still waiting to hear from the website's hosting company, so I won't have more information until Monday."

"It's worth checking out." Jackson wasn't invested in the theory, but money was one of the leading motivations to kill.

"I've got Molly Pershing's computer, but there's almost

nothing on it," Quince added. "And her neighbors didn't see her with anyone suspicious, but I haven't talked to them all yet. Now that we have a second military connection, I'll go back and show Mazari and Pittman's photos to Molly's neighbors."

The pizza arrived and they ate without much discussion. As they finished, Jackson said, "You guys might as well call it a night. Enjoy what's left of your Saturday evening."

"What are *you* going to do?" Evans narrowed her eyes at him.

"I was thinking I'd go out and see Pittman again. Find out why he lied to me."

"You're not going alone." Schak and Evans said it simultaneously.

Jackson laughed. "I guess not. Evans, I hear you have a date with Stricklyn, so I'll let Schak ruin his Saturday night."

"Netflix will be disappointed, but my wife probably won't care." Schak grinned. "I'll skip the dip in the canal in the morning and let Evans get wet instead."

"That's a shitty deal," Evans complained half-heartedly.

"Better make your date special then." Quince winked at her.

Evans pushed aside her pizza. "I will. See you tomorrow." She grabbed her shoulder bag and waltzed out.

Jackson started gathering up the remains of the pizza meal.

"Are you sure we need to do this tonight?" Schak asked. "We have a solid suspect in custody and no reason to think Pittman is going anywhere. I say we wait until tomorrow."

Jackson considered it. He had bank records to look at and unpacking to do. "Tell you what. I'll call Pittman. If he answers, we go round him up. Otherwise, we'll find him tomorrow right after we search the canal."

"Deal." Schak pulled his hands together as if in prayer. "Please let him be out drinking and not hear the phone."

Quince burst out laughing. "Are you getting too old for this?"

Schak gave him the finger.

Pittman didn't answer and Jackson didn't leave a message.


In the parking garage, he climbed in his car, put in his earpiece, and called Katie again. He started to drive out of the lot, then decided to wait. He was trying not to talk on his phone and drive unless it was necessary police business.

His daughter picked up, sounding both amused and annoyed. "I'm fine, Dad. Mom's sober, Ivan is nice, and we're all going out to a movie."

"Does that include Harlan?"

"Yes. He's meeting us there. We won't be alone, even for a minute."

"What are you seeing?"

"The Footloose remake."

"Sounds fun."

"Liar." Katie laughed. "I'll be home tomorrow night."

"Next weekend, I want to start making a different frame for the trike, one with more stability. Are you up for helping me weld it?" She'd done most of the welding on the three-wheeled motorcycle they'd built together the summer before. He'd loved working with her the way he'd spent time with his dad.

"I don't think so. Harlan and I are going to volunteer with the Stream Team on weekends."

Jackson was disappointed, but how could he argue with a

kid who wanted to make the world a better place? "I miss our time together."

"We still have Firefly movie nights."

"Let's grill tomorrow. We haven't done that in a while."

"I'd like that."

"I miss you."

She laughed again. "No you don't—you're on a case. But I love your dedication."

"Thanks, sweetie."

"Gotta go."

Not ready to quit working for the night, Jackson drove out to Pete's Pad and spent an hour asking patrons if they'd seen the guy with the shaved head and beard. Many of the same people were in the tavern from the night before—except Nikki, the one he wanted to see—and the whole activity depressed him. He'd witnessed enough drinking from his ex-wife to last a lifetime. Eventually, an older man told him the description matched one of his co-workers but that the co-worker was religious and had never been in the bar. Jackson took down the name and place of employment, but intuitively knew it was a dead end.

At home, he sat in his recliner, slipped off his shoes, and let his mind simply drift. He rarely stopped thinking, analyzing, and planning, even on weekends. Homicide cases seeped into his brain chemistry, and he thought about them even when he was working in the yard or tinkering with one of his vehicles. But he'd learned that shutting down for a while—his own brand of meditation—could inspire connections that would come to him later.

He dozed off for a few minutes, then jumped up and

grabbed a diet Pepsi. He had things to accomplish. But first he called Kera. No answer. That worried him, but he pushed it aside and left her a friendly message: "Hey gorgeous, just calling to confirm our plans for tomorrow afternoon. I'll be there around one." He resisted the urge to say something stupid like *Wear something sexy.* "I love you." He couldn't go wrong with that.

Time to unpack. Jackson started in the bedroom, shoving his clothes into the familiar dresser and the new closet. Derrick had generously vacated the master bedroom, since he wouldn't be home much. Jackson also put away three boxes of food in the kitchen, then looked at the five containers with kitchen supplies still to go and sighed. Tomorrow. This case still needed his attention.

He grabbed the stack of Mazari's account statements from his carryall and sat down at the kitchen table. This dining room was bigger than his old home, but the lighting wasn't as nice. He'd have to replace the funky overhead fixture and install some track lighting. Maybe a skylight.

The first thing he noticed was Mazari had made nearly all cash deposits and cash withdrawals. No paychecks deposited, no debit card transactions. A man who preferred to deal in cash—or simply had no choice? If Mazari didn't have a job, where was the cash coming from? The victim's name was the only one on the credit union account. Sierra claimed they kept their money separately, but she must have paid the bills, because this account only had an average balance of $283.67 for the previous month.

To keep them afloat, Sierra had been working at the veterinary clinic as well as making and selling her pet products at the Saturday market—while Rafel did what? Odd jobs for fifty dollars here and two hundred there? That must have been stressful for both of them. Was he not eligible for disability?

The deposits reminded Jackson of the donations Quince had said were made to the Veterans Relief Fund. But Mazari's cash deposits didn't seem like enough to account for all of the charity's funds. If he had been involved with the scam, where had the rest of the money gone? Had Pittman been part of it? He was a struggling veteran too. What had Evans said? That Pittman's wife had seemed scared and evasive when she asked about unexpected money.

Clearly, the seven grand the charity had stolen from Molly Pershing had never been in Rafel Mazari's account. His death might have made more sense if it had. Unless Sierra had known about the fraud and killed her husband to get her hands on the cash. Jackson rubbed his eyes and got up for a glass of water.

Mazari had been killed Thursday night, and Molly Pershing had discovered the missing money Friday morning. Jackson looked at the copy of Molly's bank transactions Quince had included. The huge transfer had been made at 1:35 Wednesday afternoon. *Damn*. He wished he had the phony charity's records so he could see where the money went.

Jackson played out several scenarios. Mazari made the audacious money grab, then Sierra found the cash, and they fought about it. She decided she'd had enough of him and plotted to kill him that evening, keeping his cash to start a new life with her lover. But who was her lover?

What if Pittman was her lover and made the fraudulent transaction? Then Sierra killed her husband to keep Rafel from ever knowing about the big money and to cut him out of the picture?

Of course, it was also possible the two cases were unrelated, and Sierra and killed her husband because he couldn't have sex or father children, but had an insurance policy in her name. Could he get a court order to search Sierra's bank records? That would be interesting.

Jackson's phone rang, startling him. It took a minute to find the device in the chair where he'd dozed earlier. *Derrick Jackson*. He still wasn't used to seeing his brother's name on his caller ID. They'd gone ten years without talking to each other, and now they were roommates. "Hey, Derrick. What's up?"

"I'm sitting in a truck stop near Waterloo, Iowa. I need to sleep but I drank too much coffee."

"I'm in the same mode."

"Did you get moved in?"

"We did. And it's a little weird to be here."

"I hope the place is clean enough."

"It's fine. But I got called out on a homicide, so I haven't unpacked much yet."

Derrick laughed. "I still have boxes of stuff in the garage from when I moved back in ten years ago."

"We can have a garage sale soon."

"Did I leave you enough space for your stuff?" Derrick had lived in the house since their parents died and had finally hauled the old family furniture off to Goodwill to make room for Jackson's things. It was another step forward for his brother.

"Everything is great. And I love your 52-inch TV. I'll feel pretty spoiled watching American Chopper on this thing."

"I'll be home next Friday, then I leave again on Tuesday. Just so you can plan."

Living with his brother was a temporary situation,

Jackson reminded himself. The goal was to fix up the house and sell it, splitting the equity.

"Okay. I'll see you next Friday. Take care."

# Chapter 18

*Sunday, Nov. 13, 6:45 a.m.*

The sun trickled through the blinds, and Jackson lay there for a moment, drifting in and out of sleep, thinking how nice it was not to be jarred awake by an alarm. He finally rolled out of bed. It was still too damn early to be awake on Sunday, but his job had no boundaries. At the least the sun was out, Jackson thought, rummaging through a box in the corner to find his jogging shoes and waterproof boots.

He drank a cup of coffee and went for a quick run, covering some of the same territory he had from his previous house. The move had been less than a mile. Except for a short stint in an apartment across town, he'd lived in this neighborhood his entire life. Sometimes it made him feel too sheltered, and he longed to get out of Oregon and see the world. Most of the time, he was happy to live in such a great year-round place with pretty, warm summers and wet, mild winters. No hurricanes, snowstorms, or tornadoes. Not to mention a population that valued progressive ideas about the environment and personal responsibility.

After a quick breakfast, he drove into the parking lot at Pete's Pad around eight and had the place to himself. He'd texted his team an hour ago and expected Schak and Evans to show up any minute. Evans was usually the first to arrive, but if she'd spent the night with Stricklyn, she might take her time getting down here. Jackson was glad she was dating someone suited to her. He'd told her more than once she'd never be happy with a civilian. He was also a little bothered—and a little relieved—that her attention was elsewhere. He chose not to examine those feelings. In the big picture, they weren't important.

While he waited, his phone rang. It was Officer Rice, the department sketch artist. "Hey, Jackson. Sorry for the delay in getting back to you. I'm in Astoria for the weekend and just saw your message this morning."

"And I'm sorry to bother you on your time off. When are you back to work?"

"Tuesday morning."

*Crap.* Jackson wanted to ask her to come back early from the coast, but he knew it wasn't reasonable. Nikki might not even be willing to come in today. "Can we set up a time for you to work with my witness?"

"How about ten? That'll give me a couple of hours to catch up."

"Okay. I'll see you then."

Jackson hung up and opened his car door. The crisp cold air and blue sky were a nice change after three days of gray drizzle. He changed into the knee-high fishing boots he'd only had on once last summer when he'd fished with Schak at Triangle Lake. An excellent day.

Schak pulled in moments later and brought him a steaming cup of Fastlane dark brew.

"Thanks. You know I was joking about the coffee yesterday."

"Yeah, right."

Jackson took a sip. "Good stuff. Shall we do this?"

"I'm as ready as I get."

They used yellow tape to mark the area along the canal that was directly accessible from the parking lot after crossing the grassy area. The assailant could have walked along the canal in either direction, but the bank was thick with shrubs and small evergreens and not easy to navigate. Besides, Prez had heard the splash, so the killer couldn't have gone far to get rid of the weapon. They would focus on the area just below where the homeless camp had been.

Evans rushed up moments later, looking bright-eyed and sexy in jeans, a snug sweater, and waders.

"Sorry I'm late. Breakfast took too long."

Jackson bit back a teasing but inappropriate comment, while Schak said, "Don't worry, we waited so you could be the first one in the water."

"Thanks." She gave him a friendly punch on the arm and rolled up her sleeves. "I brought everyone elbow-length gloves." Evans passed out bright yellow rubber gloves, then headed down the short, steep embankment. Jackson followed, pushing aside vegetation and hoping they'd get lucky.

At that particular bend in its journey through Eugene, the canal was wide and shallow but a little murky from yesterday's rain. They spread out ten feet apart on the bank and started with a visual search from there.

"Did the crime techs already search the canal?" Schak asked.

"I didn't ask Parker to, and she was on the scene by herself." Jackson realized that had been a mistake. The patrol cops had searched the trashcans behind the tavern and those of its neighboring businesses, which had seemed sufficient at the time.

"No worries," Evans said. "Now we have a good reason to." She stepped into the water, bent over, and began combing through the silt, moss, and rocks with her gloved hands. The water soaked the edges of her blue sweater sleeves.

Jackson and Schak both plunged forward, startling a family of ducks.

"Watch out," Schak called, flipping water at the fleeing fowl.

Jackson loved the good-naturedness of his team. He'd worked with some crusty old farts during his first five years in the detective unit, and they would have complained bitterly about wading in the canal on a cold Sunday morning.

"I'll be damned," Evans called out. She was directly below the easiest route from the top of the embankment and only a few feet into the canal. She held up a long silver item.

"What is it?" Jackson climbed out of the water and started toward her along the edge.

"A scalpel."

"Like a surgeon or veterinarian would use." Jackson reached for it as Evans held it out.

"The killer probably intended to toss the syringe in the canal too, but accidentally dropped it instead," Evans speculated. "Maybe they couldn't find it in the dark, so they left it, hoping it would look like junkie trash."

"I wonder if there's any chance of getting a print from this scalpel."

"It might surprise us." Evans reached for an evidence bag. "This water may be too cold to break down body oil in only a few days."

"Good work, Evans."

She scoffed. "I got lucky. They didn't throw it far."

Schak made his way over, stepping through some low-growing, willow-like branches. "What now?"

"Evans will check the evidence into the lab, while you and I find Jake Pittman." Jackson started up the embankment, and the others followed. When they were back on the flat grassy strip, Jackson said, "Pittman's reason for lying about that night could be minor, but we still need to know. If Sierra's the killer, she may not have acted alone."

"What do you mean?" Evans cocked her head.

"What if Sierra was cheating with Pittman? What if they colluded to kill Mazari?"

Schak gave him a look. "I know Pittman lied, but what makes you think this is more than a spouse-on-spouse homicide?"

"The money," Jackson said. "Mazari's recent cash deposits look suspiciously like the donations Quince said were made to the phony veterans' charity. We'll know more when we get the charity's bank records. And Pittman's wife recognized the name of the charity. What if the two ex-military guys were operating the scam together? What if this murder is about the seven grand?"

"Interesting," Evans said. "You think Sierra was involved with Pittman and knew about the theft?"

"It's just a theory. But if she had a lover, we need to figure out who he is."

"Let's go ask Pittman." Schak moved toward his car.

Jackson did the same. "We'll check his house first, then we'll start calling the people he knows."

"The lab is a quick stop," Evans said. "What else can I do?"

"Stop by the Animal Care Clinic and see if you can interview Sierra's boss. Mazari seemed to think she was sleeping with him. After that, take the afternoon off. I plan to as soon as we wrap this up." Jackson smiled to himself, remembering his plans with Kera.

Pittman's home in Northeast Eugene was a small L-shaped duplex on the corner of Kentwood and Kings, with his unit on the Kentwood side. Jackson parked on the street and, out of habit, checked his cell phone for the time: 9:45 a.m. Still early. In the driveway was an older-model truck with beat-up pumpkin-colored paint. Good, Pittman was home. The yard on the Kentwood side was thick with ornamental shrubs, and the lawn was tidy. Around the corner, the other half of the duplex had a neglected look. Jackson remembered Pittman was a landscaper.

He climbed out of his cruiser to stretch his legs while he waited for Schak. The comforting smell of sizzling bacon drifted in from somewhere, and his stomach growled. As he walked toward the truck to note the make and license plate, a cat skittered across the driveway and a cold wind cut through his suede jacket. Jackson took down the information and got back in his vehicle to wait. No point in making Pittman nervous before they confronted him.

Schak arrived five minutes later and parked behind him. In unison, they climbed out of their cars and moved up the driveway, the only path to the front door. Subconsciously, Jackson touched his Sig Sauer under his jacket, then pushed the fabric behind the weapon, making it visible and accessible.

With Schak a step behind him, Jackson gave the metal door three brisk knocks. He heard no sound and sensed no movement in response. He pounded again.

The house stayed quiet. A dim light glowed through the

opening between the drapes on the front window.

"I'm going to look in," he said softly.

Schak moved out of his way, and Jackson stepped down the sidewalk to the window. He leaned over the low shrub to peer in. The living room, nearly empty except for a couch and a TV, was unoccupied.

"He's not in the front room."

Jackson stepped back to the door and pounded again. Pittman's vehicle was here, so he wanted to believe the man was too. But he could have left with someone or gone out for a run, Jackson's analytical side countered.

He took his notepad from his bag, found Pittman's phone number, and called it. After five rings, it went to voicemail: "This is Jake. Leave me a message."

He didn't hear it ring in the house, but Jackson's instinct told him Pittman was home. On impulse, he tried the doorknob, and the door swung open a few inches. Now what? What was their legal position here? Pittman was wanted for questioning in a murder.

He looked at Schak. His partner nodded.

Jackson pushed open the door fully and called out, "Eugene Police."

No response. With the front door wide open, they could see the living room was empty and the couch covers were askew. Low light came from the kitchen.

"Pittman, we know you're in there. It's Detectives Jackson and Schakowski. We just want to ask a few questions."

The house stayed quiet. He thought about Pittman's military background, and a vivid image of Mazari's slit throat flashed in Jackson's mind. He said softly to Schak, "Pittman is ex-military and likely has a weapon. If he's home, he's either hiding or sleeping. This could get sticky."

"Want me to call for backup?"

Jackson wasn't sure. Pittman had never made any kind of threat, and they had a primary suspect in custody. "It's your call. I just want to be prepared to take him down if he gets aggressive."

"I'm good. Let's do this."

They drew their weapons and moved quickly across the small dark living room. To the right, the space opened into a short hallway with two doors. Ahead lay a small dining area, with baskets of laundry on the floor and no table they could see. To the left was a long narrow kitchen.

Jackson flipped a light switch near the opening. In the dull yellow glow of the overhead bulb, they saw the rest of the dining room. Behind the laundry baskets lay a body. Jake Pittman was face up on the floor, his throat slit open in an ugly gash.

## Chapter 19

"Holy shit." Schak looked stunned.

"He's been dead for a while." Jackson knew congealed blood even from a few feet away. "Goddammit! We should have come out here last night."

"I wish we had, but we didn't have any reason to expect this."

Jackson was too upset with himself to respond. What time had this happened? Could they have prevented it by bringing Jake Pittman into the department?

"We have to secure the building," Schak said. He glanced at the hallway, where an attacker might hide.

Jackson shoved aside his regrets, and they both moved into the parallel hallway, weapons drawn. Schak went to the right, and Jackson pushed open a door to the left. The bedroom was as sparse as the rest of the house, with only a bed and a dresser. Pittman's wife must have taken most of the furniture when she left him. The mattress was pulled half off the box spring, and everything from the closet had been yanked out, leaving clothing, shoes, sports equipment, and photos scattered on the floor. Jackson checked the back of the closet, then retreated to the hall, where he noticed the linen cabinet had been ransacked too, leaving a pile of towels on the floor.

Schak came out of a second bedroom. "All clear."

"The assailant was searching for something," Jackson said.

They checked the attached single-car garage, which held only landscaping tools and no place for a killer to hide. Re-entering through the kitchen, they stopped by the body in the half-empty dining area.

Jackson picked up his carryall, dug out paper booties, and handed Schak a pair. It was a little late, but security came first. As they put them on, Schak said, "I've been called out to a lot of dead bodies, but this is the first time I found one."

"Me too." Jackson reached for his phone. "I have to call Lammers."

His sergeant picked up after two rings. "This must be critical, Jackson."

"We have another homicide. Jake Pittman, close friend of Rafel Mazari who was murdered on Thursday. Pittman's throat is also slit."

"Oh, for fuck's sake. What the hell were these guys into?"

"Maybe fraud. A love triangle gone wrong. We'll figure it out."

"What do you need from me?"

"I need Evans out here now and Quince full-time on this case." He gave her the address and cross street. "Will you also check the jail and see if Sierra Kent is still in custody?"

"You've got it. Do you want the command unit sent out?"

The big white RV would give them a place to interview witnesses and suspects and make video recordings on the scene—but he'd be lucky to find a witness. "Thanks, but I don't think it'll help."

"I'll send out the ME and the techs. Keep me posted."

Jackson hung up, took a deep breath, and forced his brain into crime-scene mode. He pulled out two sets of gloves and both cameras. They needed to photograph the floor before walking on it again. He and Schak donned the protective gear, and Jackson handed his partner a camera.

"Let's look for footprints leading out or any drops of blood. Photograph and mark everything." Schak knew the drill, but they both usually verbalized their process to keep from skipping steps. Jackson regretted touching the doorknob with his bare hand on the way in.

"The door showed no sign of forced entry," Schak said. "He probably knew his attacker and let him in."

"Likely." Booties on his feet, Jackson stepped toward the body and squatted. The victim wore the same jeans and sweatshirt he'd had on Friday afternoon when Jackson questioned him. Had he not been home Friday night? Or had he been too busy to change clothes?

The wound in Pittman's neck was wider and more jagged than Mazari's had been, but there was very little blood. The killer had cut his throat after he was dead. Was it meant as a mutilation? Or a distraction? Pittman also had reddish-purple abrasions on his right eye and cheek, as if someone had punched him a few times first. But what had caused his death?

Jackson gently lifted the victim's hands, one at a time. They were stiff with rigor mortis. He'd been dead at least twelve hours, but less than thirty. A cracked nail on Pittman's left index finger held a tiny shred of fabric. Had Pittman grabbed his attacker by the shirt? Jackson dug out tweezers and a two-inch evidence bag, then carefully transferred the fabric. The victim's right hand had two swollen knuckles.

"I think they were in a fistfight," he said loud enough for Schak to hear.

"Not surprised." Schak looked up from the coffee-stained

beige carpet. "We'll need the UV light and luminol to find blood in this filthy mess."

Jackson assumed Parker would have the tools in her van. He slipped his gloved hands into the victim's front jeans pockets, hoping to find a cell phone, even though it hadn't rung when he'd called minutes ago. Two quarters came out of one pocket, and a small receipt was in the other. The paper had been damp at one point and was smudged, but it looked like Pittman had purchased beer at a nearby convenience store.

Where the hell was his cell phone? Mazari's killer had taken his cell phone, now it looked like Pittman's killer had taken his. To destroy the evidence of their calls to each other? They would get the records eventually. Or did the phones have links to the phony charity? One of his team would visit Judge Cranston tomorrow with subpoenas for both phones. Finding Sierra's prints so early had been a huge breakthrough, but it had also derailed certain elements of the investigation that might have been completed already. Jackson would have kicked himself in the ass were it physically possible. Then he remembered it was the weekend, and getting paperwork was nearly impossible, which had hampered their investigation. And because of budget cuts, he was working with a small team that could only do so much.

Tires squealed in the street. The first patrol unit had arrived. Or maybe it was Evans. If she drove like she did everything else, then it was likely her. Jackson wasn't ready for her level of energy on the scene just yet. Something quiet yet disturbing was nagging at the back of his brain but he couldn't connect with it. He needed time to think.

"Schak, if that's Evans, send her out to question the

neighbors about what they saw and heard last night. Maybe we'll get lucky and get a vehicle description."

The arrival was a patrol officer who went right to work securing the perimeter of the house. Jackson rolled up Jake's body at the hip and found his wallet lying under him. Had the killer removed it from his pocket? He flipped it open, noting there was no blood on it. The worn leather held a woman's photo, a car insurance card, and voter registration, but his driver's license was missing, and so were his bank cards. *Crap!* Despite the search the killer had conducted, this clearly wasn't a random robbery. But why take his ID and credit cards? What the hell was going on?

Jackson shifted closer to the victim's upper body and stared at the wound. Not as long as the gash in Mazari's throat and not as deep. And clearly post-mortem. The man's hazel eyes were open and stared back at him. An unexpected jolt of angst stabbed Jackson's gut. Another young life gone. Could he have prevented this?

Jackson forced himself to focus. He had to stay sharp, make note of everything, and find the killer—or killers— before anyone else ended up dead. He was in a unique position to be the first one on the scene. Usually by the time he arrived, witnesses and patrol cops had walked all over the area and often destroyed evidence. His gaze shifted to the corpse's scalp, where blood had dried on his ear. With two gloved fingers, he eased Pittman's head to the right and saw the abrasion just above and behind his ear. Something sharp had penetrated the skull, leaving a tiny portion of his brain exposed.

Jackson let the victim's head roll back. What would the ME and the pathologist say about this death? A fistfight, followed by a blow to the head, followed by the slit throat was his prediction. The cut concerned him. Was the killer imitating Mazari's murder in an attempt to throw them off? Or had he intended to slit his throat all along, but Pittman had fought back? And why did he assume it was a man? Because of the fistfight? Sierra was a big woman and she seemed aggressive. But she was also likely still in jail this morning. They didn't hold arraignments on Sunday.

Jackson reached for his camera and snapped a dozen pictures of the body. He photographed the cream-colored vinyl floor surrounding the corpse, as well as the walls. He could detect no blood spatter, but the vertical print of the pale green wallpaper might be camouflaging it.

Schak, who'd been crawling on the floor between the front door and the dining area, stood and came over. "I found a little piece of fresh mud, and I got photos of a partial muddy shoe print."

"Excellent." Jackson stood. "The man's ID and bank cards are gone."

"Cell phone too?"

"Yes. It's odd."

"What's odd?" From the doorway, Evans pulled on booties, then hurried in. Behind her, another patrol unit screeched to a stop on the street.

Jackson repeated the information as she joined them in the dining room.

"His wife must have taken most of the furniture," Evans commented, looking around at the sparse furnishings. "What's your working theory?"

"Without the Mazari murder, this would look like a home invasion, with the ID and credit cards taken for future fraudulent use. But I'm starting to think both murders were committed for the seven grand stolen from the old woman's account."

"Molly Pershing," Evans supplied. She squatted next to the body. "He took a beating first. And that cut in his throat looks almost like an afterthought."

"An imitation of Mazari's murder," Jackson added.

Schak shook his head. "Do we still think Sierra looks good for the first one?"

"I don't know." Jackson felt like they had to rethink everything.

"Did they release Sierra five minutes after I booked her in?" Evans hands balled into fists. "If they did, she could have done this."

"Lammers said she'd check the jail and call me." Jackson scrambled to form a plan. "Evans, talk to the neighbors. The killer probably came and went in a vehicle. Schak, start searching the house for a cell phone, computer, and personal information. I'll keep examining the body and the surrounding area until Gunderson gets here, then we'll start on subpoenas. We need banking and cell phone information for both victims."

"You really think it's about the money?" Evans looked skeptical.

"Do you have a better idea?"

"Not yet, but I think this could be a personal falling out. Pittman's knuckles are swollen." She pointed at the corpse's hands. "They fought each other with testosterone flowing. I think Sierra might be a factor in this death too."

"I don't doubt it. We'll get back to this discussion later. Let's process the scene now."

"I'm on it." Evans turned and bolted from the house, nearly running into Rich Gunderson.

The ME crossed the living room with his tool bag in hand.

"What the hell is going on? Two murders in three days? And why are you in my crime scene?" Eyebrows furrowed, black shirt wrinkled, Gunderson looked like a man who'd had a late night.

Schak headed for the hallway, and Jackson stepped back into the narrow kitchen.

"We found the body when we came to question him," Jackson explained. "I think he's been dead since last night."

"I'll let you know." Gunderson's tone was curt. He set down his bag and began to take photos.

Jackson didn't feel contrite about examining the body. Being first on the scene was a rare opportunity. He looked around the kitchen. The attacker had searched the cupboards, leaving them open and the contents disheveled. Only a few dishes were in the sink but empty beer bottles filled the space next to the sink. Two bottles sat apart near the end of the counter. One was still half full. He left them for the technicians to transport to the lab. The killer's fingerprints could be on one.

Jackson noticed a small collection of medicine bottles on the shelf above the sink. He picked them up one at time: Relafen, an anti-inflammatory, Sonata, a sleeping pill, and Trexall, which he wasn't sure about. He bagged them individually as evidence. As he started around the end of the counter to backtrack to the living room, a red spot caught his eye. The sharp-edged corner of the pale-green laminate counter had dried blood on it. He stepped closer. A bit of white goop was stuck on the point. *Was that brain tissue?*

"Gunderson? You need to look at this. I think our vic may have hit his head on this corner."

Jackson took close-up photos of the counter's edge while the ME stood up, grunting a little as he did.

Gunderson grabbed a magnifier from his bag and held it over the corner. After a long moment, he said, "Definitely blood. Could also be brain tissue." He grabbed a tiny vial and tweezers and carefully collected the material. "I didn't see a matching wound, but I'm just getting started."

"It's behind his right ear," Jackson said.

Gunderson lifted an eyebrow. "You moved his head?"

"Only a bit."

The ME rolled his eyes and kneeled back down by the body.

"Have you taken his temperature?" Jackson asked.

"Yes. He cooled a little slower than our last victim, but the T.O.D. frame is nearly the same: between eight-thirty and ten-thirty last night. That's my best guess until we know more about what's in his bloodstream."

"Thanks." Jackson moved on to search the living room.

# Chapter 20

Evans started with the other side of the duplex. The homes shared an adjoining wall, but the other front door was around the corner. Patrol officers had blocked off the street in front of the victim's house, but cars occasionally moved past on Kings Street. The only decent thing about working cases on a Sunday morning, Evans thought, was that people were often home. Oregon was the least churchgoing state in the nation.

A teenage girl answered the door wearing plaid pajama pants and a rumpled white T-shirt. Evans had seen an Albertson's clerk in the same outfit yesterday. "I'm Detective Evans, Eugene police. Are your parents home?"

The girl's eyes went wide, and she grabbed the end of her long blond hair and began to twist. "My mom's working. Why do you want to see her?"

"We're investigating something that happened next door." Evans decided if the girl was old enough to look that guilty about something, she was old enough to answer questions. "May I come in?"

"Is this about the party at Josh's house?" The girl was near tears.

"No. It's about your neighbor on the other side of the duplex."

"You mean Jake?" Her shoulders slumped in relief, and

she stepped back to let Evans in.

"What's your name?"

"Hannah Burke." She sucked in a noseful of snot.

Evans resisted the urge to suggest she find a tissue.

The living room was filled with floral prints, knickknacks, and scented candles, so she nodded toward the dining room. "Can we sit at the table?"

"Want some coffee?" Hannah plopped down on a chair, as if exhausted.

"No, thanks. Were you home last night?" Evans joined her at the round wooden table, appointed with pale-blue fabric placemats. The woman of the house was really trying.

"Yeah. I've got a cold, so I didn't go out."

"Did you see or talk to Jake?"

"No. He keeps to himself."

"Do you know if he was home?"

"He was home. I heard the TV. And the shouting."

*Now they were getting somewhere.* "What time did you hear shouting?"

"It was about halfway through Desperate Housewives, so around nine-thirty, I guess. I had to turn the volume up."

"You were home by yourself?"

"Yeah. My mom's a waitress, so she works all weekend."

"What time did your mom get home?"

"I was asleep. But on Saturday night, she usually works 'til eleven or twelve."

*Probably no help to them.* "Did you recognize the voices you heard?"

"I know Jake's, but not the other guy's."

Evans jotted down *male visitor*. "Did you hear a car? Do you know when the other guy arrived?"

"No." Hannah scratched her head. "You know we can't see

the front of his house, right? It's around the corner."

Evans ignored her sass. "Could you tell what they argued about?"

"No way." She let out a short laugh. "I've learned to tune it out. Before she moved out, Jake and his wife argued a lot too. We just ignore it."

"Did you hear any names? Any specific words?"

Hannah blew her nose on a tissue she'd had wadded up in her hand. Evans tried not to cringe.

"It was kind of muffled, but I did hear the other guy say, 'I'll never forgive you.'" Hannah dropped her pitch to imitate a distressed man. With her head cold and nasal tone, it was comical.

"Were those his exact words?" Evans made quick notes.

"I think so."

"What else did you hear?"

Hannah shrugged. "Nothing really. I went to sleep after that cuz I drank a bunch of NyQuil."

Evans gave Hannah a business card. "I may have more questions later. For now, is there anything else you can tell me about Jake that might be important?"

"Sometimes he wakes up in the middle of the night screaming. It always freaks me out. Mom says it's probably PTSD."

Evans thanked her and left, noting the young woman had not bothered to ask what had happened to Jake. She trotted back around the corner, passed Pittman's place, and tried the house on the other side, but no one was home.

Directly across the street, she knocked on a white Craftsman house with a large covered patio. An older woman answered the door, wearing a magenta caftan. She had a light purple rinse in her gray hair too. Evans liked her style.

Suppressing a smile, she introduced herself. "I'd like to ask some questions about last night. May I come in?"

"I'd rather sit on the porch. That way I can smoke." The woman stepped out the door, closed it behind her, and pulled a pack of smokes from a pocket deep in her caftan.

Evans reluctantly sat on the edge of a damp deck chair, notepad in hand. "What's your name?"

"Rose Middleton." She lit a cigarette and inhaled like it was oxygen after an underwater swim.

"Were you home last night?"

"I'm always home, except for lunches with my sister." Rose kept her upper lip rigid. She was likely hiding stained teeth, and it made her a little hard to understand.

"Did you know Jake Pittman, who lived directly across from you?" Evans gestured at the duplex.

"You make it sound like he's dead." Rose made a weird sound in her throat, then started hacking up phlegm. "Is that what's going on over there?"

Evans longed for a witness who didn't make her wish she had a mask over her face. "Jake was killed last night. Do you know anything about it?"

"I didn't know him. He'd only been in the neighborhood a few years."

"Did you see or hear anything across the street last night? Maybe see a vehicle parked over there?"

"I did see a truck. It was light-colored. And loud. That's why I looked out the window. It sounded like it was parking in my front yard."

"What time?"

"Around eight-thirty, I think. I was reading, so I lost track of time."

"Did you see anyone get out of the truck?"

Rose shook her head. "I just glanced out, saw it across the street, and went back to reading."

"Did you hear any shouting?"

"No."

"Did you hear the truck leave?"

"I did hear it start up again. As I said, it was a loud piece of crap. But I have no idea what time that was."

"How long would you say it was there? Twenty minutes? An hour? More?"

"I really don't know. But probably less than an hour."

"Had you seen the truck there before?"

"Maybe once before, a month or so ago."

Evans was eager to get back to the crime scene. The truck owner might not be hard to track down. "Thanks for your help." She handed Rose a card. "Call me if you think of anything else."

Evans crossed the blocked street, noting that the crime lab's white van had arrived. Nothing like a homicide to disrupt a neighborhood for the day.

Jasmine Parker and Joe Berloni, two crime scene techs, had joined the group in the small house. Jasmine was using the UV light to search for blood, while Joe took fingerprints from the beer bottles.

Her partners stood in the living room, looking frustrated.

"What have we found?" she asked, joining them.

"Not a damn thing," said Jackson, who rarely swore. "No cell phone, no computer, few personal papers. There's a power supply in the bedroom that indicates Pittman owned a laptop, but it's not here."

"The perp either wanted to find something in the victim's devices or hide his connections from us," she offered.

"Or both. What did you learn?"

"The teenager next door heard arguing around nine-thirty. Pittman and another guy. The only specific phrase she heard was the other guy yell, 'I'll never forgive you.'"

Schak said, "That sounds personal. Not like a money issue."

"That's what I think." Evans put her notepad away. "More important, the woman across the street said a loud, light-colored truck parked in front of this house around eight-thirty. She's not sure when it left, but she thinks it was less than an hour later."

"So our perp was here between eight-thirty and, say, ten, but the shouting didn't start until nine-thirty." Jackson pulled off his gloves, apparently ready to leave. "He drove a light-colored truck and left with a laptop and whatever paperwork was in this house." Jackson scowled. "And possibly seven thousand dollars, *if* these cases are linked."

"He shouldn't be too hard to find," Schak said.

"This is interesting," the ME called out. "He's got a long blond hair stuck to the back of his sweatshirt."

# Chapter 21

*Earlier Sunday morning*

Sophie spent a leisurely hour in bed with her smooth-skinned lover, Jasmine Parker, drinking coffee and reading the paper. Hunger finally forced them to get dressed and drive across town for breakfast at her new favorite, the Pantry & Pub. The little restaurant was worth the trip out of her riverside neighborhood. They made the best omelettes and burgers and offered a great selection of microbrews.

"Do you have plans for this afternoon?" Jasmine asked, after their food arrived.

"I do. Why?"

"I can tell you're distracted. What's going on in that wicked brain of yours?"

"I'm thinking about the feature I'm writing. You know, Rafel Mazari and the whole 'soldier/hero survives a tour in Afghanistan, then is murdered in his hometown.' I promised my editor I'd work on it over the weekend."

"You're getting ready to ditch me?" Jasmine gave her a playful look.

"Yes, and I also need information."

"I can't tell you anything about the crime scene. Not yet."

"I want to know about motive."

A tiny smile played on Jasmine's face. "Cops always look at the spouse first."

"Even in a parking lot murder?"

"Some spouses are more clever than others."

"Good to know. Speaking of spouses." Sophie lowered her voice. "I have an interview this afternoon with Laura McKinsey, the sister of Rafel Mazari's first wife. She thinks he killed Joanna Mazari."

"That's wild. How did she die?"

"She was stung by a wasp in her car, went into shock, and drove off the road."

Jasmine gave a tiny eye roll. "Where do you get this stuff?"

"It's in the newspaper archives."

"But it doesn't sound like part of a sympathetic soldier/hero story."

"I know. But Hoogstaad won't care as long as the story is juicy. Besides, just because a guy joins the military doesn't mean he's a saint. Someone may have had a good reason to kill Rafel."

Jasmine's cell phone rang quietly in her black silk blazer. She reached for it with a tiny scowl. "I have to take this."

"I know." They both had on-call jobs.

Her lover listened for a moment, then said, "I can be there in forty minutes." She clicked off and looked at Sophie. "There's been another murder. I can't tell you who or where, so don't ask. After I finish my breakfast, I'd like you to drive me back to your place, so I can pick up my car."

Sophie's nerves hummed with excitement. She could follow Jasmine to the crime scene. She'd be the first reporter on the scene—unless the TV people had already picked up a radio transmission. "Let's eat then. I expect you to give me some details eventually." Sophie took another bite of egg and cheese, but could barely swallow it. What if this murder was connected to Rafel's death? This story could be so much bigger than a hero feature.

After watching Jasmine drive away, Sophie waited a minute, then jumped in her Scion, a graduation present from her parents. They'd given her the car, she'd told them she was bisexual, then they'd sold their home and jetted off to China to teach English. Just another adventure in their wacky lives. Sophie loved them for raising her to always see the possibilities out in the world, but she had also resented them a little for never putting her first like other parents did with their kids. She liked to think she was over that now.

She pulled out of her small apartment complex, which sat thirty feet from the Willamette River, and drove toward the main street. Up ahead, she saw Jasmine's car turn left on River Road. Regardless of where the crime scene was, Jaz would have to stop at the crime lab and swap her car for the van with the equipment. Sophie didn't have to worry about sticking close until after the swap. Did Jasmine know she was following her? Had she expected it? She should have.

Sophie couldn't get close to the crime scene house because patrol cars blocked the street, but she was able to take some long-shot photos and figure out the address based on the street's numbering system. She keyed the address into the reverse White Pages on her iPhone and came up with Chester Freeman. Was he the dead guy or just the owner of the property? Most duplexes were rentals, but this was a quiet, older neighborhood, so home ownership was probably high.

Sophie climbed back in her car and called the number listed for Chester, pleased when he picked up.

"Hello. This is Sophie Speranza with the Willamette News. Do you own the duplex on the corner of Kentwood and Kings?"

"Yeah, why?" He sounded old and crusty.

"I'll tell you what's happening at your rental right now if you give me the names of the tenants living on the Kentwood side."

"What do you mean? What's going on?" Chester was a little more alarmed now.

"Tell me who lives there, and I'll tell you what I know. That's the deal."

A long silence. Finally, he said, "Jake Pittman. Now what the hell is this about?"

"I think he's dead. We've got four cop cars out here, the crime lab van, and the white station wagon they use to haul away bodies. Can you tell me anything about Mr. Pittman?" Rain started to hit her windshield, and Sophie checked the car to see if she had her umbrella.

"No." He covered his phone and yelled to someone nearby, "The tenant on Kentwood is dead." When he came back on, Chester was worried. "You won't use my name in the paper, will you?"

"I don't see any reason I should have to. Thanks for your time." Sophie hung up.

Where had she heard the name Jake Pittman recently? Sophie called her friend who'd gone to school with Rafel and left a message: "Do you know who Jake Pittman is? Any connection to Rafel Mazari? Call me as soon as you can." As soon as she hung up, she remembered. Sasha Altman had mentioned Jake as one of Rafel's childhood friends. How bizarre that two of the three friends had been killed in such a short time. Something ugly was going on. Was the third friend in danger?

Sophie checked her iPhone: 12:35 p.m. Time to get moving. In an hour, she had an interview scheduled with Laura McKinsey, sister of the now-deceased Joanna Mazari, and Laura lived in Corvallis. Sophie could have interviewed her over the phone, but she preferred to talk to people in person when she could. Besides, she'd been meaning to make a trip to the neighboring college town soon to pick up some Passion tea and chocolate biscotti from her favorite shop.

Clear and cold, the weather was decent for a short drive, and Sophie loved getting on the road. She grew restless if she didn't get a change of scenery every few weeks, so she loved it when assignments took her out of town, even a few miles. She'd only planned on living and working in Eugene for a few years, then moving on to a bigger newspaper, maybe in Seattle or San Francisco. But the digital revolution had kicked print publishing's ass and newspapers were shrinking, not hiring. Sophie was grateful to still be employed, and if she had to be stuck somewhere, Eugene was pretty damn special. An hour from both the ocean and the mountains, it was geographically perfect. It was also funky and had a great art and theater scene. Not to mention the general acceptance of people with nontraditional sexual orientations. Still, she kept her eye on job opportunities in bigger West Coast cities.

In Corvallis, she made a quick run into Tina's Tea Shop, then ate a piece of biscotti in her car while looking over her interview questions. She checked her directions, drove out Northwest Buchanan, and easily found Laura McKinsey's address.

She parked in front, snapped a quick photo, and assessed the place. Over the fence, Sophie spotted the top of a swing set, then noticed the sign: *McKinsey Daycare.*

*Please let this be her day off,* Sophie thought, walking up the sidewalk. She rang the bell and listened for the sound of children. All was quiet.

A woman in her late twenties opened the door, and Sophie's eyes were immediately drawn to the large red birthmark enveloping her right eye and cheek. The marking was substantial, but didn't detract from the woman's classic features and bright smile. Sophie quickly shifted to meet Laura's gaze and introduce herself.

The woman offered her hand and stepped aside to let Sophie in.

"Thanks for agreeing to meet with me." Sophie glanced at the living room and rejected it as a place to talk. None of the seating faced each other, and the carpet smelled like crayons and yesterday's lunch. "Can we sit at the kitchen table?"

"Sure." Laura led her to a room at the back with tall windows, natural daylight, and a clean vinyl floor.

Sophie made small talk for a few minutes, learning that Laura was married but unable to have children of her own, so she ran a daycare. "I love kids, don't you?" Laura said.

Sophie gave her a tight smile. "I don't know yet, I don't have any." She set her digital recorder on the table. "Let's get started. Tell me what you know about Rafel Mazari."

"He was a jealous, murdering bastard, and I'm glad he's dead."

Sophie choked down a laugh. "Don't hold back now. You can tell me how you really feel."

Laura managed a brief smile. "I know I don't have any proof, but I'm certain he killed Joanna."

"Her death seems like a tragic accident. How could Rafel have been responsible?"

"I think he put the yellow jackets in her car and took the EpiPen out of her purse." Laura met Sophie's eyes. "My sister was highly allergic and very careful to always have the EpiPen with her. I know they found it under the seat of her car, but she wouldn't have put it there or lost track of it."

Sophie wasn't convinced and needed to think it through. "You're saying Rafel took the epinephrine out of her purse and put it under the seat of her car. And he put some wasps he'd captured in the car at the same time. He must have conducted his mission right before she left for work, and she couldn't have checked for the pen that day."

"Or," Laura countered. "Joanna expected the EpiPen to be there because it had been the last time she checked." The sister's eyes misted with tears and she began to pop her knuckles, one at a time. "I'm not paranoid or crazy, but Rafel was a little of both. He was excessively jealous and constantly accused Joanna of cheating. He followed her around sometimes and once threatened her boss because he thought she was having an affair with him."

"That doesn't make him a killer."

"There's more. Joanna wanted to leave him, but she was afraid to. She discovered he'd been looking at internet sites for various poisons and toxic cleaning combinations."

"Maybe he was just mentally unbalanced."

Laura's eyes lit up with little fireworks. "Oh, he was unbalanced, all right."

Sophie wondered a little bit about Laura. Maybe the woman just wasn't dealing with the loss of her sister well.

Laura pushed to her feet. "I have something I want you to see. I'll be right back."

A minute later, she returned with a stiff piece of clear plastic. Inside was a sheet of lined white paper, now laminated. The handwritten note was wrinkled, as if it had been wadded up and straightened out. But the cursive writing was neat, small, and clear.

"This is a *poem*." The word oozed from Laura's mouth with disdain. "Rafel gave it to Joanna right before she died."

Sophie read the haunting lyrics:

> *A true woman's love knows only one heart.*
> *A shamed woman is like a cancer and must be cut from the soul.*
> *Her death frees the bonded heart and carries her to Jahannam for eternity.*
> *—Rafel*

"What is Jahannam?"

"It's the Arabic term for hell."

"That is creepy. Did you show it to the police at the time of her death?"

"I didn't find it until weeks later when I went through Joanna's clothes. It was in a pocket of one of her jackets. By then, the state police had called it an accident and moved on."

"May I take a picture of it?"

"Sure."

Sophie moved the note out of the bright light from the window and took a few shots. She might only use the photo in the feature's online version, where they had nearly unlimited space. One of the few upsides to digital news.

"What else can you tell me about Rafel? His sister Sasha seems to think he was a terrific guy."

"He could be charming, I grant you that. I liked him at first. He seemed so respectful of women. Opening doors, never swearing in front of females, very protective. But it's all a mask for deep-rooted distrust. Maybe it's from feeling abandoned by his mother." Laura looked away. "Or maybe it's the Islamic background."

"Rafel was Muslim? His sister said they weren't religious."

"They're not. But Rafel's father, Zain Mazari, was born in Pakistan and raised as a Muslim until his parents died and he came to the United States to live with an uncle. The uncle was Americanized and raised him with a mix of cultural traditions, which he passed on to his children. So Rafel may not have been overly religious, but he had some embedded old-world ideas about women."

"What are you saying? You believe Joanna's death was an honor killing?"

"Some version of it, yes."

Sophie was skeptical. If she had been shot or strangled, it would be easier to swallow. *But yellow jackets*? "I didn't think honor killing was that widespread. I thought it was only practiced in small pockets, within tribes and families."

Laura was silent.

"Do you have a photo of Rafel and Joanna? A digital file would be best."

"Sorry, I only have some prints."

"I'd love to take one with me. I'll scan it and mail it back to you."

Laura looked uncertain. "The photos are all I have left of Joanna."

"I understand. I'll just take a picture of the picture."

"No, I'll give you one. I never look at pictures of them together." Laura retrieved an envelope from the back of a photo album, sorted through the stack, and handed her a print.

Sophie stared, rather stunned. Joanna had blond hair, wide-spaced blue eyes, a slightly upturned nose, and abundant sensual lips. She looked so much like Sierra's Facebook photo they could have been sisters.

## Chapter 22

After hours at the homicide scene, feeling like they'd accomplished next to nothing, Jackson assigned Schak to round up Pittman's bank, credit card, and phone records, which likely wouldn't happen until Monday. In the meantime, Schak would look for Cody Sawyer. They either needed to bring him in for another round of questioning or keep an eye on him in case he was next on the killer's list. Jackson sent Evans to the jail to question Sierra again and ask specifically about her relationships with Pittman and Sawyer. It often took several interrogations for a suspect to admit to an affair.

Jackson worried that the second, similar killing while Sierra was incarcerated would cast doubt on whether she had committed the murder of her husband. At least that's what a good defense lawyer would argue, and he might be right. But despite their connections, the homicides were distinct, and looked like the work of different people. The long hair found on Pittman's back was unusual, Jackson thought, but it could have belonged to a lover or a prostitute and be irrelevant to the case.

He left the crime scene, driving past the onlookers and the KLSR news van. It no longer surprised him how quickly the media heard about a homicide and sent a reporter with a camera. They usually only managed to get distant shots of the house and the activity in front, but TV reporters needed footage for the viewers and would settle for anything.

He was headed to see Hailey Pittman, Jake's former wife. If their divorce wasn't final yet, she was technically his widow and his heir. She was also likely the person who knew the victim best and would know who else to notify. Her address on Concord in the Barger area seemed like it would be easy to find, but the street stopped and started, and it took him a few tries to find the right section. Now that his house had sold, he vowed to buy a GPS unit for his vehicle since the department couldn't afford one.

Several cars were parked in front of the bright yellow house, and his gut tightened. Hailey had company, making this situation more complicated and emotional. He was not only here to inform her of her estranged husband's death, but also to question her. As polite as it would be to wait for a better time, it was also counterproductive. Every hour of delay gave the killer time to hide evidence, set up an alibi, and possibly leave town.

Jackson rang the doorbell and suddenly had a nagging sense that he was forgetting something. Loud laughter came from inside the house—the cheerful sound of women enjoying each other's company. *Oh crap.* This was the absolute worst part of his job, but as much as he'd like to, he never assigned it to anyone else.

A thirty-something woman with a narrow but attractive face opened the door. Her smile disappeared the moment she saw him.

"Hailey Pittman?"

"Yes." Her lower lip trembled, and he noticed she had ash-blond hair that fell below her shoulders.

*Was that her hair on Jake Pittman's back?* "Detective Jackson, Eugene Police. I need to talk to you in private."

She glanced back at the two women in her living room, then stared at Jackson, as if trying to read his mind. "We'll go in the study."

While Jackson stood in the foyer, probably looking as grim as he felt, Hailey whispered to the women, who cast furtive glances at him. With a quick nod, she moved down the hall and Jackson followed. The back bedroom had been converted into an office with a sliding glass door leading into the yard. Jackson sat and willed himself to be patient, to not rush this because it made him uncomfortable.

"I understand you moved out of the home you shared with your husband, Jake Pittman, several months ago. Is that correct?"

"Yes." Her eyes blinked rapidly. "Why?"

"Have you filed for divorce?"

"Yes, but it won't be final until next month. What's going on?" Her voice pitched higher.

"We went to question Jake this morning, and I'm very sorry to tell you that we found him dead."

She took a quick gulp of air, then sat perfectly still, eyes closed, breathing deeply. After a moment, Hailey sobbed a few times, then caught herself. "I don't want to cry for him." She went still again, and Jackson gave her a moment to do whatever meditation or self-talk she needed.

Finally, she asked, "What happened?

"The evidence indicates he was assaulted." He was always careful about releasing details, even to the widow.

"I knew he was into something stupid or dangerous. That's why I left him. Well, that's one of the reasons."

"Do you know who might have killed him?"

"No." She gave a tiny shake, then looked down.

"Please tell me about Jake's activities." Jackson wanted to

get more out of her before he mentioned the loud truck. Her new boyfriend could have been the one driving it. In any death, he'd learned to suspect the spouse or the third member of a love triangle.

"I don't know much. He was very secretive in the months before I left. And he suddenly seemed to have money, but he didn't have enough work to explain it." Hailey shifted in her chair. The subject clearly made her uncomfortable.

"Did he talk about the money?"

"No."

"What did he say when you asked him about it?"

"He would say he'd done a job for someone. Cut down a tree or did some landscaping, but sometimes he didn't look dirty or sweaty. He looked guilty, and irritable with me for asking."

"Do you know anything about the Veterans Relief Fund?

Hailey's eyes registered recognition. "I heard him mention it once on the phone. I think he was talking to Rafel." Her face crumpled. "Is that why Rafel was killed too? Were they stealing from someone?" She burst into tears.

Jackson willed himself to wait it out. He knew what it was like to process the news of someone's murder. It could take a while to sink in and become real.

One of her friends called from the other side of the closed door, "Hailey, are you all right? Should I come in?"

Jackson opened the door, gave her a brief update, then asked her to return to the living room. Hailey was under control when he sat back down.

"Where were you last night between eight and midnight?"

A startled noise escaped her lips. "I had dinner with my parents. We played cards afterward until ten o'clock, then I came home." She met his eyes, showing him she wasn't bothered by his question, despite her initial reaction.

Jackson wanted to believe her, but part of him wondered if she was involved in the fraud ring. Had the wives killed their husbands to silence them? "Did you and Jake have a joint bank account when you were together?"

"We did, but we also had separate savings. We were both putting equal money into the joint account, then Jake lost his job. He started his own business, but he didn't make much money."

"Did you ever see the bank statements for his personal account?"

"No."

"Do you own this home?"

"No. I live here with my friend, Lisa. Jake and I sold the home we owned after our son died. We lived in a rental after that, thinking we'd buy another house someday, but then the recession hit."

"Last night a neighbor heard someone say to Jake, 'I'll never forgive you.' Do you have any idea what that's about?"

"No. I'm sorry." Hailey twisted the corner of her sweater. "Jake was a good man, a proud soldier. But then he did a tour in Iraq, and when he came back he was forgetful and sometimes angry for no reason. He got counseling and started to get better, then our son got sick and died of cancer. It was horrible." Tears rolled freely down Hailey's face, and she struggled for control.

"I'm sorry about your son." Jackson couldn't imagine how that would feel as a parent, and now was not a good time to think about it. He looked down and scribbled notes as fast as he could.

Haltingly, she continued. "We were both depressed for

about a year, but we pulled through. Then the recession hit and Jake lost his job. It was like the last straw. Something inside him snapped, and he became a stranger to me. He started going to the bar with his friends and drinking every day. Then suddenly he had cash to spend, and it made me suspicious. We fought a lot and I finally left him."

"We didn't find any paperwork in the house. No bank statements, no personal documents. Did Jake keep a safe deposit box?"

"No, but he shredded papers all the time. He was a little paranoid."

"Did he have a computer?"

"I gave him a laptop, but I don't think he used it much."

"Do you know where the laptop might be?"

She looked puzzled. "If it's not in the house, I have no clue."

"Did you ever hear of the group Territory Defenders?"

"No."

"Did Jake have explosives in the house?"

Hailey jerked back, eyes wide. "Not that I ever knew. He had a handgun, but that was it."

They hadn't found any weapons in their search. One more throwaway question. "Was Jake having an affair with Sierra Kent?"

"No way." She pursed her lips. "Jake didn't think Sierra was good for Rafel. In fact, he really didn't like her."

"Which one of Jake's acquaintances drives a loud, light-colored truck?"

Concern flashed across Hailey's face. "Why?"

"Just tell me."

"His ex-boss, Matthew Dolan. He owns Evergreen Landscaping."

"What was Jake's relationship with Dolan?"

"They used to be friends. After the layoff, Matt cosigned a loan for Jake so he could buy some equipment to start his own tree-cutting business. But Jake had trouble making the payments." Her shoulders slumped. "Matt eventually paid off the loan so it wouldn't ruin his credit."

"So Matt had hard feelings toward Jake?"

She nodded.

"Did he ever threaten him?"

"Not physically. He said he planned to take him to small claims court. But I left Jake soon after that, so I don't know what happened."

"Where can we find Matthew Dolan?"

"He lives on Silver Lane, off River Road. He runs his business out of his home." Hailey scooted to the edge of her chair and leaned toward Jackson. "I can't believe Matt would kill him. Are you sure it wasn't an accident?"

"Do you know Matt personally?"

"I went to a couple of backyard parties at his house. He seemed nice."

"Do you know Jake's family?"

"Only his mother is here in Oregon, but yes, I know her."

"Will you give me her contact information?" Talking to the victim's mother was worthwhile because she might know about his recent activities. Jackson took a business card from his jacket and handed it to the widow. "Please call me if you have any questions or think of anything I should know."

He nodded at the women in the living room as he left the house. In his car, he called headquarters and asked the desk clerk to run Matthew Dolan and his business through the database. Jackson learned his suspect had no criminal record, except a marijuana possession twelve years earlier. The desk clerk described him as "five-nine, one-eighty, with a wide forehead, reddish-blonde hair, and a mustache." Dolan's landline and business number were the same.

Jackson called it, and a female voice answered. "Dolan residence and Evergreen Landscaping. How can I help you?"

"I'd like to speak with Matthew Dolan."

"He's out of town today. Can I take a message?"

*Out of town? Had he run already?* Jackson hesitated. If he said 'Eugene Police,' Dolan might not ever come back to town. But if their suspect was already on the road, Jackson might need the wife's help. "Where did he go and when will he be back?"

"He had a job in Corvallis today and should be home by five. Who is this?"

"Detective Jackson, Eugene Police. It's very important Mr. Dolan call me the minute he gets back."

"You're scaring me." The woman's voice flooded with worry. "What is this about?"

"I can't tell you, but I'd like you to answer a few questions."

"If I can."

"What's your name?"

"Sheila Dolan."

"You're Matthew Dolan's wife?"

"Yes."

"What time did he come home last night?"

"I'm not sure. He was here when I got home at eleven. Why?"

*Plenty of time to have assaulted Pittman.* "We're just trying to establish a timeline. What was he driving?"

"His landscaping truck."

"What color?"

"White. Was he in an accident?" Her distress was palpable.

"Do you know the license plate number?"

She clicked off without answering.

Jackson guessed she was calling her husband on his cell phone to ask him what the hell was going on. He called the desk officer at the department again. "Jackson here. I need a state-wide ATL on a white truck that probably says Evergreen Landscaping on the side. If you can track down the license plate too, that would help." The attempt-to-locate was a step down from an all-points bulletin. He didn't know if Dolan was a danger to anyone yet. He just wanted to question him.

"For Matthew Dolan, the suspect I just ran for you?"

"Yes. I want him brought in for questioning."

"I'll notify the state police too."

"Thank you."

He hung up and texted Schak, Evans, and Quince with the update: *White truck driven by Matt Dolan, Evergreen Landscaping. Issued ATL. Will keep you posted.*

As he pushed *Send*, he realized he'd missed a call. *Kera! Oh shit.* After finding the body, he'd forgotten all about their date. This was not good.

## Chapter 23

*Earlier Sunday morning*

Kera heard the baby crying and mentally pleaded with his mother Danette to respond. Kera was in the middle of a fifty-minute workout on the elliptical machine, and little Micah was about the only thing that could make her quit before her allotted time was up. After a minute, the crying stopped and she heard Danette talking to the baby. Kera breathed a sigh of relief. Danette didn't seem as bonded to her child as many women were, but she was slowly becoming a responsive, caring parent.

Kera checked her pulse, which had slowed down while she thought about her grandson, and pushed herself back up to pace. Moments later, Danette came into the workout room, carrying Micah.

"Where is the new box of baby wipes?"

"Top shelf of the bathroom cupboard."

Micah turned and grinned at the sound of Kera's voice. God, she loved that baby. He looked so much like his father it hurt sometimes. She still had trouble thinking of her son as a father. Nathan had still seemed like a boy to her when he'd shipped out to Iraq, only to be killed by a roadside bomb on his second day. He'd left behind a pregnant girlfriend, and now the little family he'd never known was living with Kera and making her life complicated, but also joyful.

"Do you still have plans to see Brian this afternoon?"

"Yes, don't worry. We'll get out of here so you and Jackson can be alone." Danette winked, making Kera smile.

"Thanks. Is this the first time Brian will meet Micah?"

"He's seen him, but he hasn't spent any time with the baby. We'll see what happens." Danette patted Micah on the back as she left the room.

Kera sympathized. Dating was tough with a baby still in diapers. Not many young men wanted to take on that kind of responsibility. Danette would likely be in her home for a long time. A sense of dread shot through her, followed by a wave of guilt. As usual, the situation produced conflicting emotions. She loved having the baby here, and at one point when Danette was missing, Kera had thought she would end up raising Micah. She and Jackson had briefly talked about what that would mean to their relationship, but he'd made no commitment. She'd been prepared to lose her lover to take care of her grandson. Family came first. What else could she do?

But Jackson had investigated and rescued Danette, and Kera had taken the traumatized young woman and her baby into her home. Since then, Kera's relationship with Jackson had somewhat stagnated. He was always working or spending time with his own daughter, and she was either at the birth control clinic, volunteering with veterans, or looking after Micah while Danette took college classes. They just couldn't make enough time for each other. After his surgery, they'd talked about him and Katie moving in with her, but when Jackson announced he would move into his brother's house, he'd made it clear he wasn't interested in living with her. The news had been crushing. Jackson didn't know that, and she didn't blame him for his decision. She didn't enjoy living with Danette all that much either, so how could she expect him to?

Kera pushed aside the negative thoughts, finished her last five minutes, and headed for the shower. Jackson was coming over this afternoon, and they'd have a few hours of alone time. She would make the most of it. The thought made her stop in her tracks. Was she settling for a part-time relationship? For how long?

She made a quiche for their lunch, put on a sexy skirt and sweater, and sat down to read while she waited. By two o'clock when he didn't show, she got a little worried. Jackson often cancelled their plans at the last minute because he got called out on a homicide case or had to testify in court, or because Katie changed her plans, but it wasn't like him to simply not show and not call. She hated to bother him if he was working, but it wasn't fair of him to keep her waiting. She'd done too much of that lately, and it was a lonely pastime.

At two-fifteen, she called him anyway and he didn't answer. She left a message. A half hour later, he called back, sounding stressed. "Kera, I'm so sorry. There's been another homicide. I found the body and got completely caught up in the investigation. I had no idea what time it was."

"Another murder! Good grief. Who is it this time?" Yet she didn't really want to know. The shock of Rafel's murder was still with her, and every death she heard about stirred up grief, anger, and helplessness. Another drawback to dating a homicide detective.

"He's a friend of Rafel Mazari's. Schak and I went to question him and found him dead."

"I'm so sorry." Kera knew he couldn't talk about the case

and wouldn't be able to think about anything else for the next few days. She knew it was unreasonable, but it irritated her that she'd end up on the back burner again. "I'll let you get back to work, but I'll miss you."

"I'm headed over to see you now. I can't stay long, but I might as well ask some questions about Rafel while I wait to pick up my new suspect."

"I don't know if I can help, but I'll see you soon." Kera hung up. He was coming over to question her. It was a little weird, and she resented it. She knew her feelings weren't rational, but she was human. If she hadn't volunteered with a veteran who'd ended up murdered, she wouldn't have seen Jackson today. How long would it have gone between dates? Ten days? Two weeks or more? How much of this was she expected to take? She wanted a partner who would be present in her life.

Jackson showed up twenty minutes later. He wrapped his arms around her and held her close. The warmth and pressure of his body against hers was delicious and comforting, like a massage after a long day of hard work. She felt him breathe in the scent of her hair and knew he'd missed her too. They loved each other. Why couldn't they make this relationship work?

"God, I've missed you." Jackson kissed her deeply, and little sparks of pleasure shot through her. But he quickly pulled back, like a man on duty. "This last week has been crazy," he said, grabbing her hand and leading her to the kitchen.

He started to make coffee, but she took the bag of beans from him and gestured for him to sit. "I'll make it."

"I had all that packing to do after work each night, then

when we were in the middle of moving, I got called out on a homicide Friday morning. And now we're dealing with another connected homicide. And I've only got Schak and Evans on the case full-time."

Lara Evans would spend more time with Jackson this week than she would. Kera couldn't help but feel jealous of a woman she'd never met, and she resented being pushed to that state.

She waited for the coffee to brew, poured them both a cup, and sat down across from him. "I know you want to question me, so let's get this over with."

"Okay." He sat up straighter and pulled his notepad from his jacket pocket, a shift into work mode. "How well did you know Rafel Mazari?"

"I only saw him once a week for an hour, but he'd started opening up to me, and I felt like I was getting to know him."

"What were you doing for him?"

"Some physical therapy as well as teaching him pain control methods." She'd taken an intensive course so she could volunteer with wounded veterans, but she hadn't earned a PT degree and wasn't a specialist. Still, her time to them was free.

"Was he in a lot of pain?"

"The physical pain was easing for him, but his stress wasn't."

"What was he stressed about?"

"Everything. He was bitter about losing his leg. Bitter about not being able to find work and support himself. He also thought his wife was cheating on him." Looking back, Kera realized Rafel had been challenging to work with. It took a lot of energy to keep her own thoughts positive when she was around him, let alone help him stay positive. But she'd done her best.

"Did he ever say who he thought she was cheating with?"

"He mentioned her boss at the veterinary clinic."

Kera watched him take notes and smiled at his focus. She had to admire his dedication, even if it left her feeling like an outsider.

"Did Rafel ever talk about money?" Jackson asked. "Or mention a new source of income?"

"He'd mention his gratitude for my volunteer help, and he complained about his medical bills, but he didn't discuss specific finances with me."

"What else did he talk about?"

"His friends, Jake and Cody. He reminisced about growing up with them and told me stories about jumping off the train bridge into the water at Clear Lake Reservoir. About how Cody practically lived with him and his dad during the summers." Kera hesitated, not sure how to explain Rafel's tone. "Sometimes he sounded like the friendships were over, but I think he still spent time with them."

"Any sense of a falling out?"

"No, but he talked like his marriage was over. He was just waiting for Sierra to leave him."

"Did Rafel ever talk about his son?"

Kera had to give it some thought. "At first he did, but now that you mention the boy, I can't even remember his name because Rafel quit mentioning him."

"When was the last time you saw Rafel?"

"Tuesday afternoon."

"Did he seem different?"

"Maybe more at peace. But that could have been the pain medication. I think he was using more of it again."

"Why do you think that?"

"He was losing weight and his teeth were looking discolored."

Jackson slumped a little, as if he were near the end of his patience. "Can you tell me anything about Rafel that would explain why someone would want to kill him?"

"Not really." Kera decided to share a perception she had. "I think Rafel had a lot of guilt. I had to step out of our session once to take a phone call, and when I came back Rafel was on the floor, praying for forgiveness."

"On the floor?"

"He never talked about it, but I think he was Muslim. He referred to Allah sometimes."

"Okay." Jackson slipped his notepad in his pocket. "I should probably get going. I have to meet with my task force soon."

"Can we talk for a minute?"

"Should I be worried? He smiled, and she remembered how his dark eyes and dimples had seduced her the first time they'd met. She missed that feeling and worried that it wouldn't come back.

It was time to say it. "I think we should stop seeing each other."

The words hit him like a punch in the chest, stealing his breath for a moment. Jackson wanted to plead his case, to convince her he could do better, but all he could think was: *You don't love me anymore.* Finally, he said, "I know I don't make enough time for you, Kera, but I try. My job is crazy sometimes, but I love you."

"And I love you. But I don't think it's enough. I want to move my life forward." She pushed her long bronze hair back and wouldn't meet his eyes.

"Why can't we just let it be and enjoy the time we have together?" He knew it was lame, but it was all he had right now.

"Because we have different expectations. I committed to this relationship after the first time we slept together, but it feels like you've always kept the door open, like a man looking for an exit."

"I'm not looking to get out." *Why did she think that?* "If it was just you and me, we'd probably be married by now. But we both have baggage."

"I have more. I have a baby in my life who could need another twenty years of emotional and financial support. I don't blame you for not wanting to sign on for that."

"But?" Jackson sensed there was something she hadn't told him yet.

"I either want a partner who's committed, no matter how messy my life is, or I want to be alone with the freedom that comes with it."

There it was. An ultimatum. In or out. Jackson drew in a deep breath. "What are you asking? To move in together? To get engaged?"

"I don't know." His lover's eyes watered with unshed tears. "I just don't want to be an afterthought."

"I'm sorry I've made you feel that way." Jackson stood, not sure what came next.

Kera stood too, her tall, muscular body taunting him. He wanted to grab her, hold on for dear life, and tell her to be patient. But Kera's arms were crossed, and she wouldn't meet his eyes.

"I hope you'll reconsider. Things will settle down for me, and I will have more time. Soon."

"You've been saying that for a year." She glanced up for a second, but didn't smile.

"I know. I've had a lot going on with separating my life from Renee's, and we've had a huge increase in violent crime, combined with diminishing resources." Jackson thought Kera had understood this. He couldn't believe he was losing her.

"Your work and your family will always come first. I respect that, but it's not good for me."

He couldn't blame her. After a long moment of silence, he said. "I have to go back to work."

"I know. I hope you catch a break in the case."

Unwilling to say goodbye, for fear it would make the separation final, Jackson spun around and left without speaking.

## Chapter 24

*She's just upset because I blew our date*, Jackson told himself. As soon as he had a breakthrough in these homicides, they'd talk it through. He would make some kind of commitment, and he and Kera would be okay. For now, he had to put it out of his mind. Or give up being lead on the case. He'd never done that before. Jackson sat in his cruiser, still parked in Kera's driveway, and couldn't move forward. Couldn't think straight. Finally, he sent Kera a text: *This isn't over. I love you.*

She didn't respond.

Jackson forced himself to focus on his investigation. Two men were dead. Best friends since childhood, but despite their murders being two days apart, most of the evidence pointed to different killers. Rafel Mazari had probably been killed by his wife to get out of an unhappy marriage, and Jake Pittman had likely been killed during an argument with a man he owed money to. Jackson's next move was to question Matthew Dolan . . . whenever they found him. And he couldn't forget Cody Sawyer. The third friend in the trio might be the key to the whole mess. He hoped Schak had located him and brought him in.

He started the car and drove away, his sense of loss expanding in his chest with every mile he put between him and the woman he loved. How had he messed this up so badly? Was it really all his fault? His life had been hectic lately with his house on the market and him in court, testifying in hearings about his parents' murders.

*Let it go for now*, Jackson coached himself. Give Kera a little time. Focus on the case. Come back to it when you're settled and sure of what to do.

With his earpiece in, he called his partners and asked to meet at the department. They needed to regroup and update. Jackson wanted to bounce ideas off his team, because he didn't quite trust his own thinking and judgment at the moment. He swung by Dolan's home on Silver Lane before heading back downtown, but the white truck was not in the driveway. It could have been in the garage, but he knew if they were running a landscaping business they needed every inch of space for equipment. Nobody but the wealthy who owned oversized garages kept their cars indoors. The weather in Oregon just wasn't extreme enough to justify it.

The sun dropped in the sky as he drove across Chambers. The looming darkness reminded him he was supposed to pick up Katie and have dinner with her. Guilt stabbed him in the gut as he called his daughter and asked her to stay with her mother another night. *Anyone else he could disappoint today?*

Katie took it well, and he promised to pick her up and take her to school in the morning. Jackson hung up the phone, understanding why cops sometimes wanted to beat confessions out of suspects. Maybe they just wanted to go home and see their family.

As he turned on 7th Avenue, his phone rang. "Jackson here."

"This is Sheila Dolan. I need your help."

The tone of her voice made Jackson pull off the street into a motel parking lot. "Is it your husband? What's going on?"

"Matt came home and he's freaking out. A police officer followed him here, and now two more cop cars are parked out front. Matt locked himself in our bedroom, and I'm worried this situation will get out of control."

Jackson's pulse accelerated with a familiar surge of adrenaline. Police officers hated situations like this, but they also lived for them. They were all adrenaline junkies. It was a lot of what kept them on the job. "Does he have a weapon?"

"We have a small handgun for protection, and it's in the bedroom where he is."

"Are you still in the house?"

"Yes."

"I want you to leave. Your safety is critical."

"No. I'm not abandoning Matt. He didn't kill Jake." She was borderline hysterical. "Hailey called me and told me what happened. She said the cops would be coming for Matt. But he didn't do this!"

"Please stay calm. Tell Matt I just want to talk him, then I want you to get out of the house. I'll tell the officers to back off, and I'll be there in five minutes." Jackson hung up his cell phone and got on the radio, ending his communication with "I repeat, do not enter the house. I'm on my way."

He used his cruiser's lights and siren, something he rarely did, as he sped out River Road, noting that many of the people involved in this case lived in the Santa Clara neighborhood. Even on a late Sunday afternoon, the traffic was thick and slow. A bus pulled out in front of him, and Jackson swerved around it. He had to get to Dolan's home and defuse the situation before it got ugly. When he'd put out the ATL, he had no idea this would be the result. Dolan's reaction seemed extreme and signaled either guilt or instability, or both. But dammit, no one was going to get hurt today because he'd wanted to talk to a suspect.

He made a left at Silver Lane, siren wailing briefly to stop the cross traffic, and flew down the narrow street, passing North Eugene High School. The road ended at North Park, which formed a T with Silver Lane. The Dolans lived just off to the left, and Jackson spotted patrol cars parked in front of the address. Like many of the older homes in the area, the house sat back from the road on at least a half-acre of property. Two dark-blue units blocked the long driveway, and another patrol car sat in a gravel strip separating the park-like front yard from the road. Jackson pulled in behind it on the gravel strip and jumped from his car. He wished he had Schak with him, but he hadn't had time to notify his team. He'd text them at the earliest opportunity, if they hadn't heard about the incident already.

Jackson trotted back to his trunk and pulled on his Kevlar vest, another item he rarely used. He touched his Sig Sauer and Taser, just for reassurance.

The three officers stood near the lead patrol car, and the sinking, late-autumn sun cast an ominous light over the scene. "Detective Jackson here," he said, as he approached. "This is my suspect, and his wife called me out to intervene."

Officer David Meadows stepped forward and shook his hand. He was about Jackson's age and height, but bulkier. "Is the suspect dangerous? I'm a SWAT member, and we can call out a partial team."

"No SWAT." Jackson nodded at the other officers. "Matt Dolan has no criminal history. He may have killed someone recently, but we don't know yet. If I can't talk him out, we'll call a crisis negotiator."

He turned toward the home. The driveway blacktop opened into a wide parking area in front of the garage, and the white landscaping truck sat next to a small silver car. The house was a single level and L-shaped. "The wife says Dolan is locked in a bedroom and has access to a handgun. Has anyone talked to Sheila Dolan in the last few minutes?"

"No. She told us she would call you, which is the only reason we waited." Officer Meadows hummed with tension. "I think we should go in. His wife could be in danger."

"No! I could be wrong about his involvement with the murder victim." Jackson heard his own voice get loud, but couldn't hold back. "Remember Courtney Slaven? She wasn't the pharmacy robber, and we trashed her house by breaking in and setting off a flash-bang grenade. Remember the Willamette News reporter? He wasn't suicidal just because he'd purchased a helium-hood suicide kit. The Springfield Police trashed his house too. Either one of them could have been hurt, and the lawsuits may still be pending. We're moving slowly here today."

"What if he injures or kills his wife?" Meadows challenged.

"What if *we* injure or kill his wife?" Jackson shot back. "She's not a hostage, he hasn't threatened anyone, and I'll get her out of there." He sounded more confident than he felt. "I'll call Sheila now and let her know I'm here. I want this to end peacefully. I believe we just have a misunderstanding." Jackson walked away from the officers and toward the house. He wanted Sheila to see him.

She answered in the middle of the first ring. "Thank god you're here. I want you to talk to Matt. Hailey says you were calm and nice when you questioned her."

He would be calm and nice with Matt too. Unless the suspect threatened him in person. Then he would be fast with his Taser. He could see the suspect's wife through the living room window now. "Sheila, tell me something about Matt. Do you have kids? Does he have any hobbies? What does he do to relax?"

"Our kids aren't here, thank god, and I don't want you to talk about them." She took a quick breath. "Matt forgot to take his Zyprexa this morning, and I just shoved a pill under the door, so he should calm down in a while."

"Good to hear. What can I talk to Matt about to help him trust me?"

"His trike makes him pretty happy."

"Even better news. I also have a trike. Brothers of the Third Wheel." Jackson hadn't joined the group, but he'd visited the website. "Tell Matt to call me, then you come out here. I can't guarantee your safety in there." He clicked off.

While he waited for the call, Jackson texted his three team members, grateful for the backlit screen on his cell phone. He keyed in the address, followed by: *At Dolan's. Suspect is resisting. Bring the CU.* The command unit was a big white RV with interview areas at each end and equipment in the middle. The front area held a camera so he could record a video statement. Jackson wanted to give Dolan a way to sit down for an interview that wouldn't intimidate him or force him into custody. He had no reason to arrest him yet. They could take this slow and easy. Dolan wasn't going anywhere, and if they played this right, he probably wasn't a danger to anyone but himself. If Dolan had killed Pittman, it was likely a one-time crime of passion.

Standing in the driveway, with the sky darkening like a bruise and the cold air biting his face, Jackson had an eerie sense of doom. His job had always been dangerous, but the last few years seemed increasingly harsh. People seemed on edge, unpredictable, often desperate. Without optimism, ordinary citizens could feel like they had nothing left to lose. If the economy didn't pick up soon, he worried that rioting would break out here like it had in Europe. He never wanted to wear a shield and square off against the people he had sworn to protect.

Jackson shook off the gloom. He had to stay focused and positive. After a painfully long five minutes, his cell rang. He answered, keeping his voice low key.

"You're the cop who's looking for me?"

"Yes. I just want to talk for a few minutes."

"Hailey Pittman says you think I killed her husband Jake. That's crazy."

Jackson's jaw clenched. Hailey shouldn't have called these people and riled them up. "I don't know who killed Jake Pittman, but I am investigating. Someone saw your truck at his house last night, so I want to talk to you. Just talk."

"I know how the police work. You'll try to pin this on me."

"I just want to take your statement so we can clear you." *It was mostly true.*

"Send all the other cops away. They make me nervous."

"They won't leave me here alone. Especially if you have a weapon. Do you have a gun?"

"There's one here, but I'm not holding it and I'm not violent. I just don't want to be handcuffed and shoved in the back of a cop car like some criminal."

"I understand that, and it's not necessary. Sheila tells me you ride a trike. Did you build it yourself?"

"I did. Why do you ask?"

"I built a trike last summer too. I used a Volkswagen squareback. What's yours?"

"Type-3 engine with an automatic transmission."

"I wish I'd gone with an automatic, but I was totally new

216

at it. I plan to take the thing apart and redo the frame soon, make it more stable."

"You should just buy a frame. There's a guy here in town named Hutchison who has an excellent design. I finally bought one and I love it."

"Does he have a website?"

"Yeah. Hutchison Trikes."

"I'll check it out." Jackson knew it was time to make progress. "Will you sit down with me and answer questions?"

"Where? I'm not coming out with all those cops here. Some itchy-fingered asshole will shoot me."

"I won't let that happen. The command unit is on the way. It's a big RV with an interview room." Jackson scrambled to work through the logistics. "First, send Sheila out with the weapon, so we know your wife is safe and you're unarmed. Then when the command unit is here, the patrol cops will leave. You'll come out with your hands in the air and let me search you. Then we sit down in the RV and take your statement. "

"Just the two of us?"

"Another detective will be watching from the back. It's policy."

"Let me talk to Sheila."

Dolan clicked off before Jackson could respond.

Another five long minutes passed, then Sheila Dolan pushed out the front door. A halide floodlight lit up the yard, triggered by her movement. She clutched her jacket closed with one hand and held a weapon down at her side with the other.

"It's me, Sheila. Everything is okay."

She walked past her husband's truck and down the driveway toward him. Jackson had his hand on his weapon from the moment he saw the door open. "Put the gun on the ground."

"Okay." She did as directed. "It's registered and legal, and Matt didn't threaten anyone with it."

"We'll just take it temporarily." Jackson strode quickly toward her and scooped it up. "Why don't you wait in my car where it's warm?" He pointed at his unmarked cruiser.

"I'll stay here until Matt comes out. I want him to feel safe." Sheila trotted into the middle of the yard where her husband could see her from the bedroom. The blinds moved a little as Dolan peeked out.

While they waited, Jackson checked his text messages. Quince had responded with: *In Cottage Grove, talking to more fraud victims. Get there when I can.*

A few minutes later, they heard the rumble of the CU's engine idling in the street.

"Let's get these patrol cars out of the driveway, so the command unit can park close to the house." Jackson hollered orders, not wanting to take any flak about his decision. The two officers moved quickly to their cars, backing out of the driveway. He watched them pull down the street and park a few houses away. He turned to Officer Meadows. "My team is inside the CU, and that's all the backup I need. This will go better if you all leave."

"Your call."

"I appreciate your responsiveness in getting here and keeping Dolan detained."

"Good luck."

Meadows waited for the giant RV to pull down the driveway, then he drove down to rendezvous with the other patrol officers. Jackson wondered how their reports would read. He felt confident he'd handled this well. The last thing the department needed was another news story about officers breaking through a door or setting off a flash-bang grenade near an innocent citizen. Not that Dolan was necessarily innocent, but Jackson preferred to use a subtler approach. He wanted information, and relaxed suspects talked more than terrorized suspects.

Schak climbed down from behind the wheel and stood next to Jackson. "First time I ever drove that rig. You made my day, pal."

"Then my work here is almost done." Jackson glanced at the rig. "Is Evans coming?"

"She'll be here in a minute."

"Okay. Let's get Dolan out here." Jackson called the suspect again. "We're ready for you. Hands in the air and move slowly."

"I'm not armed and I plan to cooperate. Just don't cuff me."

"Okay." He hoped the man's meds kicked in soon.

A moment later, Dolan stepped out the door. In the halide light, he looked pale, thin, and young, but as he moved closer, with his hands on his head, lines appeared at the corners of his eyes and a deep furrow creased his forehead.

Sheila started to rush over.

"Not yet! Stay back, please."

She froze, but blew a kiss to her husband.

"Stop and turn around," Jackson instructed.

"I thought you weren't going to cuff me."

"I'm not. This is just a weapons search. Standard procedure."

After patting him down, Jackson stepped back. "You can put your hands down. Follow my partner into the RV." He turned to Sheila. "I'd like to interview you as well. You can wait in the house for now, but don't make any calls."

"I have to call my sister. I don't want my kids to come home until this is over."

"Fine." Jackson would have liked to call his daughter too, but it would have to wait. He had a viable murder suspect about to make a statement. If Dolan would admit to being in the victim's house at the time of death, that was half their case.

The fluorescent light of the command unit made Jackson blink. As he turned on the camera and the video feed, his stomach growled and he couldn't remember the last time he'd eaten. The food he could get by without, but he would have given just about anything for a cup of coffee.

Dolan appeared ghostly white under the harsh lights, and his leg vibrated under the small table they shared. He wore a blue shirt and jeans, both dirty from yard work. The tips of his fingers were stained a permanent shade of mud brown, and he smelled like damp earth. The scent made Jackson think of camping trips he'd taken with his brother.

Jackson sat across from the suspect, their faces only four feet apart. Being inside a vehicle, the space they shared was about twelve feet square. It would have been just as bad as the interrogation room back at the department except for the hallway opening. That two-foot escape route kept Jackson's claustrophobia at bay. With no room for a second interrogator, Schak stayed in the back of the RV, sitting on a comfortable couch, watching the live feed, in case Dolan went squirrelly again.

"This is Detective Jackson, Eugene Police, speaking with Matthew Dolan," he said for the camera. He announced the date and time, advised Dolan of his rights, then paused while

Schak brought them each a bottle of water and left.

"Let's talk about last night, Saturday, November 12." Jackson planned to keep the questioning informal for as long as he could. Dolan clearly had authority issues, and he wanted him to stay relaxed. "How do you know Jake?"

"He used to work for me, until business slowed down and I had to lay him off."

"Did you visit Jake Pittman at his home on Kentwood last night?"

Dolan hesitated for a long minute. "Yes."

"What time did you arrive at his house?"

"I think it was around eight-thirty. He called me earlier and asked me to come over."

Dolan's cell phone was sitting on the table in front of Jackson. He'd taken it when he patted him down, but he had no right to search it without Dolan's permission. "Show me the call." Jackson pushed the phone across the table.

Two seconds later, the suspect pushed it back. Showing on the screen was a list of incoming calls with Pittman's registering at 7:43 p.m.

"Did he leave a message or did you talk to him?"

"It surprised me, but I took the call."

"Why did he want to see you?"

"Jake said he had the money he owed me." Dolan's gaze was steady and so was his voice.

Jackson hadn't expected it to go this way. Dolan was craftier than he looked.

"Out of the blue, Jake called and said he had money for you?"

"Believe me, I was surprised too."

"Did he say where the money came from?"

"No, and I didn't ask."

"How much did he owe you?"

"Nearly four grand."

"Why did he ask you to come to him? Why not bring it to you?"

Dolan shrugged. "I didn't think about it at the time. I was too stunned. But he'd probably been drinking and didn't want to drive."

Jackson didn't buy it. Was Dolan lying through his teeth or had it been some kind of setup? "What did you do after the call? It didn't take forty-five minutes to drive over."

"I finished what I was working on, took a shower, and left." Dolan's voice stayed even, but the vibrating under the table increased, as though he were growing impatient, eager to tell his story.

"What happened when you arrived?"

"Jake gave me $3,800 in cash. Then he apologized for not paying the loan and offered me a beer." Dolan didn't blink or look away.

Jackson had a flash of doubt and felt the squeeze of a headache coming on. "What happened next?"

"We sat down, drank a beer, and talked for about twenty minutes. Then I left."

"Hold out your hands for me."

Dolan looked down at his hands, shook his head a little, then held them out, palm up.

"Turn them over." Jackson studied the backs, noting a few small white scars in addition to the brown stains, but saw no bruises. But three of Dolan's knuckles on his right hand looked swollen. "What did you and Jake fight about?"

"Nothing!" Dolan yanked his hands back. "I slammed my hand against the side of the truck yesterday when I was loading branches. My hands always look like this."

*Was Pittman's DNA under those dirty nails?* Even with a subpoena, they might not find it. They also needed to search Dolan's house for the clothes he'd worn the night before and examine his truck for bloodstains. Jackson hoped Evans was working on a search warrant. He remembered what Evans had said about yelling, after questioning the teenager next door.

"Jake's neighbor heard loud arguing, so we know things didn't happen the way you just described. What did you argue about?"

"Nothing!" Dolan pounded his fist on the table.

Jackson instinctively shot to his feet. "Calm down."

"Sorry." The suspect slumped and crossed his arms. "This upsets me. I didn't do anything wrong. Jake was fine when I left him."

"What time was that?"

"Before nine. I was only there for twenty minutes."

It still fit the window of Pittman's death. But to get Dolan to move toward a confession or a plea bargain, he needed to catch him in a lie. "What did you do after you left?"

"I went home and finished my bookkeeping."

"Was your family here?"

Dolan sighed. "No. My wife and the boys went out to a movie and didn't get home until after eleven."

"What did you do with the money?"

"I deposited most of it in the bank this morning on my way out of town."

"Which bank?"

"The Chase ATM inside Fred Meyer. Right up the street on Division. I have the receipt in my wallet." Dolan produced a piece of paper that showed he'd made a $3,800 deposit at 9:17 that morning.

Jackson's mind scrambled to come up with a new scenario. "Here's what I think happened. You heard Jake had come into some money, so you stopped to see him and collect what he owed you. He denied it and wouldn't give you any." Jackson watched Dolan's face carefully as he talked. "You got physical with him, maybe grabbed his shirt and pissed him off. So he punched you, and you hit him back. After a few blows, Jake lost his footing and fell against the counter, hitting his head."

Dolan shook his head back and forth, the movement growing in intensity as Jackson talked.

"Then you searched his place until you found the cash. You thought it was your money and you were entitled to it." Jackson lowered his voice. "But you didn't mean to kill him. It was an accident when he fell. That's what it looks like." Jackson left out the information about the victim's slit throat. He had to keep something back only the killer would know. Especially since it looked like they couldn't arrest Dolan just yet.

"No." The suspect pushed his hands through his hair. "Someone else must have shown up after I left."

"You were there at the time of death, Matt. You can't change the evidence. Tell me your side of it, and I can get you a deal for manslaughter. I don't believe you meant to kill him."

Dolan leaned forward and put his face in his hands.

Jackson waited.

His cell phone rang and he quickly silenced it. Dolan looked up and shook his head. Jackson cursed himself for forgetting to shut off the phone.

New tactic. "Did you know Rafel Mazari?"

Dolan started to hyperventilate. "I didn't kill anybody!

You can't pin these murders on me."

"So you did know Rafel?"

"I'd met him, but I didn't hang out with him. I know Sierra because I know her mother." Dolan was talking rapidly now. "Our families have been friends for decades. I landscaped that yard before Sierra turned it into an overgrown mess."

"The house on Santa Rosa?"

"Yes. It belongs to Vanessa Kent. She moved to Seattle a few years ago and let Sierra and Rafel move in."

The connections were interesting, but not likely relevant . . . unless Dolan knew Sierra well enough to be helpful. "Was Sierra cheating on her husband?"

"I don't know her that well." A flush of pink appeared on his pale cheeks.

"I think you do." Jackson leaned forward. "You just blushed, your eyes won't focus on anything, and your leg is vibrating harder than ever. Just tell me about her affair, and I won't have to subpoena the phone records of everyone you both know."

Dolan swallowed hard, but didn't manage to clear his throat, so he gulped from his water bottle. "My wife can't find out, please. It was long ago when Rafel first left for Afghanistan. It only lasted a few weeks. She was gorgeous and horny, but I couldn't take the guilt."

# Chapter 25

After another ten minutes of intense questioning, Jackson had to get out of the closet-like space. "Let's take a break, Matt. You can stand and stretch but don't go anywhere." He left the camera running, stepped outside into the dark driveway, and pulled in long breaths of cool night air. The pounding in his head eased, but the hollow pit in this stomach was growing.

A moment later, Schak and Evans stepped out of the back of the unit and joined him. Evans spoke up. "I saw most of the interrogation. What do you think?"

"He's consistent and makes good eye contact. If he's lying, he's damn good."

"But he was in Pittman's house during the time-of-death window, *and* he admits to an affair with Sierra." Schak wasn't really arguing, just verbalizing his own internal struggle.

"He also came into a load of cash yesterday," Evans added. "Dolan is a very viable suspect." She handed him her cup of coffee. "You look like you could use some caffeine."

"Thanks." Jackson took a long slug of the lukewarm brew. "We need a search warrant for his house and truck."

"I'll write the paper," Evans said. "But what about Pittman's slit throat? We haven't released that information about Mazari." She gained confidence as she talked. "Whoever killed Pittman likely knew Mazari had his throat cut. Either because they killed both men or because they wanted us to think the deaths were connected. We're pretty damn sure Sierra killed her husband, and since she was in jail last night, I'm starting to think she conspired with whoever killed Pittman."

"What's the motive?"

"Seven thousand dollars." Evans and Schak said it at the same time.

"Pittman admitted to having an affair with Sierra," Jackson said. "If they're still sleeping together, he's probably our man."

"Which explains why Dolan locked himself in his bedroom when they tried to bring him in for questioning." Evans started to bounce a little. "Pittman may have known about their affair. They may have killed him to silence him as well."

"I'll go question Dolan again," Schak offered. "You guys talk to the wife. Look around the house while you're in there."

"It's a plan." Jackson was ready to get out of the cold and wrap up this scene. "After this, we'll head back to the department and pull our information together. This has been an eventful day, and I don't want any details to fall through the cracks."

"What are we going to do with Dolan?" Evans asked.

"Release him and keep an eye on him if we can. We don't have enough to arrest him."

"We need to get his DNA too." Evans reached out, wanting her coffee back.


Sheila had little more to offer except to say her husband had been under a lot of financial stress, and the news of

Jake's murder had pushed him to the edge. Jackson had no reason to mention her husband's infidelity with Sierra, but he intended to find out if the affair was still going on. Dolan had vehemently denied seeing her recently, and his wife probably didn't know about the affair, so Jackson had no idea where to go for the information.

Sheila Dolan let them do a cursory search of the house, and they found no guns, no cash, and no explosives.

As he and Evans walked out to the command unit, Jackson's legs felt like lead. Yet his brain was still jumping between connections in these cases. When his mind stopped for a moment to rest, thoughts of Kera flooded in, making him doubt everything. What could he do to win her back?

"What are you thinking?" Evans asked. "You stopped in your tracks."

"Kera broke up with me today." He couldn't believe he'd said it out loud. It was nobody's business.

"That sucks. Why?"

He didn't want to admit it was his lack of commitment, and he was sorry he'd said anything. "I'm not sure and I don't want to talk about it. Please don't repeat it to anyone."

"I won't. I hope you're okay."

"I'm fine. Let's round up Schak and get on with this investigation."

Assuming his teammates had eaten long ago, Jackson bought a burger on his way downtown. Neither Katie nor Kera was there to give him grief about it, so he sat in his car in the Dairy Queen parking lot and thoroughly enjoyed every greasy, cheesy bite. He had a flash of worry about how the cholesterol would affect his retroperitoneal fibrosis, but quickly let it go. No one had any idea what caused the damned disease, so they didn't know what made it worse or better. Except the steroids. They worked, at least for a while.

Had his diagnosis and surgery scared off Kera? Was that part of it? Was she worried about having to take care of him after all the surgeries he might face? He wouldn't blame her for that. Kera was a nurse and had seemed to take the development in stride, but maybe she'd given it a lot more thought.

Jackson picked up the last few days' worth of debris from the floor of his car and hauled it to a trashcan. Sipping his coffee, he drove to headquarters, wondering if he should transfer to a position that didn't require him to work on Sunday nights. Would that save his relationship—or was it too late?

He stopped at his desk to check emails, saw nothing critical to the case, and headed for the conference room. Schak and Evans were already seated at the table, watching Sierra's interrogation again. Evans got up and turned it off.

"You stop and feed your face on the way?" Schak asked, pointing to Jackson's chin. "You've got cheese there, I think."

Jackson made a face, pulled a tissue from his carryall, and wiped his mouth again. "Let's make this meeting fast. I'm exhausted." He realized who was missing. "Oh crap, I forgot to contact Quince."

"I texted him," Evans said. "He's coming."

"Thanks. Will you take the board too?"

"I'm on it." Evans jumped up. "We need a second board, and I know where to find one."

A minute later, she was back, pushing a smaller wheeled version. "This was in the storage room. I think Internal Affairs stashed it, but they haven't gotten around to sneaking it out."

"You're stealing your boyfriend's pilfered goods?" Schak let out a grunting laugh.

"We'll call it a loan." Evans parked the second white board next to the first and wrote *Jake Pittman* at the top. "We have to keep these separate until we know for sure they're connected."

"But you think they are?" Jackson wanted to hear every side and every angle. These cases were stumpers.

"They have to be." Evans wrote *Connections* on the board and started a list: *best friends, ex-military, money problems, wife problems, died 48 hours apart.* She looked back at the group and asked, "Anything else?"

Quince came through the door and peeled off his wet jacket. "Where are we?"

"We're establishing connections between the two homicides," Jackson said.

"That's quite a list." Quince scanned the second whiteboard. "How does Sierra Kent figure into the second death? I thought she was in jail."

"She is, but we think she has a partner, maybe her lover."

"She wouldn't say much when I saw her in jail," Evans reported. "Except to threaten to sue us for emotional damages. And she vehemently denied having an affair with anyone. The animal clinic was closed when I stopped by earlier, so I still haven't talked to Dr. Davidson, the veterinarian, yet."

Jackson collected his thoughts, then summarized for Quince. "We have a suspect for Jake Pittman's murder. His name's Matt Dolan and he used to be Pittman's boss. He also loaned Pittman money and got burned, so Pittman owed him nearly four grand." While he talked, Evans wrote Dolan's name on the board and listed the details. Jackson continued,

"Dolan admits to visiting the second victim last night during the time frame for his death, but he claims Pittman called him over and paid back the money. He showed me an ATM receipt for the deposit."

"He could have killed Pittman and taken the money," Quince offered.

"Yes, and here's the interesting part. He also admits to having a brief affair with Mazari's wife more than a year ago. But if Sierra and Dolan are still lovers, they could have conspired to kill both men—with the cash from the charity scam being the motive."

Evans cut in. "We need to know who took the seven grand out of the charity's bank account after they transferred it. If that's where Dolan's money came from."

"None of the money was ever in Mazari's account," Jackson added. "I looked at his statements last night. Now we need Pittman and Dolan's records. I think tracking the money will show us what really happened."

"I should have information about the charity's bank account tomorrow." Quince looked frustrated and a little guilty. "Maybe we'll even get a name."

Evans looked at the board. "What else do we know about Pittman? Did you get anything interesting from his wife today?"

Jackson summarized the conversation he'd had with Hailey Pittman, focusing on her husband's financial troubles followed by his unexpected money. "She also heard him mention the Veterans Relief Fund while on the phone with Rafel Mazari. Which links both men to the fraudulent charity."

"Any other connections?" Evans looked back over her shoulder, after making rapid notes.

"Not that I know of. I asked Hailey Pittman if her husband had been sleeping with Sierra and she said no, that Jake didn't even like Sierra. I sensed she might not like her either." Jackson glanced at Schak. "What have you got?"

"Nothing yet. I couldn't reach Cody Sawyer by phone, so I stopped by his house, but no one was home. I'll keep trying." Schak rubbed his face, looking tired. "I wrote the subpoenas, but I can't get bank or phone records until the businesses open again tomorrow."

"Let's get Pittman's cell phone company to ping his phone and see if we can locate it. Mazari's too. If the killer took them, he or she may still have them in their possession. Even if they tossed the phones, the location should help us."

"Will do."

Jackson added, "I'll attend Jake's autopsy, then we'll meet here as soon as we have the bank and phone records. We'll be up to our asses in paperwork, but we'll find the trail."

"Mazari's funeral service is tomorrow at ten," Evans said. "That's another thing Sierra told me. She's hoping to be arraigned first thing in the morning so she can attend. I think I'll go and see who Sierra leans on. Maybe her lover will be there."

The information surprised Jackson. "That seems soon for a service."

"Sierra said Rafel's sister set it up. Apparently, it's a cultural thing to bury their dead as soon as possible."

"Text me with the location, in case I get out of the autopsy in time." Jackson turned to Quince. "Call me tomorrow if anything breaks on the charity's website or bank account."

"I will."

Schak closed his notebook. "Are we giving up on the guy

at the tavern who had the shoving match with Mazari?"

"No. But our sketch artist won't be back until Tuesday morning, and our witness won't return my call, so it's on a backburner." Jackson looked at his cell phone: 9:45. "Let's call it a night."

## Chapter 26

*Monday, Nov. 14, 5:30 a.m.*

Jackson woke from a nightmare and sat up, heart pounding. In his sleep, his ex-wife had murdered Kera, and Jackson had found her body in a ditch near the stadium. Somehow, in the dream, he'd known where the body was, as if he'd conspired with Renee to kill Kera.

*Jesus.* He shook off the horrific images, jumped out of bed, and rushed to splash cold water on his face. A sense of guilt and dread hung over him as he showered and dressed for work. Sitting down with a cup of coffee and the newspaper, he texted Katie first: *I'll pick you up at 7. We can stop for a bagel.* He knew his daughter was up and dressed for school, because she'd been getting herself ready in the morning since she was eight, when she realized her mother was not dependable.

A front-page story in the paper caught his eye. *Homicide Victims Were Longtime Friends* read the large-font headline. He knew the media would make the connection eventually, but he hadn't expected it this soon. Had Hailey Pittman talked to a reporter? Jackson glanced at the byline: *Sophie Speranza.* Of course. Sometimes he thought she followed him around. With a jolt, he remembered she had once followed him all the way to Newport to report on a missing person story.

He read the brief article, relieved Sophie hadn't mentioned that both victims had slit throats, only that they had been friends since childhood, had both served in the military, and had died forty-eight hours apart. The news story also mentioned that Sierra Kent, wife of the first victim, had been arrested for theft, but gave no details about the charge.

Good, Jackson thought. The reporter had probably picked up just the basic data from the jail's inmate-information website. Thinking about Sierra's theft of the sedative reminded Jackson to check in with the crime lab to see if they'd compared the syringe with Mazari's toxicology report, but he suspected the tests might not have been completed yet. Blood work went to the state lab, which was always backed up.

Katie texted him back: *Harlan's driving me to school. C you 4 dinner.*

He set down his coffee with a little too much force, slopping some on the paper. He texted back: *No. I told you yesterday I'd pick you up. Be there soon.*

Too irritated to read more of the paper, he went to the kitchen to grab his travel cup, so he could take coffee with him to headquarters. He couldn't find the mug. Was it still in a moving box? He thought he'd unpacked the important stuff. And why was this kitchen so damn dark even with the lights on? Jackson looked up at the ancient light fixture and realized one of the bulbs was burnt out. He'd change it later. Eventually he'd replace the fixture with something modern and recessed. Damn, he missed his old house. He'd put a lot of sweat equity into it.

He strode to the bedroom, pulled his Sig Saur from its fingerprint-activated case, and strapped it on. Grabbing his jacket and carryall, he rushed from the house. Rain soaked his hair and jacket in the twenty feet to the car, and he swore as he climbed in. He'd looked forward to having breakfast with his daughter and now she would be pissy with him. But making her stick to their plan was the right thing to do—wasn't it?

Yes, he decided. Spending too much time with a boyfriend at the age of fifteen was not a good idea. Jackson started his cruiser, and while it warmed up, he took a couple of calming breaths. It didn't help.

Renee's apartment was in an upscale quadplex across from Skinners' Butte Park, only a half-mile from the river. Harlan's little Honda Accord was parked in the visitor space. Jackson's chest tightened in a painful squeeze. *Don't blame the boy*, he coached himself. *Katie is responsible for this situation*. He pounded up the stairs.

After one rap, the door flew open. Harlan looked groomed and cheerful as ever. "Good morning, sir. I apologize for being here. I think there's been a misunderstanding." The boy took a step forward.

Jackson moved out of his way, too surprised to speak. As Harlan walked away, Jackson said, "Drive safe." *Lame!* But at least the boy would know he wasn't blaming him. He stepped into the living room and called out, "Katie."

His ex-wife greeted him from the kitchen. "We're in here."

*Crap.* He didn't want to make small talk. Normally, when he was here, he waited in the car for Katie. He dragged himself into the bright kitchen. "Good morning, Renee. Katie, are you ready?"

She didn't look at him—simply put her empty juice glass

in the sink, grabbed her backpack, and pushed past him toward the living room.

He gave Renee a tight smile and spun around.

"Wade."

Not fast enough. He turned back. "Yes?"

"You could have let her ride with him since he was already here."

"That's like saying 'Might as well let them have sex since they're already naked.'"

Renee rolled her eyes. "You still overreact to everything."

"No, I'm teaching Katie that it's not okay to go behind my back to get what she wants. And I don't want her riding with young teenage drivers. It's dangerous." He wanted to add so much more, but bit his tongue.

Renee shrugged and changed the subject. "Did you know she quit drill team?"

"Because of Harlan?"

"She says it took too much time."

"I'll talk to her." He left while he felt he was still in control.

Katie was quiet in the car and declined an offer to stop at Off the Waffle, which she loved. The restaurant had moved to Willamette Street and was now much closer to her school. Jackson asked questions about what she'd done over the weekend and she gave one- or two-word responses without looking at him.

He took a deep breath and plunged in. "Katie, I'm not trying to interfere with your friendship with Harlan. But it has to have limits."

"Oh bull. You don't like him, and you're trying to break us up."

The first half was true—or it had been until that morning—but the second half wasn't. "I just found out you dropped out of drill team, and I suspect it's because you want more time to spend with Harlan. That's not healthy for relationships. You both need to have your own lives and interests."

"We hardly ever see each other! We have no classes together, and he's at church a lot. Should I start going to church with him?" Katie turned and dared him to respond.

"I don't think that's the answer. Just be patient. You're only fifteen."

He turned into the familiar parking lot. He'd gone to high school in this building, and so little about it had changed, at least from the outside.

"Don't pull up front. Just let me off here."

The words cut him like a knife. His daughter had never acted ashamed of being seen with him before. Too hurt to even be obnoxious, he stopped and let her out.

"See you later." It was all he could say.

Katie mumbled something he didn't understand and hurried away. With every receding step, she seemed more like an unfamiliar young woman than the child he'd loved and raised. Jackson took a long sip of coffee and warned himself not to start thinking about Kera too. If he did, he'd become a basket case, and he had an autopsy to attend, where emotions had to be checked at the door.

Jackson took the elevator to the basement and strode down the hall, the sound of his footsteps echoing in the empty corridor. Few hospital visitors came this way, except those unfortunate souls who had to identify the dead. Still feeling on edge, he braced himself for the bright whiteness of the room and the coolness of the giant stainless steel drawers. It was odd to be back in Surgery 10 after only two days.

"Good morning," Konrad said, looking up from his microscope.

"Good morning. Where's Gunderson?"

"He's running late. He's picking up preliminary tox screens from the Mazari case."

"Excellent."

"Let's get started. I have another autopsy this afternoon."

Jackson pulled on a gown, hairnet, and gloves, while Konrad examined his work tray to make sure his tools were handy.

The pathologist removed the white sheet covering the corpse, and Jackson gave the body a once-over. After this point, he would listen more than look, unless the pathologist called his attention to something. Jake Pittman's stomach and legs had never seen the sun, and nearly every inch of white skin was covered with hair. His tanned arms were equally furry, and his privates were intact. It was the first time Jackson had made note of that in an autopsy, but after seeing Mazari's body, he'd never take a penis for granted again.

The pathologist moved to the end of the table and began a methodical search, starting with Pittman's toes and working his way up. Jackson zoned out for most of it, hearing only Konrad mutter something about a "chainsaw scar."

"Healthy skin and good muscle tone," the pathologist added. "And see this?" He pointed to faint grooves in the corpse's upper arm. "This man was vaccinated for a tour of duty in the Middle East. The anthrax vaccine sometimes leaves that mark."

"He was in Iraq years ago."

The medical examiner rushed in, and Konrad waited while he suited up.

"Do you have the toxicology report?" Jackson wanted to know what had been pumped into the first victim.

"I have a preliminary analysis. They tested for sedatives and barbiturates first. Mazari had ketamine in his blood."

"That's what Sierra took from her clinic."

"Do you mind if we conduct one autopsy at time?" Konrad looked over his glasses at them.

They stopped talking, and the pathologist continued his examination of the neck area, probing with his fingers.

"No puncture marks in this victim, in case you were curious."

"Good to know." With the bruising on Pittman's face, Jackson hadn't considered that he might also have been drugged.

The pathologist took measurements of the gash across Pittman's throat. "This wound is superficial. The trachea is damaged, but the carotid arteries are mostly intact. And it was clearly made after the man's heart had already stopped beating."

Jackson wanted to blurt out, *What about the head wound?* But he waited for Konrad to get there.

The pathologist spent ten long minutes examining facial bruises with his magnifier, then turned the head to the side. Finally he said, "This looks like pre-mortem bruising, but what's interesting is this abrasion behind his ear."

Jackson bit his tongue and waited.

Konrad used thin, jeweler-type tweezers to remove tiny pieces of evidence that Jackson couldn't even see. He assumed they were bits of skin and hair.

"I need a closer look." Konrad reached for a pair of hair

clippers and shaved a two-inch circle around the raised wound. After a moment, he said, "Something sharp but shallow struck him with substantial force."

"Like falling on the corner of a kitchen cabinet?" Jackson asked.

"Could be. I noticed the reference in the ME's report. We'll test his brain tissue to see if it matches the sample from the counter."

Jackson turned to Gunderson. "Did you find any trace evidence under those dirty fingernails when you brought him in?"

"I took the debris to the state lab this morning, but it'll take a week to get a DNA report."

"I'll open him up if you two are ready." Again Konrad looked over his glasses at them, Stryker saw in hand.

Jackson kept his eyes on the corpse's toes as the whine of the saw cut through the sternum. When Konrad flipped back the Y-shaped flap of skin, it made a slapping noise as it landed on Pittman's face. The sound always made Jackson jump a little, no matter how many times he'd heard it.

After a few minutes of extracting organs and sampling tissue, the pathologist grunted. "That's quite a tumor on his liver."

"Cancerous?" Jackson asked.

"We won't know for sure until we send out a biopsy," Konrad said. "Either way, it must have been causing him some pain."

Jackson wondered if Pittman had seen a doctor for it. Right now, he needed to get going. "Are you ruling his death a murder?"

"I can't say yet. I have more scope work to do on the trace evidence and tissue retrieved at the scene. Gunderson and I also need to study the crime scene photos and determine if the angle of a fall could match up to the mortal head wound." Konrad set the engorged liver on a tray to weigh it. "Considering the beating this man took, it was likely more than just an accident, but the death may not have been premeditated."

# Chapter 27

*Monday, Nov. 14, 5:45 a.m.*

Evans woke a little later than usual and jumped from bed feeling anxious. She drank a cup of high-octane coffee while she checked the news online, then went out for a five-mile run. Heart pounding, brain buzzing, she ran through the winding cul-de-sacs on the other side of Barger. In these moments, she felt stronger and happier than at any other point in her day. The homicides occupied her thoughts, and she kept coming back to two dominant questions: Who was Sierra sleeping with? And why did the second perp slash Pittman's throat to make it look connected to the first? If the killers were working together, how did it benefit them to highlight the connection between the deaths?

She rounded the corner, and her next thought was so jarring it almost made her slow down. Had the second killer tried to make the murders look connected to throw suspicion off Sierra? Because she was in jail and therefore couldn't have done it? Only a smitten lover would have done something so pointlessly protective. Which brought her back to the first question: Who was Sierra's lover? Dolan seemed like a good bet, but they couldn't rule out Cody Sawyer, even though he claimed he had a girlfriend. And she hadn't questioned Sierra's boss at the animal clinic yet either. The second murder had thrown them off some of the second-level interrogations they would have normally conducted by now.

Only in the home stretch did Evans let herself think about Jackson. Kera had broken up with him, and he'd made a point to tell her about it. Did that mean something on its own, or was it just part of a pattern of him opening up to her more in the last few months? The bigger question was: Should she do anything about it? She loved Jackson and probably always would, but she didn't want a rebound relationship. She didn't want to date a man who was still in love with someone else.

Slowing to walk the last block, Evans smiled at the irony. Of course, that was her exact situation with Ben. He was dating a woman who was still in love with someone else. Was that fair to him? But how was she supposed to get over Jackson without dating someone new?

Evans slipped her key out of her sock, entered her tidy little home, and headed for the shower. She had a funeral to attend.

The cemetery was nestled between an orchard and a new suburb in the Santa Clara area, an unincorporated chunk of Eugene. The sky threatened rain, and many of the mourners carried black umbrellas. Evans wore a hooded, knee-length black coat and stood near the back, where she hoped to blend in. She was strangely pleased by the opportunity to wear the coat, which had been collecting dust in her closet. The group at the graveside was small; she counted about eighteen people.

She recognized only a few: Sierra, who must've barely had time to change into black after being released from jail; Cody Sawyer, Rafel's other friend, whom she'd interviewed on Friday, and Sheila Dolan, whose presence surprised her.

Did the woman know about her husband's affair with Sierra? Matt Dolan had stayed away. Another woman, who looked a bit like Rafel, stood with an older man, whose facial skin was the color and texture of a walnut. Evans assumed they were Rafel's family, likely his sister and father. Sierra stood near the two, but they didn't speak to each other. A tall older woman had her arm linked with the widow's, and Sawyer stood behind them with a young woman Evans didn't recognize. Likely the girlfriend he'd mentioned.

A short redheaded woman, carrying a large red bag, trotted up at the last minute and stood next to Evans. She recognized her from photos posted on the newspaper's website. Evans turned and stuck out her hand. "Detective Lara Evans. You're with the paper?"

"Yes. Sophie Speranza. I'm writing a feature about Rafel Mazari and covering the homicides." She kept her voice low. "I'd love to talk with you after the service."

"Sorry. I can't give you anything." Evans looked her over. Sophie was shapely but soft, and pretty, but only with makeup. And damn good at her job, Evans remembered. "Do you know any of these people?"

"Sure." Sophie made small gestures to point out individuals. "The woman in front with long black hair, that's Sasha Altman, Rafel's sister. I suspect the old guy next to her is their father, Zain Mazari. Their mother disappeared when Rafel was twelve."

Evans reached in her pocket for her notepad. She hadn't known that, and the names were important. "Do you know the family's nationality?"

"Pashtun. The old man was born near the Pakistan border." Sophie continued identifying people. "And that woman with the red birthmark on her face? That's Laura

McKinsey. She's the sister of Rafel's first wife, and I'm rather surprised to see her. She hates Rafel."

Evans struggled to keep her face impassive. "Why?"

"I'll tell you later, it's starting."

Disappointed to have the flow of information cut off, Evans planned to corner Sophie afterward the service to see what else she knew.

Parts of the service were in another language and Evans tuned all of it out. Moving slowly and subtly along the back, she watched the crowd, looking for unusual reactions, maybe guilt or glee. Discovering an unexpected person at a funeral service had helped an investigation in the past, so they always tried to attend if the case was still unresolved. Their presence was also supportive for the victim's family. Evans would make a point to speak with Rafel's family before she left.

His sister wept openly throughout most of the service, but Sierra was stoic, head down and her thick dreadlocks covered by a large dark scarf. At one point, Evans saw Sawyer put his hand on Sierra's shoulder and squeeze, but his other hand remained locked with his girlfriend's. By the end of the service, Evans was restless and ready to start asking questions.

She approached the sister and father to ask for some of their time, but they brushed past her with polite nods and hurried to their vehicle. Evans turned back to Sierra, who was still arm-in-arm with the older woman, but also taking condolences from friends.

Evans caught a sudden movement to her right and spun toward it. Laura McKinsey, the woman Sophie had mentioned was an ex-in-law, was charging toward the burial site. The woman cursed Rafel to hell and spit in his grave as the cemetery workers moved in to fill it. Evans rushed toward her instinctively, in case the situation escalated. Fortunately, the dead man's family members were already walking away and didn't see it.

A young man rushed over and grabbed the woman's arm. "You bitch! What are doing?"

She jerked free of his grip as Evans reached the two.

"Eugene Police. Back away from her. It's over." Evans used as much authority as she could muster without shouting and drawing more attention.

The man cursed and walked away. Evans wanted to know who he was, but more important, she wanted to talk to Laura McKinsey, who had just unknowingly stepped into the role of suspect. She turned to the woman and introduced herself. "I'd like to talk with you, Ms. McKinsey. Let's go sit in my car where it's warm and dry."

"I'm sorry to be disruptive. Are you going to arrest me?" She looked near tears.

"This is an emotional time. We understand that. I'd just like to talk to you about Rafel."

"There's nothing to say. He's dead now, so it's over."

"What's over?" Evans touched her elbow, gently steering her away from the gravesite.

McKinsey, wearing a sky-blue jacket in contrast to all the black, moved with her. "The injustice is over. For the last three and a half years, my sister Joanna has been dead while Rafel was alive. Now he's dead too, and I have to let it go."

Evans wished like hell she was recording the conversation, but she didn't want to stop the flow. "Do you believe Rafel was responsible for your sister's death?"

"Yes, but there's no way to prove it and now it doesn't matter."

They reached the parking lot, and Evans tried to steer her toward her car. "I'd like you to come in to the department and make a statement. Perhaps the investigation into your sister's death can be reopened." It was a classic bait-and-switch. Get her in to talk about her concerns, then ask her about Thursday night when Rafel was killed.

McKinsey stopped and squinted at her. "I didn't kill Rafel, if that's what you're thinking. I was home with my husband in Corvallis."

"I'll want to corroborate that."

"Why would I wait three years to kill him, then show up at his funeral?"

*Good question.* "I need ten minutes," Evans said. "Just sit down with me and tell me your story."

## Chapter 28

As Jackson headed to his desk, Sergeant Lammers stepped out of her office. "Jackson. Just the guy I was looking for. Got a minute?"

"Sure." Sixty seconds was about all he had. The task force was meeting at twelve-thirty.

He stepped into her office and left the door open. His boss didn't ask him to close it. A good sign. Lammers dropped her two-hundred pound bulk into a custom-fitted office chair she'd purchased herself. Jackson sat too, once again putting them on eye level.

"You've had a hell of a weekend. Be sure to take some time off after this thing breaks."

"I will." He noticed she'd used the singular form, assuming the cases were related.

"I thought the wife looked good for the first homicide," Lammers said. "But she was locked up during the second. What the hell is going on?"

"These murders might be about money. Quince is investigating a phony charity that we think both victims were involved in." Jackson tried to sound confident. "We're looking at bank records this afternoon."

"What kind of charity?"

"It's called Veterans Relief Fund. The site has been taken down, but we subpoenaed the hosting company, and we're waiting to hear back."

"Good luck with that." She rolled her eyes. Smart criminals rarely used legitimate hosting companies or legitimate names to commit fraud. "What else have you got?" she asked. "We're taking some heat over this one. As soon as the media identified the first murder victim as a veteran, we started fielding a flood of calls from the public. They seem to think it's our fault, like we should have had a cop in that parking lot, standing watch over him."

The lengthy complaint was rare for Lammers. She took most flak in stride, and when she let loose, it was usually short and foulmouthed. Jackson had a flash of sympathy for her. Veterans evoked all kinds of emotional reactions from the public.

"We have a possible witness for the first murder, and we think we found the weapon." Jackson tried to give it a positive spin, but he had to be honest. "The weapon was in the canal, so we're not likely to get prints."

"Possible witness?"

"A homeless man who saw the killing but was too far away to identify the assailant."

Lammers made a harsh sound, a cross between a bark and a laugh. "Any real evidence?"

"We have a syringe found near the first victim with the wife's prints on it. Her husband had ketamine in his blood when he died, and I'm still waiting to hear from the lab about what was in the syringe. But I believe it will be ketamine."

"That sounds like something that will hold up in court. What's the theory?"

"I think the wife had an accomplice, a lover. She killed her husband—by drugging him and slitting his throat—and her accomplice killed Pittman, the best friend. They did it for the seven grand the charity stole from Molly Pershing." It was the first time he'd put it together exactly like that, and it seemed solid and logical.

"Speaking of Molly Pershing, do we have any more fraud victims?"

"A couple dozen here locally, but probably a lot more online. Quince spent the weekend tracking them down. But all of the others voluntarily gave small amounts to the fake charity in response to an email."

Lammers pounded a fist on her desk. "We spend so much time and effort on crime prevention, and old people still get victimized."

"It's a shame," Jackson agreed. "Too many seniors don't have anyone looking over their shoulder."

"I wish I could give you another detective for this case, but we just don't have anyone available."

"Any chance of getting some patrol cops to keep an eye on our suspects, Sierra Kent and Matt Dolan?"

"I'll try. As soon as you have something solid, I want you to make a statement for the media. Sometimes the public needs reassurance from officers on the job."

Jackson cringed. "Not a press conference, right? Just pick a reporter and give them a quotable statement?"

Lammers rolled her eyes again. "I'll settle for that."

At his desk, Jackson made another call to Zain Mazari, the first victim's father, and again got no answer. He didn't bother to leave a message this time. Eventually, when he had an extra hour, he'd find the address and make a trip out there to interview him. He wouldn't feel like he'd really gotten to know Rafel Mazari until he talked to his parent. Had Sophie Speranza interviewed him already? Jackson thought about calling her, then changed his mind.

He ordered food for the group, then made two trips to the conference room carrying stacks of paper. American Heritage had faxed three months of transactions for the business account of Veterans Relief Fund. All he really wanted to know for now was: Who opened the account? And who transferred the seven grand?

Quince was in the room when he came back with the second load. His teammate jumped up. "Is there more?"

"No, thank god. This may help you prove the fraud case, but it's giving me a headache already."

"Better than not enough." Quince started thumbing through the stack. "Where's the account holder information?"

"I didn't see it. Let's hope it's in there somewhere."

Schak and Evans came in together, laughing at something Schak had said. They stopped when they saw the stack of printouts.

"Holy crap." Schak dropped his carryall on the floor. "We'd better have food and coffee coming."

"We do." Jackson made a quick call to Full City and asked them to deliver four tall house blends. To his team, he said, "Anything significant I should know before we dive into these?"

"Nothing yet," Evans said, and Schak shook his head.

"Let's divide the stacks then, and search for the account holder information first. We need the names of the fraud perps. We also received phone records for Mazari today, and I'll start with those."

"You can use my Netbook," Quince offered and pushed the silver laptop toward him. "Unless you want to go back to your desk."

"Thanks. I'll work here. We'll keep each other awake."

Quince shoved a stack of paper at both Evans and Schak, then turned his pile over and checked the last two pages. "Here it is. The account has three names on it. Terrance O'Dell, Brice Farley, and Omar Guiterrez. I'll run them, but I wouldn't be surprised if they're all fake."

A wave of disappointment hit Jackson. How would they track three ghosts?

As if reading his mind, Quince said, "They could be real people, and these cases might not be connected. We'll run the IDs and see what comes up. Even if the perps used fake ID to open the account, we may still find some leads."

"Sounds like a long shot." Schak started scanning his pile.

"If it's an online bank, how did they access the money?" Evans wanted to know.

"Plastic," Quince said. "They had debit cards issued to each person on the account. All the perps had to do was stick the cards into universal ATMs and pull out the cash."

"We need to find where the seven grand was pulled from," Jackson said. "It had to involve several machines, maybe over the course of several days."

Quince warmed to the scenario and began to pace. "The money left Molly's account early Wednesday afternoon. Mazari was killed around ten the next night."

Evans scooted to the board to make notes.

"The cash didn't show up—that we know of—until Saturday night, approximately around the time Pittman was killed." Quince turned and paced back. "So they had plenty of time to make stops at ATMs, taking $300 or $400 a pop."

"Most ATMs have video," Schak reminded them.

"But hiding your face is easy," Quince shot back.

"But who are *they*?" Evans asked. "Did Mazari take the money, and Sierra killed him for it? Then Pittman stole it from her, so her lover killed him?"

"Or were Sierra and her lover working together from the beginning to simply cut out the others from the cash flow and keep it to themselves?" Jackson still liked his conspiracy idea.

"Or is Cody Sawyer the third man in the charity and Sierra's lover?" Quince offered.

"I'm still looking for him," Schak said. "I talked to his mother this morning, and she says Cody is devastated by the deaths of his friends. She thinks he's out at Clear Lake grieving."

"We need to bring him in." Jackson looked at Evans. "Have you talked to the veterinarian Sierra works for? Mazari seemed pretty convinced he was Sierra's lover."

"When I called this morning, they said Dr. Davidson plays golf on Mondays. I tried his cell phone but haven't reached him yet. I'll keep at it."

"Look at these deposits," Schak said, tapping his printouts. "Up until recently, they were all small amounts; $50 here and $100 there. The money was withdrawn in similar amounts as fast as it came in. Then bam! Suddenly $7,000 flushes into the account, and two days later, two of the scammers are dead."

"The money must have been the catalyst." Jackson picked up the thread. "One of the scammers violated the rules of their scam and grabbed a risky windfall. Maybe he tried to keep it for himself. So they killed him to minimize their risk and get the money for themselves."

"Don't forget Pittman supposedly gave $3,800 to Dolan, a man he owed," Evans commented. "How does that fit in?"

"Or Dolan is the third man and simply took it from him." Jackson's adrenaline was flowing now. "We need to find the third scammer, and even though Cody Sawyer isn't military, he also looks like a good bet. He could be one of our killers, or the next victim."

The food arrived and Jackson was glad. They needed to spend time with the data and see if any patterns or answers emerged. Everyone grabbed a sandwich and dug in, eating quickly. The coffee came a minute later, making the room smell like a Starbucks.

"Oh yes." Schak pulled up the lid and inhaled deeply, but didn't drink it yet. They'd learned not to burn themselves on the piping hot stuff.

When they'd polished off the last of the pickles and chips, Jackson turned to Evans. "Let's get back to the whiteboard. Anything interesting from the funeral service today?"

"You mean like someone spitting in the man's grave?"

They all turned, mouths open.

"Laura McKinsey is the sister of Joanna Mazari, Rafel's first wife. McKinsey thinks Mazari killed her sister and made it look like an accident. She's so happy he's dead, she drove down from Corvallis to spit in his grave."

"Where was she Thursday night?" Jackson didn't need another suspect, but he couldn't ignore her either.

"At home with her husband. I talked to the husband and he verified it. I think the sister's a kook, but probably not a viable suspect. She did give me another idea." Evans paused for a drink of coffee. "If it's true and Mazari killed his first wife because he thought she was cheating"—Evans paused and turned to Jackson—"Mazari might have been planning to kill his second wife too. Again for cheating. Only Sierra went proactive and cut him down first."

"That's intriguing." It also made Jackson's head hurt. They had too many players, too many possibilities. At its core, this case was probably simpler than they thought. "Let's finish this update, then look at the bank data. I didn't learn much at the autopsy, except that Mazari had ketamine in his system, and Pittman had a tumor on his liver, likely cancerous."

"Maybe he needed the money for treatment," Evans offered.

"As an Iraq veteran, wouldn't he get free medical care?" Schak countered.

Evans wrote *Cancer?* on the board under Pittman's name. She turned to Jackson. "What did the pathologist say about the cause of death?"

"Undetermined, so far. More than an accident, but maybe not premeditated. The slash to his throat was superficial and after the fact, as we surmised."

"I thought so. Maybe Sierra's lover came looking for the money and tried to beat it out of Pittman." Evans faced them from the board. "This morning I had the idea that her lover cut Pittman's throat to make it look similar to the first crime and throw suspicion off her. That still works."

"We need to find her lover," Jackson said. "How are we doing on Sierra's phone records?"

"I've got the subpoenas signed, sealed, and delivered, but the phone companies are taking their sweet-ass time." Schak tapped the table. "I'll call them both again as soon as we're done here."

"Don't forget we want the companies to ping Mazari and Pittman's phones too. The location of the damn phones might tell us more than what's inside."

"Sierra's mother was at the funeral," Evans said. "Maybe I should talk to her about Sierra's lover."

"I wouldn't be hopeful, but put her on your list." Jackson tapped his pile of phone records. "Let's dig into this data."

After twenty minutes of cross-checking numbers in Mazari's phone records with numbers in the database, Jackson learned the victim had made fewer calls than average, and that his calls went to friends and family. Jake Pittman was the most frequent person Mazari spoke to, with several calls going each way in the days and hours before Mazari's death. Surprisingly few calls were to his wife in his last few days, except Thursday night when he'd called her from the bar. That was the last time Rafel Mazari had ever used his cell phone. Did he have any inkling he was about to die? Kera had mentioned that Rafel thought his wife wanted him dead.

Jackson wondered about his own mortality. Would he die on the job, facing off against a lowlife with a gun or a knife, heart pounding, vision blurred, knowing it was last thing he'd see and feel? He hoped the hell not. If he could choose his own exit, what would it be? Lying in bed with Kera, both too old and tired to get up, but holding hands and smiling. The image almost crushed him with sadness, and he had to shake it off.

In his notepad, he created a timeline of Mazari's calls for Thursday, stared at it, and hoped it would be useful somehow. At the moment, it meant nothing to him. He really wanted to pry open Sierra's phone and see who she'd been chatting with while her husband lay bleeding.

Twenty minutes later, Schak called, "Bingo."

Jackson shot out of his chair, eager to stand and stretch.

"On Wednesday and Thursday, the card ending in the number 0532, issued to Terrance O'Dell, made eighteen withdrawals." Schak stood too, his voice a little excited. "Most were for $400, and they came out of three machines. One at a Safeway, one at ShopKo, and one at a US Bank. All within a half mile of Jake Pittman's home."

"So Pittman could be the one who fiddled with Molly Pershing's account and made the $7,000 transfer." Jackson began to pace. "Where were the smaller, earlier withdrawals made?"

"All over. Campus, Santa Clara, West Eugene. The other guy was smart and didn't create a pattern." Quince touched his forehead, pondering. "The third card was never used. One of the guys on the account didn't access the money."

"That's odd." Jackson turned to Quince. "Can you track these three IDs and see where they came from?"

"I'll do my best, but I'm not optimistic." Quince leaned forward and his words came in a rush. "We need to get the videos from the ATMs where the withdrawals were made. Maybe one of the perps didn't bother to cover his face."

"I don't know." Evans shook her head. "They were smart about getting fake ID and using an online bank. And they probably used phony identification to set up the web hosting account. They may be ghosts."

"Scammers get sloppy," Jackson countered. "Especially if things go smoothly, and they think they're getting away with it." He turned to Quince again. "Find out who owns the ATMs and get videos. We need to see their faces."

Evans spoke up. "I'll find out who Sierra was sleeping with, even if I have to bribe her co-workers."

"Good." Jackson turned to Schak. "Keep calling everyone connected to this case until we find Cody Sawyer, then call me. After that, work with Quince on tracking down the fraud perps." Jackson started gathering up the stacks of bank printouts. "I'll head out to Sawyer's house and see if he's there. We have three people involved in a charity scam, and we have a trio of friends who grew up together. Two of those men are dead, so Cody's starting to look like a man who might have some answers."

Jackson went back to his desk and took two aspirin, glad it was just a headache and not the usual gut-stabbing pain. He pulled out his cell phone and stared at it. Should he call Kera or give her some space? While he worried over that, his phone rang, startling him a little. He didn't recognize the number and almost didn't pick up, then decided just to get it out of the way, whatever it was.

"Jackson here."

"This is Dr. Meyer. How are you doing?"

"I'm fine." A little flutter of panic. Why was his urologist calling him?

"I wanted to remind you to schedule your next MRI. We need to keep an eye on the fibrosis, and these scans are critical."

"Okay. I'll do it."

"I'll call Oregon Imaging next week to get your results."

That was doctor code for 'I'm going to check up on you and make sure you do this.' Jackson wrote himself a note. "Thanks for the reminder."

"You're welcome. Is everything fine? Kidneys working well?"

"I'm good."

"Excellent. We'll talk again after I see the MRI scans."

Jackson felt a little less fine than he had before the call, but he was grateful his doctor was thorough and compassionate. He'd make the appointment a little later in the week.

Instead of calling Kera, he sent a brief text: *Thinking about you. Missing you.* What he needed was a grand gesture.

Not flowers or balloons or anything superficial. Kera wasn't impressed with such things. In fact, she was so low-maintenance, he'd taken her for granted and blown the relationship.

*Should he propose?* The thought sent a bolt of fear up his spine. Yet earlier that day, he'd envisioned growing old with Kera and dying in her bed. What the hell was wrong with him?

*Focus!* He found Cody Sawyer's number, called, and got a friendly voicemail message. The man didn't sound like a killer, but that was irrelevant. Jackson left a message, asking for an immediate call back. Looking back through his notes, he found that Sawyer worked at Royal Caribbean Cruise Lines. He'd stop at the call center first. There was a good chance Sawyer would be at work on a Monday afternoon.

The cruise line center, located on the outskirts of Springfield, had a twenty-foot white anchor coming out of the building. Jackson pulled into the circular parking lot, noticing that without the goofy anchor, the nearly new building would be aesthetically pleasing.

The receptionist informed him that Cody Sawyer wasn't at work because Monday and Tuesday were his days off. Jackson thanked her and left, regretting the trip. He called Sawyer again, was routed to voice mail, and hung up without leaving a message. Where to now? Jackson checked his list of phone numbers and addresses for the case and found Sawyer's. The home was in south Eugene, and he remembered Evans had said Sawyer lived with his parents.

Before starting his car, his phone rang in his hand, and the call came from Parker at the crime lab. *Finally!*

"Hey, Parker. What have you got for me?"

"A few things. First, the syringe from Mazari's crime scene contained traces of ketamine."

"Excellent news. One more piece of evidence to help convict Sierra. Anything else from the first crime scene?" So much had happened since then, it seemed like a week ago.

"The sticky substance from the side of the victim's car was tree sap."

"Huh." Jackson had no idea what to make of that. He couldn't picture any trees near the driveway of Mazari's home. Had Sierra, or someone, accidentally transferred the sap to the Jeep? He needed more information. "Anything on the second homicide?"

"The long hair found on the victim is synthetic, so I can't send it out for DNA."

"Like a wig?" That was puzzling.

"Yes. Some hair pieces are real, but not this one."

Jackson's first thought was that Pittman had been with a prostitute. But his killer could have worn a wig or the hair could have been on the dirty carpet for months. He would have to give it more thought. "Thanks for the update."

He took Beltline to Delta and crossed the downtown area. A large group of protestors were gathered in front of the county courthouse, carrying anti-establishment signs. A dozen officers stood around the perimeter, keeping an eye on the situation. *Crap.* The presence of those officers at the protest meant their resources were stretched and he wouldn't get any help keeping tabs on his suspects.

He drove south on Hilyard and twenty minutes later pulled up in front of a two-story house sitting in the shade of giant fir trees. No cars were in the driveway, and no lights were on in the house. Feeling frustrated, Jackson checked his watch: 4:27 and already starting to get dark. He wanted to talk to Cody's parents too and wondered if anyone would be home soon. He strode to front door and knocked loudly, just to make sure. No one answered, so he decided to sit in his car and wait for a while. If no one showed up in the next hour, he'd leave and try again after dinner. Schak had said Sawyer might be out at Clear Lake grieving, but he had to come home eventually. Unless the young man was already heading out of town. Jackson wondered if he had probable cause to issue an attempt-to-locate. So far, they didn't have a single piece of evidence connecting Sawyer to either death, or even to the fraud case.

He pulled out his compiled notes and started reading through them. The nagging feeling that he was missing an undercurrent in this case was still with him.

A few minutes later, a silver Miatta pulled into the driveway. A sixty-something woman with shoulder-length gray hair got out of the car and stood looking at him. He shoved his notes back in his carryall and stepped out to greet her.

"Detective Jackson, Eugene Police." He held out his hand, hoping she would offer her name.

"Susan Sawyer. What can I do for you?"

"I'd like to talk to you about your son Cody."

Her face tightened with worry, a reaction he'd seen from many parents.

"I just have a few questions." He wanted to smile and reassure her, but he couldn't.

"What is this about?" A tiny quiver in her voice.

"The deaths of Rafel Mazari and Jake Pittman, friends of Cody's."

"We're all devastated by this. I've known both those

young men for decades." Her eyes were puffy from crying.

"Can I come in?"

"All right."

She led him into the house and took a seat on the couch. Jackson sat across from her on the edge of a padded chair. The home was nicely furnished, with a walnut hardwood floor and a collection of expensive-looking pottery. Cody Sawyer probably didn't lack money in the same way his friends had. "Do you know where Cody is?"

"It's his day off, and he's grieving so I'm not sure."

"Does he have a girlfriend?"

"Sort of. They used to be a couple, but now they're just friends."

The timing was interesting. "Why did they split up?"

She gave a little shrug. "I think they just grew apart."

"What's the girlfriend's name?"

"Melissa Jenkins." Mrs. Sawyer squeezed her hands together. "You don't think Cody had anything to do with these horrible murders, do you? Rafel and Jake were his best friends since grade school, when we all lived in Junction City. If you knew Cody at all, you'd know he couldn't hurt anyone. He's the sweetest young man." Her eyes begged him to believe her. "Cody did volunteer work the whole time he was unemployed, just to feel useful."

"What kind of volunteer work?"

"He spent a lot of time at Southside Senior Center. He read to old people and helped them learn computer skills."

A jolt of energy shot through Jackson's tired body. Was Cody the mastermind of the charity fraud? "Cody has good computer skills?"

"Sure. Most young people do."

"Does he know how to build websites?"

"Of course. The templates make it easy for anyone."

She obviously stayed current on technology and thought people who didn't were Neanderthals. "Have you ever heard Cody mention Veterans Relief Fund?"

Mrs. Sawyer shook her head, puzzled. "What does this have to do with the murders?"

"Where was Cody Saturday night?"

"He went over to Melissa's."

They heard a car outside and both looked toward the window. A red Dodge Charger had parked behind Susan's car in the driveway. A young man climbed out and stood for moment, looking at Jackson's cruiser, much the way his mother had.

In the silence of the large house, they both watched to see what the young man would do, on edge for different reasons.

Finally, Cody strode toward the house, gave a small wave, and came inside. Jackson and Mrs. Sawyer both stood as her son entered the living room. Jackson put Cody at six feet, with short dark hair, a soul patch on his chin, and a thin build.

Jackson introduced himself, then said, "I'd like you to come into the department and answer some questions."

"He can answer them here." Mrs. Sawyer moved toward her son.

Protective parents could be the worst roadblocks, and Jackson worried that if he pressed the issue, they'd lawyer-up and he wouldn't learn anything. "Can you leave us alone for a moment then?"

She hesitated, and Cody said, "It's okay, Mom. Maybe you should call Dad though."

Mrs. Sawyer quickly left the room, and Jackson wondered what he'd missed. "Let's sit down."

Sawyer took the spot his mother had occupied. "I've lost two friends in the last four days," he said. "And I'm very upset, so I'd like to keep this short." His eyes had a tired look that didn't quite make direct contact.

Jackson nodded, but intended to keep to his own agenda. "Where were you Saturday night between nine and midnight?"

"I was with my girlfriend, Melissa. We watched a movie at her house."

"What time did you leave?"

A slight hesitation. "Around eleven."

It was outside Pittman's time-of-death framework. "Give me Melissa's phone number so I can verify it."

Sawyer didn't hesitate, and Jackson wrote the number next to the girlfriend's name.

"What about Thursday night between nine and ten?"

"I was right here, and my parents can vouch for that."

Jackson decided to step up the intensity. "Are you having an affair with Sierra Kent?"

Sawyer's eyes came open, startled by the question. "Of course not. Rafel was my good friend."

"We'll have her phone records tomorrow. If you're in there, we'll know you lied."

"She called me a few times. We were friends. So?"

"May I see your cell phone?"

"No." He offered no explanation or excuse.

"What have you got to hide?"

"Private messages that have nothing to do with this."

"What did you do as a volunteer at the Southside Senior Center?"

"A variety of things. Mostly just kept old people company."

"What about Molly Pershing? Did you keep her company?"

Jackson thought he detected a flicker of recognition.

"I don't know the name."

"Are you sure? Molly's dead now. She had a heart attack."

"I don't know why you're telling me this." Sawyer's shoulders hunched forward a little, as if he were cold.

"Molly was a victim of fraud. What do you know about the Veterans Relief Fund?"

"Nothing."

At the sound of another car, Sawyer looked visibly relieved. Jackson started to ask another question, but he realized he'd lost his suspect's attention. A few moments later, an older version of Cody walked in the door. Jackson stood to acknowledge him.

"I'm Jim Sawyer, Cody's father and lawyer, and I'm advising him not to answer any more questions."

*Oh boy.* A lawyer father. It didn't get any worse. "I'm just trying to clear Cody as a suspect, so we can resolve a couple of homicides."

"I appreciate that you're just doing your job. So am I."

Jackson handed the father a business card. "If your client is innocent, I suggest you bring him in to make a statement. Call me when you're ready." He nodded at both men and left.

Sitting in his cruiser in front of their house, frustration building, Jackson called the girlfriend. If she corroborated Sawyer's alibi, his team would have to work a lot harder to get a subpoena to search Sawyer's phone and bank records. They would also have to keep looking for a third man in the fraud ring—who might not be a man at all. If the charity debit card were only used to pull cash from an ATM, the gender of the fake ID didn't matter. Sierra could be the third person, or even Hailey Pittman.

The girlfriend's phone rang five times, then went to voicemail. Jackson identified himself and asked Melissa for an immediate call back. He started his car and considered going into the department to check in with his team. Then he changed his mind. It was time to go home, cook a meal in his new kitchen, and spend a moment with his daughter.

Deep in thought, Jackson turned down his old street out of habit and didn't realize his mistake until he saw a strange car parked in the driveway of his old house. He wondered how many more times he would do that until the new route was automatic. That was one problem with staying in the same neighborhood.

Once he made it home, Katie came out of her bedroom and greeted him cheerfully. "Hey, Dad. How was your day?"

"Not bad. How about you?" Apparently, the morning's unpleasantness was forgotten.

"Good day for me. I got a B on my algebra test."

Jackson grabbed a diet Coke from the fridge. "Congratulations on the test. You must have studied while you were at your mom's."

"I did."

"Let me get out of this jacket and I'll be right with you." They both knew that was code for 'I need to put my weapon away.' Katie didn't like to be around it and wouldn't let him hug her if he was wearing a gun.

Back in his bedroom, he pulled off his jacket, locked away his Sig Saur, and took off his shoes. Tension drained from his body. Damn that felt good. Could he take the night off and sit and watch a movie with Katie? The thought made him laugh a little. As good as it sounded, he knew he couldn't do it. Not as long as this case was still tied in knots.

Jackson headed back to the kitchen, where Katie was marinating pork chops. She turned to him. "I know it's dark and cold out, but you said we could grill."

"Sounds good. What else are we having?"

"You pick."

"I'm not even sure what is here." Jackson rummaged through the cupboards, noting his brother still ate Captain Crunch cereal, and finally found a box of instant mashed potatoes. "We'll smother them in gravy," he said, holding up the box for her approval.

"I'll pass, but you go ahead."

Dieting again. Jackson didn't comment. "What else is new with you?"

"I thought about what you said this morning, and I'm thinking of signing back up for drill team. I would have to wait until next term though."

He couldn't help but grin. "I look forward to seeing your next performance." He decided to push his luck. "Will you also make time to work on the trike with me?"

"Sorry, I'm just not into it anymore."

"That's okay. We'll find something else we can do together."

She gave him a funny smile. "Sorry about this morning."

"Thanks for saying that."

"Don't get too excited. I'm not breaking up with Harlan." Katie grabbed the meat tray and headed out the back door.

The word *breakup* made him think of Kera. Should he tell Katie about it? Or wait and see if he could salvage the relationship? His daughter had held Kera at arm's length until she'd accepted that her parents were never getting back together. Then Micah, Kera's baby grandson, had come to live with Kera, and Katie had bonded with the baby in a way that surprised him.

Jackson decided to wait. He wasn't giving up Kera without a fight. He would call her after dinner.

# Chapter 29

*Tuesday, Nov. 15, 9:35 a.m.*

Quince hurried into the Southside Post Office, subpoena in hand. Before the Veterans Relief Fund website had gone down, he'd made note of the post office box listed as a place to mail checks. The 97405 zip code indicated this post office, and he was determined to walk out of here with a name—and hopefully a real one. To open a mailbox, the post office required a photo ID and one other solid piece of information, such as a vehicle registration or insurance policy.

The line was short and he quickly stood in front of the clerk, an older man with crazy-curly gray hair. Quince pulled his eyes away from it when the clerk greeted him. He gave his name, presented the subpoena, and waited while the clerk checked his records.

"The box was opened by Brice Farley on July 27 this year."

*Damn.* That was one of the names on the charity's bank account, which he'd learned yesterday was fake and belonged to a young man who'd died in a car accident. The person who'd set up the charity and all its accounts had been very careful, smarter than most of the desperate or drug-stupid criminals who usually committed this kind of fraud.

"You don't have a copy of his ID, do you?" Quince knew it was wishful thinking.

"We ask to see ID, but we don't keep it on file."

"Will you check and see if there's anything in the mailbox?"

"Sure." The clerk turned and headed into the bowels of the processing center. In a moment, he came back and shook his head. "It's empty."

"Thanks." Quince strode to his car. He had just enough time to make a quick stop before the task force meeting that morning.

He entered the Rosehill Estates, waved at the receptionist, who'd seen him a few times by now, and headed down the long corridor toward Molly Pershing's apartment. He'd found nothing helpful in her paperwork or on her computer and he'd talked to most of her neighbors over the weekend. But the woman who lived directly across from Molly hadn't been home any of the times he'd been here. Her name was Gloria Hastings, or so said the pretty plaque on her door.

He heard someone inside moving slowly, and Quince was relieved to be able to check this task off his list. A tiny woman who looked at least ninety opened the door a few inches and peered out. "Who are you?"

"Hi, Gloria. I'm Detective Michael Quince, Eugene Police Department. I'd like to ask a few questions about your neighbor, Molly Pershing."

She opened the door a few more inches. "Let me see your badge."

Quince pulled it from his pocket and showed her. "Can I come in? I only need a minute."

"I'm still in my bathrobe, and I just got out of the hospital. Can you come back later?"

"I wish I could, but I'm running out of time. Did you know

Molly died on Friday?"

The door opened a few more inches. "Yes. My friend told me when she visited me at the hospital."

Quince felt bad about keeping a sick old woman standing in her doorway, but he had to get this done. "Someone accessed Molly's bank account and stole her money. I'm trying to find that person. Have you seen anyone new with Molly lately? Possibly a young man?"

Her cloudy eyes registered fear, then anger. "I did see a strange young man leaving Molly's apartment about six weeks ago. At first I thought it was her grandson, then I realized he was too tall."

"How tall?"

"A little taller than you."

Quince was five-eleven, but he often said "six feet" just to round it off. "What color hair?"

"I'm not sure. He was wearing a knit cap."

"What else can you tell me about him?"

"He was skinny and he wore glasses."

The glasses didn't sound like any of their suspects, but he pressed forward anyway. "What about facial hair?"

Gloria made a face. "He had one of those tiny little beards on his chin."

A soul patch, Quince realized, as he jotted down the description. Was that Pittman or Sawyer? "Did you catch his name or any of their conversation?" Quince pulled out his Netbook while he talked.

"I heard Molly say thanks."

He opened Facebook, found Cody Sawyer's page, and showed the photo to Gloria. "Is this the guy?"

She pulled up her glasses from where they hung around her neck and peered at the digital page. "I think so."

# Chapter 30

*Tuesday, Nov. 15, 9:15 a.m.*

Sophie deleted the last sentence she'd written and tried again. She struggled to find a new way to report the same information she'd had yesterday. Jackson hadn't called her back, so she'd called Detective Evans and left a message. And Jasmine still wouldn't tell her anything, so she'd learned almost nothing new about Jake Pittman's death. Still, her editor wanted daily news stories about the homicides until she was ready to run her full-length feature, so she was trying to give him something. The more she learned about Rafel Mazari, the less Hoogstad was going to like her article. He wanted a piece about the tragic civilian death of a soldier who'd survived a tour in Afghanistan, but that wasn't the *real* story. Jake Pittman, Rafel's best friend, was ex-military too, and he'd been murdered two days later. She had to assume the men had been involved in something illegal and likely dangerous. After a dozen phone calls the day before, trying to dig up something, all she'd learned was that Rafel had been well liked by men, but some women thought he was controlling and sexist.

It was time to tell her editor she needed a few more days on Mazari's feature and that the story had morphed into something else. Sophie got up from her desk and walked past a row of cubicles to Hoogstad's glass-walled office. The carpet kept her pumps from making a clicking noise, which would have been about the only sound in the building. The salespeople, usually more talkative than the reporters and editors, were out on calls, leaving an empty echo.

Leaned back in his chair with his eyes closed, Hoogstad looked like he was sleeping. She rapped softly on his open door. "Karl?"

He shot forward, drool hanging from his lower lip. "Jesus. Don't scare me like that when I'm thinking."

"Sorry. Do you have a minute?"

"Sure. What's on your mind?"

"These two murders." Sophie paused, wondering how politically correct she had to be. "Both men were military veterans, but I don't think they were heroes—or least not anymore. I'm not sure I can write the fallen-hero feature you originally mapped out."

He stared at her for a long moment. "So find out what they were involved in and write that instead."

"Thank you." She started to turn away.

"What's on your schedule today?" Hoogstad asked.

"Visit the animal clinic where Mazari's wife is employed and talk to her co-workers. She's out of jail, but I'm sure the police still consider her a suspect." Sophie also hoped to interview Rafel's father. Laura McKinsey had given her the number and mentioned that the old man lived out River Road on a secluded farm. Sophie had called him, of course, but he hadn't returned her call.

"Get a statement from the police too. I know you have contacts there. Work 'em."

"I'll do what I can."

Back at her desk, she called Jackson on her landline, and he surprised her by picking up. "Good morning, Sophie. Do you realize you've left me four messages in the last three days?"

"And now you're talking to me. Thanks for answering."

"How did you get Jake Pittman's name so fast?"

"I know people who went to high school with Rafel and his friends."

"Like who?"

"Someone who knew Rafel's first wife." Sophie wasn't about to admit she'd followed Jasmine Parker to the crime scene. "Can you give me a statement that includes both murders?" Sophie clicked on the recorder attached to her desk phone.

"How about this? Rafel Mazari and Jake Pittman were best friends, so the timing of their deaths two days apart is not likely a coincidence, and we're pursuing that angle."

"That's not exactly a breakthrough."

"I know, but now it's coming from the department instead of you."

"Do you have any physical evidence linking the crimes?"

"We're still waiting on lab reports."

"You arrested Sierra Kent on theft charges. Is she a suspect in her husband's death?

"I've got to go. I have a lot to do before my task force meeting."

"Thanks, Jackson. Call me when you have more time."

They both laughed, and Sophie hung up. He hadn't really given her anything but a useless quote, but useless quotes from politicians, experts, and law enforcement were what often passed for news. She tried to do better, but it wasn't always possible.

Sophie keyed Jackson's quote into her brief news story, then shut down her computer. Sierra Kent's theft charge intrigued her, and she hadn't pursued it yet. On her way out of the building, she called the police department and asked for the report of Sierra's arrest. For a small fee, they said they'd mail it to her, but she told them to hold it and she'd pick it up in a few minutes.

Sophie found a parking space behind Full City coffee, across the street from the county courthouse and only a block from City Hall. She decided to run into the county building and look up the property record for Zain Mazari. If she found the address, she'd drive out there later and see if Rafel's father would talk to her. If nothing else, she'd get some photos of the place where Rafel grew up. His sister had said his friends spent a lot of time on the farm when they were young, so it could be a poignant part of her story about the two murdered friends.

Her search took five minutes and cost $15—doing her part this morning to keep both the county and city afloat. The property records department also gave her a plat map that showed the address off a small side road, which might have been easy to miss. She could always get directions from her iPhone, but she hated stopping to do it.

Pleased to be moving forward on the story, she hurried one block over to police headquarters and picked up Sierra's arrest report. Back in her car, Sophie scanned the information. The one significant word in the whole report was *syringes*. Why the hell had Sierra stolen syringes from the veterinary clinic where she worked? And what did it have to do with her husband's murder? Had she drugged him? A rush of excitement flooded her stomach. Sophie shoved the report in her oversized bag, started her car, and headed for Willamette Street.

On a late Tuesday morning, the parking lot at the Animal Care Clinic was nearly empty. Great news. The staff would have time to talk to her. Sophie checked to make sure she had her recorder, notebook, and a pen, then straightened her messy bangs. She stepped out of her car and took a few pictures, noting the building had an odd Mexican look, with stucco and rounded windows. Inside, the small waiting area was empty, and the receptionist looked bored. Chewing gum, the young woman looked up from her oversized monitor. "How can I help you?"

"I'm Sophie Speranza with the Willamette News. I'm writing a feature about Rafel Mazari, and I'm looking for background information about him and his wife Sierra Kent."

The receptionist's boredom vanished. "Sierra called a while ago. She should be here any minute to pick up her final paycheck if you want to wait and talk to her."

Hell yes, she would wait. She'd been trying to talk to the widow for days. "Did you say final paycheck?"

The receptionist nodded.

"Did Sierra quit or was she fired for stealing syringes?"

The receptionist made a mocking gesture of ignorance. "I don't know anything about that. I just assumed she needed time off to grieve."

"Did you ever meet Sierra's husband or spend time with them together?" Sophie pulled out her notepad.

"Sure. When they first got married, Rafel volunteered here sometimes. We all liked him."

"What did he do as a volunteer?"

"Cleaned cages and helped wash the big animals. That kind of stuff."

"But not recently?"

"Not since he got back from the war."

"What kind of man was he? How would you describe him?"

The receptionist gave it some thought, knowing she might be quoted. "He seemed very much in love with Sierra at first, but he was intense in some ways and kind of quiet."

Sophie had to ask. "Can you think of any reason why Sierra might want to kill him?

The woman's eyes went wide and she made a little O with her mouth. "Goodness no. Why do you ask? Is she a suspect?"

Sophie gave a casual shrug. "The spouse is always a suspect."

The clinic door banged open behind Sophie and she turned. Sierra marched toward the counter, a bundle of dreadlocks bouncing behind her head. Sophie started to open her mouth to introduce herself, but the look on Sierra's face stopped her. Instead, Sophie stepped aside to observe.

"Can you get my check?" Sierra's tone was curt, more worried than angry.

"I have it right here." The receptionist reached for an envelope near her computer. "I'm sorry about your husband. Best wishes to you."

"Thanks." Sierra grabbed the paycheck and started to turn.

"Sierra Kent? I'm Sophie Speranza with the Willamette News."

The tall woman spun around and walked out, without even looking at her. Sophie hurried to the window, curious about Sierra. She watched her get into a red Charger with a dark-haired man at the wheel. He looked younger than Sierra and wasn't smiling. Sophie remembered seeing him at the funeral, but didn't know his name. Was it one of Rafel's childhood friends?

She motioned for the receptionist to hurry over. "Come look at this guy. Do you know him?"

The Charger backed out of its parking space, and by the time the receptionist rounded the counter and trudged over, the vehicle was heading for the road.

"Do you recognize that car?"

"No. Sorry."

Sophie considered following them, then questioned the point of it. The guy was probably Sierra's brother or some friend offering his support. Still, Sierra's coming to collect a final paycheck seemed a little odd. Sophie ran to her car, unlocking it with her clicker as she approached.

The Charger had turned right with the traffic, but it took Sophie five minutes to exit on Willamette. She finally honked at a driver to let her out, and surprisingly he did, but not without a *What the fuck?* look. She pressed the gas but got nowhere in the heavy traffic. The Charger was no longer in sight, so Sophie kept checking side streets to see if it had turned. After a few frustrating minutes, she gave up and headed back toward the newspaper.

# Chapter 31

*Tuesday, Nov. 15, 11 a.m.*

Jackson stepped into the conference room, the smell of coffee heavy in the air and anticipation running high. The file of Sierra's phone records had come through, and he was eager to see who she'd been talking to in the days before her husband had been killed.

Evans and Schak were present but Quince hadn't shown up yet. Jackson set down the stack of papers and nodded at his teammates. "We've got Sierra's phone records. Up for some more data scanning?"

"I'd love to," Schak said, "but I have to be in court this afternoon. I just stopped in to tell you I heard from Mazari's phone service. They pinged his cell this morning, and the signal bounced off a tower in Creswell. My guess is that it's in the Short Mountain Landfill."

"Crap. Thanks."

"Don't thank me. I still haven't found a damn thing about the Territory Defenders group. If anything breaks on this case, text me, will you? It'll keep me awake in court." He grabbed his coat and headed out.

Jackson divided the stack into thirds, assuming Quince would show up soon. He pushed a pile of paper toward Evans. "By the way, I heard from the lab," he said. "Three things: That sticky stuff you pulled off Mazari's Jeep? It's tree sap, but I don't know how that helps us."

Evans mulled it over. "Pittman is a tree cutter. Maybe he was present for Mazari's murder."

"Why didn't the homeless guy see him?"

"I don't know. Maybe Pittman leaned against the Jeep earlier. What else?"

"The hair found on Pittman's back is synthetic."

"Weird." Evans made a face. "I can't help but think prostitute."

"That was my first thought. But we need to ask around and see who in this group wore a wig."

"What's the third thing?"

"The syringe from the crime scene had traces of ketamine. If we can get our homeless guy into court and help him sound credible for the day, I think we can get a conviction for the wife."

"Speaking of Sierra," Evans said. "She quit her job. I was at the animal clinic first thing this morning, and her boss vehemently denied having an affair with her. Her co-workers didn't see any signs of a thing between them either, but someone told me Sierra had called and said she wouldn't be back."

"That's interesting." Jackson didn't know what to think. "She could be grieving and getting ready to make a change in her life, or she could be preparing to get the hell out of town."

Evans' eyes sparked with excitement. "Should we put out an ATL on her?"

"Definitely. And after talking to Cody Sawyer last night, I think he may be involved."

"Oh yeah? What did you learn?" Evans stood and moved toward the board.

"Sawyer volunteers at the Southside Senior Center and

has the computer skills to create websites."

Evans scowled. "That's not the center Quince mentioned."

"It probably gave him the idea, then he was smart enough to go somewhere else for marks." Jackson realized they still had much more legwork to do.

"Does Sawyer have an alibi for the time of death?" Evans asked.

"He says he was watching a movie with his girlfriend. I called her but she hasn't got back to me." Jackson looked at his notes, trying to remember what Sawyer had said about the night of the first victim's death. "Sawyer's dad is a lawyer and came home before I could ask him much. He advised his son to quit talking, and I didn't have a damn thing to justify bringing him in."

"If Schak were here, he'd grumble about the good old days when cops could act like cops," Evans said. "Sometimes I think he's right. We have to be so damn careful."

"Let's find Sawyer in this data," Jackson said. "Then we'll go get a subpoena for everything: phone, bank, and DNA."

Quince hustled into the room. "Sorry I'm late. I had to speak with a witness in the fraud case." He slid into a chair and glanced at the stack of phone records.

"Anything we should know?" Jackson asked.

"One of Molly Pershing's neighbors saw a young man matching Sawyer's description come out of Molly's apartment about six weeks ago. I showed her Sawyer's Facebook picture and she thought it was him."

A shimmer of excitement ran up Jackson's spine. Finally, they had a connection. "So the non-military guy was the brains behind the scam." Jackson stood and wrote Sawyer's phone number on the board in big letters. "This is what we're looking for in this pile of data. Or possibly Dolan's." He wrote the other suspect's number too.

Jackson sat down, and they went to work, scanning the rows of small-print phone numbers. After a page, he grabbed his reading glasses from his carryall.

Ten minutes later, Evans tapped her pile and said in an excited voice, "Got it. A call from Sawyer to Sierra at 12:15 p.m. on Wednesday the tenth, and another one at approximately the same time the day before."

"Calling her on their lunch break," Quince said.

"It's not enough," Jackson added.

"There's more." Evans flipped to another page, scanning with her finger. "They talked to each other on their lunch hour almost every day."

His phone rang, and Jackson picked up, hoping for good news.

"This is Melissa Jenkins, returning your call."

For a moment, the name meant nothing to him, then he remembered his last few calls. "Oh yes. You're Cody Sawyer's girlfriend."

"We're just friends now." She sounded a little sad.

"Did you see Cody last Saturday night?"

"Sort of. He came over to watch a movie, but he was irritated about something. Then he told me our relationship was over and left."

"What time did he show up and what time did he leave?"

"I think around nine, then he left within ten minutes. Is this about Jake?"

"Do you know where Cody is right now?"

"No. I haven't seen him since Rafel's funeral yesterday. He's pretty upset."

"Was Cody seeing someone else?"

She was silent for a long moment. "He said he wasn't, but

I think that's why he broke up with me."

"I may want to talk again later, but thanks for your time." Jackson hung up before she could ask more questions.

His teammates looked at him expectantly.

"Sawyer has no alibi for Pittman's time of death, and he lied about it. We need to put out an ATL on him and Sierra and bring them both in. We'll play them off each other until one talks to get a plea deal."

"Any idea where to find Sawyer?" Evans asked.

"Call Royal Caribbean and see if he's at work. Quince, run out to Sierra's and see if he's there. I'll check his home again."

# Chapter 32

Back at the newspaper, Sophie called her friend Kim Bradley and mentally begged her to answer. When she didn't, Sophie swore at her phone before leaving a message: "I need to know who in Rafel and Sierra's group of friends is tall and skinny with short dark hair. He's cute, has a little soul patch, and drives a red Charger. Call me ASAP if you know."

Moments later, she received a text from Kim: *Not sure. I'll see what I can find out.*

Sophie called Rafel's sister and left a similar message, but with a little more diplomacy.

Her cube neighbor on the left, an older woman who wrote food and church features, popped up. "What's the deal? You sound kind of frantic."

"It's weird. I know I'm occupationally curious and prone to wild ideas, but I have a feeling I saw something a little nefarious."

"You've got great instincts, so stay on it. I wish I could help, but I'm stuck in this Lifestyle-section rut."

"Thanks." Sophie hadn't known the woman was unhappy with her job. "Maybe we'll work on a story together sometime."

Her co-worker waved it off. "Forget it. I'm good."

Sophie checked the time. Only 11:45. Close enough. She would take lunch early and head out to Zain Mazari's place.

She couldn't sit here, waiting for someone to call her and identify Sierra's companion. Time to move forward.

River Road passed through thickly populated suburbs, with older housing on the city side of Beltline and newer divisions once she passed under the expressway. The sun popped in and out of the clouds as Sophie drove, and the thick traffic exacerbated her stress. When she finally cleared the housing developments, the roadside was suddenly lined with farm fields that had been plowed under for the cold season. A few scraggly pumpkin patches remained.

After about five miles, Sophie started looking for Hayes Lane, then made the turn a few minutes later. She passed more fields with farmhouses set back from the road. She slowed and started to watch for route numbers on the mailboxes. After ten minutes of driving back and forth between numbers that were too big or too small, she finally turned down a dirt driveway with no mailbox. The lack of address meant Zain Mazari valued his privacy, and she started to worry about how she would be received. Or more likely, not received.

A clump of oak and poplar trees sheltered a small ranch-style home on what looked like a narrow ten-acre lot. The driveway continued past the house toward fields in the back and another clump of trees. She pulled off the narrow road into an open space in front of the house. Dirty white and unadorned, with no flower boxes, no pretty window coverings, and no feminine touch. An old Chevy Apache truck sat in the sun, paint fading, and a chicken wandered through a patch of grass under a giant oak. Sophie waited in the car for a moment, hypothesizing that if Mr. Mazari was the angry-old-man type, he'd soon come running out with a shotgun and she'd get the hell away.

The house was completely quiet, and she saw no movement anywhere. Maybe he wasn't home. The truck could be his farm vehicle, and he might be at a job somewhere, for all she knew. No, Sasha had said he was retired. Sophie grabbed her camera and climbed out of the car.

The pictures would be terrific, she realized, as streaks of sunlight hit the barren home. The whole scene had such a forlorn look, almost abandoned. She worked quickly, then crunched across the gravel toward the front door. She decided she would ask to see photos of Rafel as a child. No parent could resist that. Once the old man opened up, the other questions would be easier.

Sophie knocked on the wooden door and took a deep breath, but no sound came from inside the house. She rapped again. While she waited, the faint sound of voices drifted from the back of the property. Or were they coming from the river that was back there somewhere? Sophie waited and listened for the distant sounds. After a minute, she gave up finding Mr. Mazari inside the house and decided to take a quick look around back.

She rounded the corner of the house and walked along the dirt road, noting fresh tire tracks. She passed the back of the house and saw a small patch of overgrown grass and weeds. Beyond it was a chicken coop, a well house, and several rundown outbuildings. A giant tree held a tattered rope swing and a child's fort made of now-rotted lumber.

She heard the voices again and stopped. They were coming from the clump of trees in the distance.

She caught sight of something red among the green foliage. Was that the car she'd seen earlier at the animal clinic? The one Sierra had climbed into with the dark-haired man at the wheel? If so, what the hell were they doing at the back of Zain Mazari's property? A cool chill ran up her spine. Normally, she would have jumped in her car and driven back there to see what was going on. But two people connected to Sierra had been killed recently, and Sophie had no desire to confront the two of them out here in the middle of nowhere.

She snapped a few more pictures, an occupational compulsion, then headed back to the front of the house, glancing over her shoulder as she walked. In the front yard, with the house between her and the people in the trees, she dug out her cell phone and tried to call Jackson. The call wouldn't go through. *Damn.* No service. What now? She hated to leave. If the couple in back took off while she was gone, Jackson would miss them, and she might never know what the hell was going on back there or what had really happened with the murders. Yet instinct told her this was important, and the detectives working the case should know about it. She hurried to her car, climbed in, and started it. Had Sierra and her companion heard the engine start? Would it spook them?

Sophie shook off the vibe. Sierra and her friend's presence here was probably nothing. This was Rafel's childhood home, and they'd probably come here to honor him somehow. Sophie told herself she was being paranoid and hoping for a little excitement. Still, the sense of urgency stayed with her as she drove toward River Road. Junction City was the nearest town, but there had to be a cell phone tower somewhere closer. With her Bluetooth on, she kept hitting redial as she drove. As she rounded a curve, she heard Jackson's phone ringing. He didn't pick up, and she wasn't surprised. He'd already granted her five minutes that morning and wouldn't waste any more time with her. She pulled off the road into a driveway and texted him, not bothering with punctuation, something she was normally obsessive about: *Red Charger parked at Rafel dad. Saw sierra & some guy in it this a.m. Check out?* She keyed in the address and pressed Send. How often did Jackson check his messages?

A huge farm truck rumbled past, carrying a load of pumpkins. Sophie made a U-turn in the narrow road and headed back to the Mazari property. A car coming in the other direction caught her eye. Was it Sierra and the guy? She slowed and stared at the vehicle as it approached. No, it wasn't even the right color. Chill, she told herself.

At the forlorn little house, she backed into the parking area so she'd be ready to drive off in a hurry if she needed to. Her car was visible from the road, so Jackson would see it when he came. She ran around the corner of the house and saw that the Charger was still there. Relieved, Sophie hurried to her car, climbed in, and locked the doors. She grabbed her laptop from under the seat, clicked it on, and waited impatiently for Word to open. When it did, she started typing notes from the scene. She wanted to capture the details, the colors, sights, and senses while it was all vividly clear in her mind. She paused every few seconds to look up and make sure she didn't have company and to check her cell phone. But of course, Jackson hadn't gotten back to her. Even if he had bothered, she didn't have reception here. Should she have mentioned that to him?

Sophie keyed in a few more thoughts, closed out the file, and tossed the laptop into the passenger seat. She had to get out and investigate more.

## Chapter 33

Jackson pounded on the door of the Sawyers' house again, knowing intuitively no one was home. Not one of their three cars was in the driveway, and all the lights were off. It was possible Cody's car was in the garage and he was home, avoiding the police, but Jackson didn't get that sense. Sometimes he acted on his gut feelings, especially if he had nothing else to go on. More often, he waited for the evidence to substantiate his thinking. This case was so weird and complex—compared to a typical spouse-on-spouse homicide—that he was leery about overstepping his authority. The lack of clear forensic evidence in the second murder made it even harder to sort out.

Finally, he walked away and climbed in his vehicle. He wouldn't force his way into the house without backup, but knowing that uniformed officers were now looking for Sawyer's car gave him some sense of relief. He pulled his cell phone from his jacket pocket and noticed he had a message from Sophie Speranza. He would have ignored her, but the first few lines of text started with *Red Charger.* His pulse quickened and he opened the message: *Red Charger parked at Rafel dad. Saw sierra & some guy in it this a.m. Check out? 77895 Hayes Lane. Off River R.*

*What the hell?* Sierra was with Cody Sawyer at her father-in-law's home? What was Sophie doing there? And why was she texting him about the situation rather than pulling out her little recorder and chatting with the couple? Jackson found Sophie's last call to him and pressed Callback. It rang six times, then went to voicemail. She must be interviewing Rafel's dad, Jackson thought.

He started his car, put in his earpiece, and sped away. If he got there in time, this could be an ideal opportunity to bring in both Cody and Sierra for questioning. They would put them in separate interview rooms and pit them against each other until one opened up. The tactic could be very effective.

As he waited to turn on Amazon Parkway, he started to call Schak, then remembered he was in court. He called Quince instead. "I just got word that our main suspects are together at Rafel's father's house. I'm headed out there now and could use some backup."

"What's the location?"

"77895 Hayes Lane. It's off River Road, close to Junction City, I think."

"Never heard of it, but I've got GPS on my phone, so I'll find it. What's the situation? Anything tense?"

"A newspaper reporter informed me, so it's probably civil." Jackson had second thoughts. "But they are murder suspects, so I'll get Evans on it too."

He hung up and called Evans, leaving her a voicemail message with all the details. Knowing her, she'd beat them both out there.

The drive back into town from south Eugene was slow with thick traffic in the 30th Avenue area. By the time he reached downtown where he could turn and head west, he felt jittery with impatience. River Road was even worse, with the area around Beltline congested to the point of not moving. When had his quiet little college town morphed into a busy, often frustrating, concentration of people?

Jackson finally cleared the suburbs and pressed the accelerator, passing several slow-moving cars just to blow the sludge out of his engine and his veins. Ten minutes later, moving too fast, he shot past Hayes Lane and had to turn around.

The secondary road wandered past fields and small clumps of oak trees and finally curved toward the river. He watched for addresses but also kept his eye out for Sophie's dark-green Scion.

Sophie listened for the distant voices as she walked toward the house. They were quiet now, but she heard another rhythmic sound she didn't recognize. Every fiber in her body wanted to drive to the end of the property and see what the hell they were doing, but self-preservation overruled curiosity. She would wait for the police officers and follow them back. For now, she'd snoop in some windows and take more notes.

The living room was cluttered and dusty, she noted, pressing close to the glass. But no one seemed to be home. She walked toward the driveway running past the house and rounded the corner again, wanting to check on the situation at the end of the dirt road. But first, she stopped parallel to a small window on the side of the house. A roll-up shade covered the top half of the glass, but the bottom was visible, even through the streaks of dirt that the fall rain hadn't washed off yet. She stepped through the weeds and peered in.

Sitting on the floor with his back against a bed was an old

man with his face half blown off. Sophie instinctively recoiled. Was that Zain Mazari? Shocked and sickened, she pressed her nose to the window again. A shotgun lay on his outstretched legs, as if he'd dropped it there, and a book of some kind was on the floor next to him.

Jackson spotted a Scion on a property on the left side of the road. He braked and turned, taking the corner a little faster than he'd intended. He raced up the driveway and parked next to the house, keeping his vehicle in the road to block it. He climbed out and headed for Sophie's car, and she rolled down the window as he approached.

"The red Charger is on the back of the property, and I hear two voices. I saw a similar car at the Animal Care Clinic this morning." The reporter's voice was wound tighter than usual, but she relayed the information like a pro. "Sierra picked up her final paycheck, then climbed in. The guy driving looked tall and skinny with dark hair and a soul patch."

"Cody Sawyer." The name popped out of his mouth without thinking. "Thanks, Sophie. Now you need to leave. Start your car and drive away." Jackson glanced at the road to see if Quince was coming, then turned back to his own car.

"Jackson, there's more," Sophie said softly. He spun back around.

"There's a dead guy in the house, and it looks like a suicide."

Adrenaline flooded his veins. "You went in the house?"

"No. I saw him through the bedroom window. He's obviously dead though. It looks like he put a shotgun in his mouth."

Jackson's brain scrambled to form a plan. This wasn't the EPD's jurisdiction, but it was his case. The sheriff's department would have to be notified, but he had two murder suspects to apprehend immediately. They may have killed the old man and made it look like suicide. He grabbed his cell phone and dialed Sergeant Lammers, but the call wouldn't go through. He radioed the department instead and gave the details.

While he was talking, Quince came flying down the driveway and parked behind his car. Jackson got out and trotted back to him. "They're down this road, parked in the grove. Let's both drive back."

"Right behind you."

Jackson jumped in his car and pulled forward. He made a point to drive slowly, not wanting to spook the suspects. He didn't expect them to be armed, but he'd operate on the assumption that they were. Pittman's weapon had disappeared from his house the night he died.

He drove past a fallow field and neared the clump of trees. The dirt road went through the middle of the grove, and the Charger was parked about twenty feet in. Off to the left, he saw Sierra and Sawyer. *What were they doing? Digging a grave?* His pulse escalated and he touched his Sig Sauer on reflex.

At the sound of his engine, they stopped and looked up. The couple froze, shovels in hand. Through his windshield, he saw them talking to each but couldn't hear what they were saying. Jackson parked, shut off his car and stepped out. Behind him, Quince did the same.

"Put your hands in the air," Jackson called out.

He took one step and they bolted for the Charger. *Shit!*

"Freeze!"

He had his hand on his weapon but he didn't draw it. The suspects weren't armed, and he had no reason to shoot them. They scrambled into the vehicle and fired up the engine. Jackson considered shooting at their tires but his training didn't call for it. The tactic was rarely effective and people got hurt. Blocking their escape made more sense. He jumped in his cruiser, trying to determine how far the dirt road went and what was beyond it. He hoped it would dead-end into a fence or the river.

Mud flew at this windshield as the Charger raced through the trees ahead of him. Jackson gunned his engine, staying close behind. Beyond the trees was another field, this one smaller. Jackson tried to see past the vehicle in front of him. How deep was the property? Did it have a fence across the back? He sensed Sawyer knew the area and thought he had a chance to get away. Jackson envisioned them abandoning the car and jumping into the river. The shooting pain in his gut told him this would not turn out well.

Ahead and to the right, he saw the far corner of the acreage. A wire fence ran along the back, but it leaned heavily away from them. Sawyer planned to run through the fence. Beyond it were more fields and a strip of trees running along the horizon. The river!

The Charger flew past an old hay barn, plowed over the decrepit fence, and careened to the left. Jackson gunned his engine and followed, ending up on another dirt road. They raced down a path that cut between fenced fields on both sides. He glanced in his rearview mirror and saw Quince's vehicle right behind him. He wondered where Evans was and where this road came out. Instinct told him it emptied onto a main road. Was Sawyer's plan to outrun them?

*Fucking idiot.*

As predicted, the dirt path came out on Hayes Lane, and the Charger made a wild turn to the right, headed for River Road. Jackson slowed for the corner, and the fleeing car gained ground. They rounded a curve, and a flatbed truck came into view, driving toward them from the other direction. The truck began a wide turn across the road, aiming for a tree-lined driveway, still unaware of them. Jackson slammed his brakes, steered to the right, and prayed Quince wouldn't rear-end him. He heard the squeal of the Charger's brakes as it slowed and veered off the road to avoid a head-on collision with the farm truck. As Jackson skidded through the gravel and came to a stop, he saw the sports car bounce through a shallow ditch.

A moment later, it plowed into one of the thick trees along the driveway. The air filled with the deafening sounds of crunching metal and glass and screaming truck brakes. The big vehicle slammed to a stop just before it pinned the Charger to the tree.

Jackson shut off his engine and glanced back. He saw Quince in the ditch, but both he and the cruiser seemed fine. Jackson radioed for help, then jumped from his car and ran toward the wrecked vehicle. The passenger's side was totaled, and hoped Sawyer and Sierra were still alive.

# Chapter 34

*Wednesday, Nov. 15, 3:30 p.m.*

Jackson stood in the hallway of the hospital, waiting for the double doors to open. A nurse in yellow scrubs came through and he identified himself. "I'm here to see Cody Sawyer. I cleared it with his doctor earlier."

"Follow me."

As they walked past open doors, Jackson kept his eyes straight ahead. He'd made many visits to the hospital, but it never got easier. Sick and dying people were almost harder to deal with emotionally than the dead victims he investigated. The nurse led him into Sawyer's room, where Cody's mother sat in a chair, reading.

She startled at the sight of Jackson and stood, as if to protect her son. "I don't think you should be here."

"Five people are dead, and I need answers."

Jackson glanced at the young man. He had a white bandage on his forehead, and his left arm was in a cast, but he was surprisingly undamaged after driving his car into a tree. His passenger had not survived.

At the sound of Jackson's voice, Sawyer opened his eyes.

Jackson decided to be gentle and use his first name. He wanted the suspect to open up. "I need you to answer some questions, Cody."

His mother started to protest, but Cody cut her off. "It's

okay, Mom. I didn't kill anybody on purpose, but Sierra is dead and that's my fault. I need to take responsibility." His voice was raspy and maybe a little drugged.

"Your father wouldn't want you to do this without him present." Mrs. Sawyer stepped toward her son.

"I don't care. Please leave us alone."

She looked back and forth between the men, grabbed her purse, and walked out. He suspected she would call her husband right away. Jackson took a seat by the bed. If Sawyer was ready to talk, he didn't want to be intimidating. He showed him the recorder and the suspect nodded his consent.

"Let's start at the beginning. Whose idea was it to create the Veterans Relief Fund?"

"Jake thought of it, but I set it up because Jake and Rafel didn't have the skills. I didn't want the money, and I never took a dime of it. I did it to help my friends because they were broke and miserable."

"What about Molly's money. Did you take it?"

"No! She wanted to donate to the veteran's fund, and she asked me to help her set up an automatic transfer." His distress seemed real. "Jake got the access information from me one night when we were drinking. I'm so sorry about Molly. That should never have happened."

Jackson wanted to hear every detail, but he knew he had a limited amount of time, so he went for the guts of the story. They'd found Rafel's journal near his father's dead body, and Jackson had stayed up late reading it. Heartbreak and anger had leapt off the pages, tearing at Jackson's emotions. Rafel's journal had given Jackson chunks of the story, but there were still big holes surrounding Jake's death. The best they could figure, Rafel had mailed the journal to the old man—wanting him to know the whole ugly truth—and his father had killed himself after reading it.

"What happened the night Rafel died?"

"I didn't know it then, but Rafel and Jake had formed a suicide pact." Cody squeezed his eyes closed for a moment. "They both felt like they'd lost everything. I knew they were miserable, but I didn't know how bad it was."

Jackson waited, letting him tell his story in his own way.

"Their plan was for Jake to take Rafel's life in a mercy killing and frame Sierra for it. Rafel knew Sierra was cheating on him and he wanted to punish her."

"When did learn about this?"

"Not until Saturday night." Cody took a sip of water and didn't look at Jackson. "Rafel didn't know who Sierra was cheating with though. We worried he would catch us and maybe kill her, but we never suspected he was cruel and calculating enough to frame her for murder."

"He never confronted you with the affair?"

"No. We were very careful." His eyes filled with tears. "I loved her. I can't believe she's dead."

"What happened Saturday?"

Cody shuddered. "Everything. You took Sierra in for questioning and asked her about the syringe. She realized Rafel had somehow dropped one with her prints at the crime scene, and we suspected Jake had actually killed him." Cody choked back a sob. "Now I know Jake did it out of love, but it still infuriated me."

Jackson didn't know if he could ever commit a mercy killing, but he understood why people did it. He waited for Cody to continue.

"I got a bad feeling, so I checked the charity's bank account and saw that someone had transferred seven grand from Molly's account. I freaked out. Up to that point, all of the donations were voluntary and the money really did go to a couple of veterans. It was a mostly a legitimate charity, except for being unregistered."

Jackson could have argued the point, but he wanted to hear about Saturday night. "So what did you do?"

"I tried calling Jake but he wouldn't answer. So I finally went over there and confronted him. He'd been drinking and didn't try to hide anything. He said he took the money because he had debts to pay and he thought the bank would cover Mrs. Pershing's loss. I accused him of being an idiot and tried to get him to give the money back. He said it was too late, that he'd already paid some of his debt. Then I asked him if he'd killed Rafel." Cody stopped and made a face. "I feel queasy."

"Do you want to lie back?" Jackson needed him to finish his story, whatever it took.

"I think it's the painkillers. I'll be okay." Cody took another sip of water. "That's when Jake told me about the suicide pact. He said Rafel had begged him to end his life and help him frame Sierra."

Jackson remembered some lines from Rafel's journal: *More than anything, I want to be free of this wretched body, free of the guilt about what I did to Joanna...My friend Jake has finally agreed to help me die and to make my death count for something.*

After reading the journal, Jackson had looked up some statistics online and learned that a hundred and ten off-duty National Guardsmen had killed themselves the previous year.

Cody's hands balled into fists. "He told me how he'd put on a wig, then drugged Rafel and cut his throat, leaving the syringe and scalpel to be found. Jake called Sierra a whore and said she deserved to rot in jail. That's when I hit him."

"How many times did you strike him?

"I don't know. I was furious. He punched me back, but his heart wasn't in it. He'd been drinking, and the last time I hit him he fell. The sound of his head thumping the counter was awful. I'll never forget it." Sawyer started to cry.

Jackson was unmoved. This man had made too many tragic choices. "What happened next?"

"I tried to revive Jake but he was dead. I almost called the police, then I remembered Sierra was in jail and you guys were convinced she'd murdered Rafel. With Jake dead too, I realized we'd both in prison." Sawyer paused. "So I cut his throat to make it look like the same person had killed them both. I figured it would cast reasonable doubt on Sierra's guilt." He gave a grim smile. "My dad's a lawyer, so I think like one sometimes."

"Why did you search his house?"

Sawyer looked ashamed for the first time. "After Jake died, I panicked. And it didn't make sense to leave the cash for the cops to find. Sierra and I were already talking about moving away together as soon as she was cleared, so we needed every dime we could get our hands on. But only some of the money was in the house."

"What else did you take?"

"Everything. I took his phone and his computer, so you couldn't trace the charity. I took his gun and the wig he wore the night he killed Rafel." Cody shook his head. "That was stupid. I should have left the wig. I still can't believe they tried to frame Sierra for the murder."

The wig explained what Prez thought he saw and the long synthetic hair stuck to Jake Pittman's back. "Where is all of that stuff now?"

"I put them in a dumpster behind Albertson's on 30th Avenue."

Jackson didn't look forward to that search. "What were you and Sierra doing at Zain Mazari's house?" Jackson knew part of the answer because a sheriff's team had found the bones in the bottom of the hole and he'd read Rafel's journal.

"Digging up his mother's body."

"How did you know it was there?"

"I watched Rafel and Mr. Mazari bury her when I twelve." Sawyer's eyes glazed over in a faraway look. "I was spending the weekend, and the sound of angry voices woke me up in the middle of the night. Then I heard a strange cry and Rafel got up to see what was going on. I heard more murmuring, then after a while it was quiet, so I tiptoed out to the hallway and saw Rafel and his father carrying Mrs. Mazari's body outside. I followed them to the forest, as we called it then, and I watched them dig a hole and bury her. They didn't know I was there."

He looked at Jackson for empathy. "I was scared and mesmerized at the same time. When they started filling in the grave, I snuck back up to the house and got in bed. The next morning they acted like nothing had happened, and I thought I had dreamt it." Sawyer shook his head at his own gullibility. "Eventually I blocked it out. Then Monday at Rafel's funeral as I watched them start to fill his grave, it all came back to me in a rush."

Jackson recalled another passage in Rafel's diary. He'd written something like: *I didn't kill my mother, but I didn't try to save her either. And I helped the old man bury her. The guilt never left me.*

"Why did you dig her up?"

"I thought they probably buried Mrs. Mazari with her

little locket still around her neck. We all thought she kept the key to her journal in it, or so she said. After the funeral, when I told Sierra the story of how Rafel's mother died, she was sickened. Then later, she remembered that Rafel had once said his mother had stocks she'd inherited from her family that had never been accounted for. He thought his father knew what happened to the money, but the old man refused to talk about it."

Cody paused, clearly uncomfortable with the rest of the story. "I got it in my head that the key might be to a safe deposit box and that if we could dig it up, we could find the stocks and cash them in. We needed the money to get away and start a new life somewhere." Sawyer looked at Jackson with an odd, longing expression. "I want to know if I was right." He reached for his wallet beside the bed and pulled a small rusty key from the coin zip. "Take this to Rafel's sister. If there is any money, it's hers."

Jackson resisted the urge to shake his head. Sawyer was both a dreamer and a fool. "Why did you run when we showed up?" As many times as he'd seen the reaction, it never made sense to him.

"I loved Sierra with all my heart and soul. I had for years." He choked up and had to wait it out. "I couldn't imagine seeing her locked up for something she didn't do. I couldn't imagine my life without her." His expression shifted to anger. "I thought the police would do everything they could to put her away. You can't blame me for wanting to spare her that."

Jackson understood the sentiment, but they still would blame Sawyer for Pittman's death. And Sierra's. Even two counts of manslaughter would put him away for a decade. Still, the punishment wouldn't change anything for the tragic childhood friends. Rafel's life had been ruined long ago when his father made him complicit in his own mother's murder, burdening the boy with guilt and a misogynistic view of women. Jake had been dealt some blows too, but he hadn't been strong enough to handle them. Cody, on the other hand, had had it all and let it slip away when he fell in love with another man's wife.

Jackson walked out of the hospital, feeling a little dazed. He couldn't stop thinking about Cody's declaration of love for Sierra. The man had been willing to go on the run and live the life of a refugee for the woman he loved. Even Pittman had slit the throat of his best friend because he loved him enough to put him out of his misery. Jackson wondered if he was capable of doing something irrational to save Kera. Did he really love his girlfriend the way she deserved to be loved?

Until his daughter had been born, Jackson hadn't believed he was capable of that kind of overwhelming, irrational love. But even if he didn't have that with Kera, he still loved her enough to know his life would feel empty without her. Jackson knew what he had to do. A moment later, he was running for his car.

He called Kera on the drive over to make sure she was home. She answered, sounding pleased to hear from him. "I'm so glad you called. I want to see you."

"I'll be there in a moment," was all he said. He had to do this in person.

By the time he arrived, he felt calmer, but still sure of his decision. He noticed Danette's car was not in the driveway. Good. They'd have a moment alone ...except for the baby. And that's the way it would be going forward, he told himself.

Kera opened the door, gave him hug, and pulled him into

the living room. Micah was sleeping in his playpen near the couch.

"Let's sit," she said. "We need to talk." She eased down onto the couch.

Jackson dropped to his knees on the floor in front of her and took her hands. He wished he had a ring, but this was too important to wait. "Kera, I've been a fool. I love you, and I want to spend my life with you. Will you marry me?"

At first, she looked panicked, then his gorgeous girlfriend burst out laughing.

Jackson smiled, realizing he'd been holding his breath. "That's not quite the reaction I expected."

She stroked his hair. "I love you too, but we're not getting married. At least not anytime soon."

"You're turning me down?" He didn't know whether to feel rejected or relieved.

"Not exactly. I hope we do get married someday, and I'm glad you're thinking in that direction, but we have too much family stuff to work through first." Kera smiled and patted the couch beside her. "Please get off your knees. I know it's painful for you."

Jackson let out a mock sigh and clambered up to the couch. He gently touched her face. "I don't want to lose you."

"You won't. I'm sorry I put us through that. I knew it was a mistake as soon as you walked out the door. I realize I had unreasonable expectations." She kissed him passionately, and the pain he'd carried in his chest for days melted away. Kera pulled back. "I know I'm as busy as you are, and I don't always put you first either. We both have to try harder to find time for each other."

The tension was leaving his body in great waves. "We will. Let's start with a vacation. A real vacation where we fly somewhere together and lay on a warm beach."

"That sounds lovely." Kera leaned in to kiss him again. The baby's cry cut through the moment. Kera turned reflexively to look at her grandson, then gave Jackson a smile. "Just the two of us?"

"Absolutely."

L.J. Sellers is an award-winning journalist and the author of the highly praised Detective Jackson mystery/suspense series:

> Secrets to Die For
> Thrilled to Death
> Passions of the Dead
> Dying for Justice
> Liars, Cheaters & Thieves

She also has four standalone thrillers:

> The Sex Club
> The Baby Thief
> The Arranger
> The Suicide Effect

When not plotting murders, L.J. enjoys performing standup comedy, cycling, social networking, and attending mystery conferences. She's also been known to jump out of airplanes.

*Thanks for reading my novel. If you enjoyed it, please leave a review or rating online. Find out more about my work at ljsellers.com, where you can sign up to hear about new releases. —L.J.*

17100918R00164

Made in the USA
Lexington, KY
25 August 2012